Ta

"Take me away with you right now, Roland," she begged. "Let's just run away from here and never go back."

Roland smoothed back her hair with his hand. "If only that were possible, my love. But where could we go? We're penniless, you and I. You're a powerful lady and I'm a nobody. We're trapped by what we are."

"But you can't let me marry Treadwick," Laura pleaded. "Promise me you won't let me marry Treadwick."

"I'll do everything within my power," Roland said, "but you must be patient, my sweet. We can't just run off and live like peasants in Italy or Spain."

"Why not?" Laura demanded.

"Because you were not born to live like a peasant," Roland said. "You like your beautiful clothes and your jewels."

"Jewels!" Laura exclaimed. The diamonds! She had the diamonds!

"Roland, there may be a way out for us after all!"

She broke away from him and began running back toward the house. She heard him calling after her, "Laura, where are you going? What's wrong now?" But she didn't stop.

Don't miss these other riveting sagas from HarperPaperbacks:

The Journey Home
by Zoe Salinger

Emerald's Desire *
by Paula Munier Lee

And look for **BOYFRIENDS GIRLFRIENDS** — the romantic new series by Katherine Applegate.

#1 Zoey Fools Around
#2 Jake Finds Out
#3 Nina Won't Tell
#4 Ben's In Love
#5 Claire Gets Caught
*#6 What Zoey Saw**
*#7 Lucas Gets Hurt**

* coming soon

THE SUTCLIFFE DIAMONDS

JANET QUIN-HARKIN

HarperPaperbacks

A Division of HarperCollins*Publishers*

This is a work of fiction. The characters, incidents, and
dialogues are products of the author's imagination and are not
to be construed as real. Any resemblance to actual events or
persons, living or dead, is entirely coincidental.

HarperPaperbacks *A Division of* HarperCollins*Publishers*
10 East 53rd Street, New York, N.Y. 10022

Copyright © 1994 by Janet Quin-Harkin
and Daniel Weiss Associates, Inc.
Cover art copyright © 1994 Daniel Weiss Associates, Inc.

Produced by Daniel Weiss Associates, Inc.,
33 West 17th Street, New York, New York 10011.

First printing: June 1994

Printed in the United States of America

HarperPaperbacks and colophon are trademarks of
HarperCollins*Publishers*

10 9 8 7 6 5 4 3 2 1

THE
SUTCLIFFE
DIAMONDS

Sutcliffe Family Tree

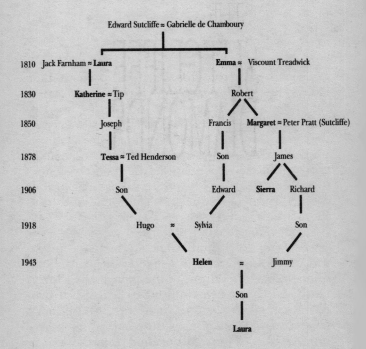

Edward Sutcliffe ≈ Gabrielle de Chamboury

1810 Jack Farnham ≈ **Laura**   **Emma** ≈ Viscount Treadwick

1830   **Katherine** ≈ Tip   Robert

1850   Joseph   Francis   **Margaret** ≈ Peter Pratt (Sutcliffe)

1878   **Tessa** ≈ Ted Henderson   Son   James

1906   Son   Edward   **Sierra**   Richard

1918   Hugo ≈ Sylvia   Son

1943   **Helen** ≈ Jimmy

                          Son

                        Laura

LONG AGO . . .

Long ago, two little girls went with their mother to visit their grandparents in France. Their names were Laura and Emma, and their father was English, but their mother was a French countess and they had never seen their French relatives before. They were amazed at the beauty of the château and the luxury of life among the French aristocracy. They were very impressed that their grandmother knew Queen Marie Antoinette and took them to visit her at her palace at Versailles.

The queen was enchanted with the two pretty little English girls and had dresses made for them so that they looked like miniature queens. The girls thought the palace was a fairyland and they never wanted to leave, but one day their mother came to them, looking very pale, and whispered that they had to go home immediately. Their father had heard rumors that a revolution was brewing in France and their lives would be in danger. He had sent a coach to take them back to England. The little girls wanted their grandmother to go with them because they had come to love her very much, but the old lady refused to leave her home. The little girls cried as they kissed their grandmother good-bye. They cried as they kissed the pretty queen.

"Don't cry, my little ones," the queen said. "See, I have a present for you. Here is the most beautiful doll in the world. Take very good care of her, for there is none like her. I may come to visit you one day, and then I want to inspect her to see that you have looked after her well."

When they had arrived safely back at their house in London, they heard that Queen Marie Antoinette had been caught trying to flee the country. Of their own grandmother they heard nothing more, but the terrible tales of revolution and the killing of the aristocrats made them fear the worst for her.

The beautiful doll sat on the shelf in the nursery and was much admired. Then one day Laura, who was older and the more curious and mischievous of the two, lifted down the doll and set her in her carriage. Emma, the obedient sister, was horrified. "You'll get her dirty, Sissy," she said. "Mama wouldn't want us to play with the queen's doll."

She tried to put the doll back on the shelf, but Laura snatched her away and danced around the room with her.

"Please put her back!" Emma pleaded, and tried to capture the doll from her sister. There was a scuffle and suddenly the doll's head came away in Emma's hands. The two girls looked in horror at what they had done.

"Maybe Papa can fix it," Laura said in a trembling voice.

They examined the doll's body to see if the head could be put back on again. It had a hollow, porcelain body, but it was stuffed with paper. Laura pulled the paper out and something sparkling fell to the floor. A diamond necklace!

When the girls showed it to their mother, she nodded as if she understood. "The queen wanted her necklace kept safe, in case anything happened to her," she said. "We'll not tell Papa about this. It will be our little secret, and we'll keep it safe until the queen is back on her throne."

But the queen of France was never to get her throne back. Soon afterward came the news that she and King Louis had been executed and France was now ruled by the people.

"What will happen to the necklace now, Mama?" Laura asked, while Emma cried for the poor queen.

The countess thought for a moment. "I suppose that it now should to go to the new government of France," she said, "but I'll give nothing to that rabble after what they did to my family and my friends. The necklace is now yours, my children. I'm sure the queen would have wanted you to have it. You may one day be in need of it."

"Will revolution come here, too, Mama?" Emma asked.

"No, my darlings. You are quite safe here,"

their mother said, putting an arm around each of them, "but you never know when it will be useful to have something of value that is entirely your own. When you grow up you will find that, as women, you have no power or rights. Your husband owns everything and makes all the decisions."

"But that is not right, Mama," Laura said. "No man is going to tell me what to do."

Their mother smiled. "That is the way of things," she said. "I have been lucky. . . . My marriage to your father has been a very happy one, but that is not always the case. Not all men are sweet and kind like your father. I want to make sure that you live happy lives. You must treasure this necklace. It is your legacy and your freedom. It is your power."

The children didn't understand then what their mother meant. The necklace was hidden in the doll on the nursery shelf, waiting for the day when it would be needed.

CHAPTER ONE

ENGLAND. THE PRESENT

"Boring!" Laura Sutcliffe sighed, hot and sweaty in the crowded train carriage. It seemed to have taken hours to cover the journey from London to the Cotswold Hills. Laura's grandmother had shown her the map the night before and it had looked like only about eighty miles. Eighty miles was nothing on the freeway back home, but this train stopped at every little station with names like Ogbourne St. Martin and Withering in the Marsh. Laura's grandmother thought they were delightfully quaint. Privately, Laura thought so too, but she wasn't about to admit it. She had made it very clear from the moment they took off from San Francisco Airport that she was coming only because she was forced to and was not, under any circumstances, going to enjoy anything about her trip to England.

"What is boring?" Grandmama asked.

"Everything," Laura said. "Every single thing since we got here. All we've done is look at boring old palaces and churches and castles and museums. I swear I'll scream if I have to look at another suit of armor. Isn't there anything fun to do in England? Aren't there any dance clubs? Is there anybody here under seventy-five?"

"I'm sure there are plenty of dance clubs and every other sort of recreation you can do back home," Helen Sutcliffe said in a clipped English accent. "But I didn't bring you here to let you do what you could do at home. I brought you here so you could experience your heritage."

Laura rolled her eyes to the ceiling of the train. "We both know very well why you brought me here," she muttered. The carriage was crowded, and she didn't want the fat little schoolboy who was sitting next to her, looking ridiculous in the weirdest cap and blazer, to hear her private conversation.

"Oh?" Helen Sutcliffe asked with the hint of a smile.

"It was my parents' idea, wasn't it?" Laura said in a low voice. "To get me away from Brian."

"Nothing of the sort," Helen Sutcliffe said. "I took your sister to England as a graduation present, and I make a practice of treating my grandchildren fairly."

"Whether they want it or not," Laura said. "I'd rather have had the money."

"And what would you have done with it?" Helen Sutcliffe smiled. "Spent it on record albums?"

"CDs, Grandmama. They don't make record albums anymore." Laura hated it when she felt that her grandmother was acting superior and laughing at her. She turned away and stared out the window. A miniature landscape flashed past: little square fields surrounded by stone walls, yellow stone cottages, tiny flower gardens—everything neat, contained, and orderly. Laura thought back to the hills at home in Northern California: sweeping grasslands that went on forever and gave her the feeling of freedom and openness. This was Grandmama's sort of countryside, neat and orderly. Laura felt totally out of place here.

Not that she felt totally *in* place at home right now. In fact, she had recently begun to feel like the invisible woman in her own house. Ever since her mother had had to take a job at the department store, she was hardly ever there. When she did come home, she was exhausted and expected Laura to fix dinner while she complained about rude customers and supervisors on power trips. Laura knew, in theory, that it must be a drag to go back to work after so many years as a happy homemaker. She also knew, in theory, that it must be a drag for her father to have lost his job after twenty years with the same company, but that didn't make him any easier to live with. He just sat around most of the day, watching game shows on TV. He hardly ever spoke, except to complain that she had left her jacket in the front hall or that she was seeing too much of Brian. When her parents did make any attempt

7

at dinnertime conversation, it was usually about Jennifer: how well she was doing at Berkeley; how she had always kept her room clean and never broken a curfew or gotten a traffic ticket in her entire life, how all her boyfriends had been clean-cut valedictorians and future Nobel prize winners.

In a way, Laura had been glad to escape from the sitcom from hell. Still, a month in England with a grandmother whose idea of a good time was wandering around drafty old castles was not the vacation she would have chosen. She wanted to see Europe. That was the thing to do after graduation. In fact, Brian was probably there right now, in France or Spain, hitchhiking from hostel to hostel or even sleeping out on beaches.

"We could head down to Spain," he had said. "I know some guys who are going to hang out on the beach down there. It won't cost a thing—we'll just buy bread and wine . . . play some music . . . sleep out under the stars. . . . Sounds cool, right?"

It did sound very cool to Laura. She imagined lying in Brian's arms under the bright Spanish stars while somebody strummed a guitar and the waves broke gently in the background. Unfortunately it didn't sound cool to her parents. They hadn't liked Brian from day one. Her father had freaked out so much at the ponytail and the earring that he'd never bothered to see Brian's intellectual qualities. And all her mother could do was compare him to Jennifer's boring boyfriends, who were either computer nerds with glasses and pens in their shirt pockets or Young Republicans. Brian was different, unique. That was what had attracted her to him in the first place. He had transferred to her school in middle of their senior year, and the first time she saw him he had taken her breath away. Here was this gorgeous guy with a ponytail sitting on the campus steps playing a guitar when everyone else was in class. Laura had been on her way to an appointment with her counselor.

"Shouldn't you be in class right now?" she blurted out, instantly feeling like an idiot.

He looked at her with raisin-dark eyes, eyes that somehow smoldered with dark inner lights. "It's government," he said. "I don't believe in government. I'm an anarchist. I believe in freedom for the people."

"Oh, right," Laura stammered. "Well, gotta go."

She could see he was smiling at her embarrassment. She could feel him watching her all the way across the quad. She couldn't stop thinking about him all day: he was so different, so free-spirited . . . and so sexy!

They finally got together when Laura was helping with costumes for the spring play and Brian had the lead. She hadn't thought she'd ever have a chance with him; he seemed so sophisticated and just out of her league, but he had one really quick change in the second act, and Laura had to help him. The tension of tear-ing off one outfit and shoving him into a new one in twenty seconds flat had made them laugh, creating a bond between them, so that he went right over to her at the cast party. "Anytime you want to tear off my clothes again, just let me know," he said, his dark eyes challenging hers.

"I'll do that," she countered, smiling, her heart beating fast at the way he was looking at her. He didn't leave her side all evening. She had never met anybody like him: He was a very talented actor, as well as a talented musician and poet, but he hadn't decided what he wanted to do with his life yet, he told her. He was just going to live one day at a time. If he felt like going to Moscow tomorrow, he'd go. To Laura, whose life was made up of such petty concerns as what she should wear to school and whether or not she would pass English comp., he was like a visit from the gods. He was heading for Europe after school, he told her. He might stay there a month, a year, or a lifetime. He hadn't made up his mind yet. But he wanted to experience Life with a capital *L*. He didn't ever want to be tied down to the dismal routines of job and suburbia.

"Come with me," he whispered, nuzzling at Laura's ear. They had driven out to the beach on Brian's motorcycle. Behind them the surf was pounding, and the wind tangled their hair together as they sat among the dunes, wrapped in each other's arms.

"To Europe?" Laura was scared and excited at the same time.

"Why not? We're great for each other, Laura," he murmured, easing her back onto the sand. "And the beaches aren't cold in Spain. Imagine making love in warm moonlight. . . ."

Laura had never wanted to do anything so much in her life. She was facing the bleak prospect of two years at junior college, while her parents spent the rest of their money paying for Jennifer to be brilliant at Berkeley. So she thought, "Why not"?

"I'd learn a lot more in Europe with Brian than I ever would at a boring junior college," she told her parents. "I'd be experiencing *Life*. I'd know what I really wanted to do and I'd be able to make valid choices."

"Valid choices," her father growled. "What sort of future could you look forward to if you don't start off with a decent college degree?"

"What good is a college degree? You got one and you don't even have a job," Laura snapped back. She regretted her words instantly, but she didn't know how to say so as she watched her father's face go blank with hurt.

That was when Grandmama Helen came up with her invitation to England. She wanted Laura to see where the family's roots were, she'd said. Her parents said it was a wonderful opportunity and she should definitely go. She said she'd rather be in Spain with Brian, and her father said over his dead body. Unfortunately she had no money to pay for her air ticket to Europe with Brian, and a month in England was definitely better than a month with two overstressed parents and a brilliant sister, so she agreed to go. Her secret hope was that Brian would come and save her, sweeping her away to a beach in Spain.

The train slowed to a halt at yet another little station. There was a dollhouse-size waiting room on the platform, edged with curly wooden trim and bordered with geraniums. The sign said TREADWICK.

Grandma jumped up. "Ah, here we are," she said.

Laura followed her down onto the platform. Other people were disembarking too, but they were looking around as if not sure which way to go, while Laura's grandmother strode out to the white picket gate at the far end.

"Come along," she said. "We'll take the shortcut across the field."

At the end of the station yard, a sign pointing through the trees said FOOTPATH TO TREADWICK HALL.

Laura sighed. "Not another old house!" she said. "What could there possibly be at Treadwick Hall that I haven't already seen at Buckingham Palace and Greenwich Palace and every other crummy palace?"

Grandma Helen smiled an enigmatic smile. "You'll see," she said.

The path led through a stand of trees. It was soft underfoot and smelled sweet and fresh. Birdsong echoed through the treetops, and they walked in dappled sunlight.

"At least it's not raining for once," Laura admitted grudgingly. "Are we going to be spending all afternoon looking at armor again?"

"Just wait and see," her grandmother said, still smiling annoyingly. Then she stopped with a wistful look on her face. "There it is," she said. "That's Treadwick."

They stepped out of the trees into a wide meadow. There were horses grazing, their manes blowing in the breeze, and at the far end of the meadow was an elegant gray stone house. It was built in an E shape with wings at either end and a pillared porch jutting out to make the middle stroke of the letter. There were stone balconies at the upper windows, and carved stonework decorated the lower windows. Laura looked at it without interest. It was not as big or impressive as some of the monuments she'd already seen but more like the sort of home a movie star would have built in California.

"So?" she said, bored and eager to get the whole painful process over with. "What's this house famous for?"

"This," Grandma Helen said, not taking her eyes off the house for a second, "used to be my home."

"You're joking," Laura said, giving her grandmother a sideways glance.

"Indeed I'm not," Grandma said. "This is Treadwick Hall, my family home. Your ancestral home, Laura."

Laura's mouth twitched in an uneasy grin. She still wasn't completely convinced that her grandmother wasn't kidding. The English had an odd sense of humor, she knew that.

"Come along," Grandma said, picking up the pace again. "We want to be in time for the three o'clock tour."

"You mean you have to pay to go on a tour of your own house?" Laura asked. "You would think they'd let you in for nothing whenever you wanted."

Grandma Helen shook her head. "Unfortunately new people bought the house a couple of years ago," she said. "I knew the previous owners but I have no knowledge of these people at all. I don't know what they've done to Treadwick or what we shall find. We'll just have to see."

She strode out so eagerly that Laura could hardly keep up with her. In spite of her gloomy mood and her determination to have a miserable time, she found herself smiling fondly as she watched the tiny woman in her mid-seventies striding along in military fashion, her face glowing with anticipation, and she told herself to shut up for the afternoon. "If Grandma really believes it was her house, then I should go along with the fantasy."

The path through the fields came to an end and they found themselves in a big courtyard at the front of the house. Just as they arrived a bus drew up and people streamed out of it. It was the first hint that Treadwick Hall wasn't a normal private house anymore.

Grandma Helen sighed. "It costs so much to keep these big houses going that they have to be turned into tourist attractions to support themselves. And to think in my day we had about ten maids and five gardeners and coachmen and stable boys. Half the village worked for us and that was considered normal."

Laura wondered if her grandmother was fantasizing again. "Then how come we're not rich now?" she said.

Grandma sighed. "Ah, it's a long story," she said. "I'll tell you sometime but not now. Now is the time for remembering how we lived in our glory days, when all this was ours."

Grandma Helen took Laura's hand and led her up the front steps behind the party from the bus.

"This way for the tour, ladies and gentlemen," a young woman was saying. "Pay at the ticket booth on your right, and the tour starts at the bottom of the stairs."

"Go and tell them that this was your house and see if we can get in for free," Laura whispered.

Grandma shook her head. "I've no wish to make a fuss," she said. "We'll pay like everyone else."

They bought tickets and joined the crowd in the high-ceilinged entrance hall. The large number of people made surprisingly little noise, everyone speaking in hushed voices, as if they were in church. They were clearly overawed by

the grandeur, the marble pillars, the giant portraits, and the inevitable suits of armor.

Laura nudged her grandmother. "Did your
father ever wear this stuff?" she whispered.
"Which suit was his? Did they make minisuits
for the kids?"

Grandma shot her a disapproving look as the
tour guide began to speak. The tour was pretty
much like all the other tours they had been on:
boring facts that meant nothing to Laura.

"Treadwick Hall was the home of the Treadwick family for over two hundred years. The
house was built by the third viscount Treadwick
in 1725 and the family continued to improve
upon the house until they sold it in 1929."

"Aha," Laura thought, smirking to herself.
"Grandma's name wasn't even Treadwick. It
was Henderson. I bet if she lived here, she was
one of the maids' children."

They passed through the salon with its elegant brocade-covered sofas, gilt-framed mirrors,
and huge marble fireplace, then the wood-pan-
eled morning room with leather armchairs and
hunting pictures on the walls. Then came the
dining room with a polished table long enough
to sit sixteen people, decorated with ornate silver candelabras. They were shown the dumb-
waiter—the little elevator that brought up
dishes from the kitchen—and then they toured
the dark, cavernous kitchens and the library,
with walls lined with matching leather-bound
books, and its little gallery reached by a spiral

staircase. When they came out of the library they continued up the curved stone staircase.

"Along this gallery you will see most of the family portraits," the tour guide said. "Some of them were painted by the foremost painters of the time. You will note the elegant rendition of Lady Emma Treadwick by Sir Joshua Reynolds."

"Big deal," Laura thought. Faces sneered back at her from the walls of the gallery, all very much the same sort of face—podgy, spoiled, expressionless, or smirking in a self-satisfied sort of way. *If they really are my ancestors, then I'm glad I don't take after them.* Not that she believed for a moment that she could have any connection with those powdered wigs and tight waists and fish eyes that stared back at her. She turned away from the ornate frames on the wall and let her gaze wander along the gallery, wondering what was behind the doors they hadn't been shown and where all the little side passages led.

"And now, ladies and gentlemen, if you will follow me into the East Wing, we will be coming to the Royal Suite, so named because the Prince Regent once stayed . . ."

The tour swung to the left and disappeared down a side hall. Grandma Helen went with them, her eyes not leaving the portraits for a second. Laura didn't follow them. She stood, transfixed, while the crowd flowed around her, jostling her and muttering as she got in people's way. The noise of feet and murmuring voices died away, and Laura snuck down a passageway in the opposite direction. She had just seen something quite unbelievable: From the shadows of a side hallway, a face was looking at her— her own face. For a moment Laura believed it must be a trick of the light and that it was a cleverly placed mirror in a golden frame. But as she stood in front of it and had time to examine it closely, she saw that it wasn't a mirror. It was a portrait. She felt the back of her neck prickling and her skin creeping as the eyes looked down at her. They were humorous eyes, slightly mocking, as the girl smiled as if she knew a joke she wasn't about to share. Laura had often seen that smile when she brushed her hair in front of the mirror and had to laugh at the hopelessness of ever getting it to go where she wanted. The portrait even had her own flyaway, untamable curls. One curl was escaping from the neatly arranged cascade. Everything was the same—the same reddish gold tint to the hair, the same green-flecked eyes, the same freckles on the nose that even a generous shake of white powder couldn't conceal. The only thing that was different was the dress. This girl was wearing a green velvet ballgown with a high waist and an indecently low neckline that exposed half her breasts. In one hand she held a fan. In the background, French windows opened onto a terrace and lawns. A spaniel was sitting at her feet.

"Incredible," Laura said to herself, now over her initial fright. "*Obviously I have an ancestor who looked just like me. Wait till Grandma Helen sees . . ."* She broke off in mid thought as she saw the writing on the small brass plate at the bottom of the frame: LAURA SUTCLIFFE, PAINTED BY SIR JAMES HARCOURT, 1808.

"Laura?"

Laura started as she felt the light touch on her arm. She looked around, half expecting to see one of those ladies from the portraits in old-fashioned costume come to life. But it was only her grandmother, standing in the empty hallway beside her, dressed in Grandmama contemporary: pleated blue skirt, white blouse, and the ever-present white cardigan.

"I wondered where you'd got to," she began. "Why, child, what's the matter?" she continued, looking at her with concern.

"I've just seen my portrait on the wall," Laura said flatly. "I thought it was just someone who looked like me, but she's even got my name. I don't understand, Grandma. I'm really freaked out. I mean, how can someone have painted my portrait back in 1800? You don't believe in reincarnation, do you?"

Helen Sutcliffe patted her granddaughter's arm. "There's nothing supernatural about it, dear," she said. "You saw a portrait of your ancestor and namesake. There was another Laura Sutcliffe. She was the one who started the whole thing . . ."

"What whole thing?"

"The whole story of the Sutcliffe diamonds,"

19

Grandmama Helen said. "She was the first of the Sutcliffe women who followed her heart and not her duty." She looked at Laura steadily. "The Sutcliffe family breeds strong women, Laura, but not always wise women. All the troubles that have come our way have been because we've been too headstrong to listen when our hearts have been involved. We don't always fall in love with the right men, Laura."

Laura glanced at her grandmother. She was wondering if the old woman was just using this as an opportunity to lecture her about Brian.

"You married the right man, didn't you?" she countered. "You and Grandpa Jimmy always seemed very happy."

Helen Sutcliffe smiled. "We were very happy," she said, "but it was only by a twist of fate that I married him. I might easily have made the same mistake as all the others . . ."

Laura wasn't really listening. "What were you saying about diamonds?" she asked. "The Sutcliffe diamonds, you called them. What were they?"

Helen smiled. "Only a legend now, I'm afraid, but within the family it's always been told that we once owned an incredible diamond necklace that came from Queen Marie Antoinette of France."

"And what happened to it?" Laura demanded.

Grandma Helen nodded wisely. "We might still have owned it if it hadn't been for Laura and her love for that scoundrel Roland. . . ."

CHAPTER TWO

LONDON. 1808

"How do I look, Emma?" Laura Sutcliffe framed herself in the doorway of her sister's bedroom and struck a dramatic pose. She was wearing a ball dress of dark green velvet, and her auburn curls tumbled loose over pure white shoulders. "Do you think I'll be the belle of my own coming-out ball?"

Emma Sutcliffe looked up from her vanity. She was trying to decide where to attach a beauty spot to her face.

"You look beautiful, Sissy," she said with true admiration in her voice. "The dark green really does wonders for your coloring. It brings out all the gold highlights in your hair and it matches your eyes. You'll have all the men fighting duels to dance with you tonight."

Laura made a face. "Our dear new mama tells me that I'm too thin—all skin and bones, and no man of taste will be interested in me, but I don't believe her." She came over to perch on her sister's chaise longue. "If you want to know, I believe she's jealous that all the men won't be fawning over her tonight. I might be skinny, but I have curves in all the right places."

"Laura!" Emma exclaimed in horror.

Laura laughed at her sister's expression. "I do," she insisted. "That old lord what's-his-name couldn't take his eyes off my cleavage at dinner the other night. I thought his eyes were going to drop into his soup." She paused as Emma started giggling. "And Roland Marshall certainly finds me desirable. I can tell from the way he's always correcting my fencing stance by putting his arms around me and maneuvering me into position. You should see where his hand lingered yesterday!"

"Laura, don't talk like that, it's not lady-like," Emma whispered. "Roland isn't a gentleman. He's only the fencing and dance master, not of our class at all."

"Oh, pooh," Laura said. "All this nonsense about who is a gentleman and who isn't. Roland can't help it if he was illegitimate. His father is as highborn as ours, only he can't acknowledge Roland as his son because of all the fuss it would cause at court. Anyway, I don't care. He's the most handsome man I've ever seen, and I'd rather have him make love to me than any of those stuffy old bores who are bound to be there tonight."

"Laura, please don't talk that way," Emma pleaded. "If Celia were to come along, you'd get into terrible trouble."

Laura frowned. "Celia isn't my real mother. She can't tell me what to do."

Emma sighed. "Unfortunately she can. You're not twenty-one for two more years, and until then she can rule over you as much as she likes."

The two girls exchanged a long, sad glance.

"I wish Mama had been alive to see you at your own real ball," Emma said softly. "She'd have been so proud."

"Do you miss her as much as I do, Sissy?" Laura asked.

Emma nodded. "Every minute. And if you find a husband tonight and move away, I don't know what I'll do all alone here with *her.* I can't understand what Papa sees in her. He must be blind."

"She's very clever, Emma," Laura said. "You have to give that to her. She snared him when he was still grieving for dear Mama. Now she's got him wrapped around her little finger and she won't rest until she has complete control of him and his money." Laura reached across and covered her sister's hand with her own. "But don't worry. I wouldn't leave you here. Wherever I go, I'll take you with me. I'll tell any future husband that I'll only marry him if there's a place for my sister too."

"Oh, Laura," Emma said. "What would I do without you?"

Laura laughed, shrugging off her sister's embrace. "Maybe you'll be the one who finds a husband tonight, not me. Then you'll have to take me with you."

"Oh, no," Emma said. "That wouldn't be right. You're older. You have to get married first. I'll get my ball next year."

"If Celia hasn't spent all of Papa's money by then," Laura said. She stood up and went over to the mirror, examining herself critically. "What this dress really needs is the diamond necklace," she said. "Don't you think I could wear it, just this once? After all, it is ours."

"But we promised Mama," Emma said. "We told her we'd keep it hidden unless we really needed it. Remember when she was dying she kept talking about it?"

"I remember," Laura said. "She kept murmuring that it was in the new doll, as if we didn't already know that. It was lucky Father didn't overhear or understand, or he'd have probably turned it over to the French government by now."

"If Celia hadn't got her hands on it first," Emma said in a low voice. "That's why we must continue to keep it hidden, dearest Sissy. It must remain our own little secret, for Mama's sake."

She broke off as there was a rustle of skirts in the hall outside.

"Laura?" came their stepmother's sharp voice. "Laura, I hope you're not trying on your new dress again when I gave strict orders that you weren't to touch it until this evening . . ."

She appeared in the doorway, a once-striking woman whose generous young curves were giving way to middle-aged plumpness and whose mouth showed lines of discontent. Her face was a perfectly made-up mask, but her eyes darted around the room, missing nothing.

"I put it on to show my sister," Laura said calmly.

Celia clapped her hands. A maid came scurrying from a nearby bedroom. "Daisy, take Miss Laura back to her room and help her off with the dress," Celia said. "Knowing you, it's a wonder you haven't already ripped it climbing out of a window or spilling tea all over it. It's time you grew up, young woman. That dress cost a lot of money—"

"My father's money," Laura interjected, "and I'm sure he was delighted to spend it on me."

"Only so that he could make a good match for you as soon as possible, and so that you will no longer be an expense," Celia shot back. "Now off with you."

As Laura walked down the hall, she heard Celia say to Emma, "Your sister sets a very bad example to you. I'm glad you haven't inherited your mother's French temperament. I'm sure it will be far easier to find you a husband when your time comes."

Laura didn't wait to hear any more. She tossed back her auburn curls defiantly and strode ahead of her maid down the hall. She toyed with the idea of slipping away to show Roland her dress. She knew he'd approve. His eyes would wander down her naked shoulders and linger at the lace on her bodice. She let fantasy take over, imagining that he would grip her bare shoulders with his strong, artistic hands as he drew her toward him. "That dress drives me mad with desire," he'd whisper. "I can no longer deny my emotions. I don't care that you are a lady and I'm only the fencing master. I want you . . ."

"Stand still, miss, while I slip off the dress," Daisy said, her rough hands taking the place of Roland's as she unbuttoned the bodice. Laura sighed. Everything was so difficult. She wasn't looking forward to tonight. She knew she was expected to find a husband from among the men assembled by her father, but she couldn't think of any one of them that she wanted in the way she wanted Roland.

Ever since he had come to Sutcliffe Hall as fencing master last year, Roland had set her pulse racing. He was different from any man she had met before, quite unlike the languid, stuffy gentlemen or the coarse slow peasants who had been the only men in her life until now. Roland spoke with a smooth, gentleman's voice, but he didn't behave like a gentleman. He had told her himself that he was dangerous. He'd had to flee for killing a man in a duel over a woman. He looked at her with frank, passionate stares, and sometimes his hands lingered on her body when he corrected her fencing stance. When he spoke to her his words often carried delicious double meanings that made her heart race. So far there had been only brief stolen minutes alone together at the end of a lesson or a ride, before Celia sent a servant looking for her. Not that her stepmother suspected what was going on in Laura's head or she would have dismissed Roland by now. Laura waited patiently, knowing that one day they would be alone and then he would take her in his arms and fulfill all her fantasies. . . .

Laura sighed as the maid slipped her day dress over her head. If only one of her suitors tonight could be like Roland, she'd be looking forward to her ball more. She knew all the men who had been invited, and she found them equally boring and unattractive. Was it possible that any gentleman her father approved of could ever make her feel the way Roland did? She twirled away from the maid's clumsy hands. "Leave me alone. I can finish this for myself," she said impatiently.

The maid backed away. "Very good, miss," she said. "I'll be back to help you with your ball dress at six."

Laura looked at the dress hanging on her wardrobe. Tonight she'd be wearing it and all eyes would be on her. And she was still young and hopeful enough to pray for a miracle. "Maybe there will be a last-minute entry to the marriage sweepstakes," she thought. "One of the guests will bring along a foreign cousin, and he'll be quite as handsome and dashing as Roland, and he'll sweep me off my feet!"

*   *   *

Laura's eyes were still bright and hopeful as she was escorted into the ballroom on her father's arm that evening. The ballroom looked as magical as she had dreamed. The chandeliers were glittering with a thousand candles. Jewels sparkled from bare necks, and the men looked tall and handsome in their white silk breeches, their cutaway coats, their bright uniforms, and their powdered wigs.

As the ball progressed, however, Laura had to admit that her afternoon fantasy was not likely to come true. Almost all the eligible men from London and the south of England were assembled in the Sutcliffe ballroom, and not one of them set Laura's eyelashes fluttering.

"Look at them, Sissy," she whispered to Emma between dances. "I'd wager that not one of them can even hunt decently. They certainly can't dance. Lord Darcy trod on my toes during a minuet, and one stands so far apart in that dance that it should be impossible!"

Emma smiled in commiseration. "If only the duke of York's son were here," she said. "I understand he is very dashing."

"He's away with the army," Laura sighed. "I'm sure all the most eligible young men are away fighting that tiresome Napoleon. All we're left with is the middle-aged and the lame ducks."

Her eyes scanned the twirling couples, and she sighed again at the truth of her words. "I do think Papa might have managed a German prince or two," she said. "There must be one or two good-looking foreign princes who are just dying to marry an English rose."

"Laura, I've been looking everywhere," came her stepmother's voice. She grabbed Laura's arm. "You are neglecting your duties as hostess. I've arranged to have Viscount Treadwick escort you in to supper. The Treadwicks have very large estates near Gloucester, and the viscount is a most amiable man."

Laura did not think the viscount at all amiable. He was overweight and middle-aged, his cheeks very red in contrast to his white powdered wig. There were bags under his eyes as he examined her, inch by inch. "Damn fine dress, Miss Laura," he said in a loud, braying voice. "It certainly becomes you. If I had a painter on hand, I'd sit you down and have you painted right now."

"Surely not before supper, Viscount?" Laura said sweetly, her gaze sinking to his middle.

He didn't detect the sarcasm. "Well, no. I'm not the sort of man to say no to a good meal," he said. "I understand I have the honor of escorting you."

He took her arm, and she allowed herself to be led into the banqueting hall, conscious of his sweaty, pudgy fingers squeezing the flesh of her forearm. All through dinner she was polite but aloof, laughing at Lord Treadwick's jokes only when she felt that it was absolutely necessary and letting her gaze wander around the table to see if there were any less boring men seated nearby. The viscount talked between mouthfuls about his travels to Italy, his close friendship with the king, the improvements he had made to Treadwick Hall. Laura had fallen into a trance of boredom and only came out of it enough to hear him say, "Of course, what it needs now is a woman's touch. I can't play the gay bachelor forever, you know. Got to think about settling down and producing an heir."

A jolt of alarm shot through Laura's head. Surely he couldn't be hinting that he wanted her to produce the heir for him? She tried not to shudder, praying for the meal to end so that she could excuse herself and take her turn with other dance partners.

The night dragged on and on, but she only had to dance with Lord Treadwick once more. This time she was so frostily polite that she hoped he had gotten the hint that she was not interested. She even flirted outrageously with a young officer as they danced by where Lord Treadwick was sitting, even though the young officer was almost as boring and talked about nothing but the latest campaign.

"Just as I thought," she confided sadly to Emma as they said good night to the last of the guests. "No prince charming to sweep me off my feet. Celia will be angry that she's stuck with me a little longer."

"I'm sorry you didn't meet anybody you liked, Laura," Emma said gently. "Surely someone better will show up during the London season. Maybe the duke of York's son will come home from the army campaign. . . ."

"Something's got to happen, Sissy," Laura said, gripping her sister's arm, "because I'm not going to marry any dreadful old bore! When I marry it will be for love, and I can only love a man who is exciting." She didn't add "like Roland," but his picture came into her head as she said the words.

The next morning her father called her into his study.

"Well, Laura, a very successful evening," he said, looking pleased with himself. "And it has produced a successful outcome too. You've had a proposal."

"Oh, really?"

"Lord Treadwick has asked me for your hand."

"Lord Treadwick?" Obviously she hadn't been rude enough to put him off. "That stuffy old bore," she said, laughing. "He described, brick by brick, about how he added another wing onto his house."

"Lord Treadwick is a wealthy, respected man," Edward Sutcliffe said, giving his daughter a serious stare. "You could do worse."

"But Papa," Laura was still laughing, not sensing as yet any danger in the situation, "I'm sure I could also do better. He must be all of thirty-five, and pompous with it."

Edward Sutcliffe interrupted his daughter, holding up his hand to her. "You didn't let me finish, Laura," he said. "I was going to say that Lord Treadwick asked for your hand, and I accepted on your behalf."

Laura gazed at him in open-mouthed horror. "No, Papa, you can't have done such a thing. I can't believe it of you!"

Edward Sutcliffe's expression didn't change. "When you come to know him better, I'm sure you'll find that you two have a lot in common, Laura," Edward said. "He loves to hunt, for one thing. You could ride together."

"Father, I don't wish to know him better and I certainly don't want to marry him. How could you have thought that I would? Please think of my happiness and don't make me marry that man," Laura begged, her voice softening.

"I *am* thinking of your future happiness, child," Edward said. "I know of your extravagant tastes. You need a rich, powerful husband, Laura. Anyway, my mind is made up on the matter."

Laura's voice grew hard. "*She* made up your mind for you on this, didn't she?"

"She?"

"You know perfectly well of whom I'm speaking," Laura said, eyeing him coldly now. "Our dear new stepmama. She hates me. She wants me out of the house as soon as possible, and she wants influence at court. She has you bewitched, Papa."

Edward Sutcliffe's voice rose in anger as his face flushed. "What rubbish, child. This was my decision, and I'll abide by it. And I'll tolerate no more rudeness from you. To your room, miss, and start studying how to be a good wife!"

Tears welled up in Laura's eyes as she ran from the room. She felt as if she were in the middle of a horrible nightmare. It couldn't be true—surely her father cared about her happiness. He couldn't want to condemn her to a life with Lord Treadwick just because the man was rich and powerful.

"That woman," she thought. "It's all her fault. She's bewitched him. She'd do anything to get us out of her hair. Well, I won't do it. I won't let them. . . ."

"Laura, what's wrong?" Emma's voice echoed down the marble hallway.

Laura pushed past her blindly.

"Laura, Sissy, dearest. . . ." She heard Emma calling after her, but she couldn't stop. She just had to get away, to escape, to get her thoughts in order. She kept on running, out of the house, across the courtyard. Then she struck out onto the footpath that led to Treadwick village. She had no clear idea where she was going, just the blind panic that if she stayed close to the house they would come for her and drag her off to be married right away.

A barking dog brought her back to her senses, and she saw that she was on the little path leading to the estate cottages. Roland lived in the first one, a pretty little thatched house with roses around the front door. She had to see him, even though it would mean trouble if anyone found out. Celia would definitely marry her off instantly if there was any hint of an attachment to Roland.

Attachment to Roland! Laura sighed. That was what she wanted more than the whole world. And more than anything she wanted to see him now, to be held safe in his strong arms. Roland would know what to do, Roland could save her if anyone could. . . . She began to run again, praying that he'd be home.

As she came through the last of the beech trees, she could see him sitting reading in his garden. His dark curls fell across his forehead, and in his white fencing shirt and black pants he looked just like a painting of a romantic poet. Her heart lurched and she called out his name. He looked up, startled, as Laura wrenched open his front gate.

"Why, Laura, what is it?" he asked, forgetting to use any title of respect before her name. "What has happened?"

"Oh, Roland, I've just come from Papa. He's told me I've got to marry Lord Treadwick," she gasped.

A smile crossed Roland's face. "You could do worse," he said. "I hear he's frightfully rich. You could take me with you as your fencing teacher and send your husband out hunting all the time. I understand he loves to hunt."

Laura looked hurt and horrified. "I couldn't stand for that horrible man to touch me, Roland. I'd rather die than marry him! How could you even suggest such a thing." She started crying again. She was hurt and confused. She had expected him to take her into his arms and promise to make everything all right.

Roland came over to her and put his hands on her shoulders. "There now, little one, don't cry," he said. "It may never happen. Treadwick isn't young. Insist on a long engagement and he may die before the wedding day. If you make the engagement last for two years, you'll be twenty-one and able to decide for yourself."

Laura moved toward him and nestled her head against his shoulder. "Oh, Roland," she whispered. "There's nobody in the world I want to marry except you. I know you feel the same way about me that I do about you. Hold me tightly."

Roland glanced around nervously to see if anyone was watching them. Then his arms slid around her until she was wrapped in his embrace. She could feel the coarse black hair of his chest scratching her cheek, the fresh, manly smell of his body. As she raised her face toward his, she saw him looking down at her. His dark eyes were cloudy with desire. "You know I want you, Laura," he whispered. "I've always wanted you." His lips crushed against hers in a demanding kiss. His hands slid down her back as he pressed himself closer against her. Laura moaned deep in her throat. This was what she had been dreaming about, this was the passion and fire she wanted in her life.

When they broke apart they were both breathing heavily.

"Take me away with you right now, Roland,"

she begged. "Let's just run away from here and never go back."

Roland smoothed back her hair with his hand. "If only that were possible, my love. But where could we go? We're penniless, you and I. You're a powerful lady and I'm a nobody. We're trapped by what we are."

"But you can't let me marry Treadwick," Laura pleaded. "Promise me you won't let me marry Treadwick."

"I'll do everything within my power," Roland said, "but you must be patient, my sweet. We can't just run off and live like peasants in Italy or Spain."

"Why not?" Laura demanded. "I understand Italy is very beautiful." She could picture it so clearly—a castle on a cliff overlooking a beautiful bay of deep blue water. There would be wisteria growing over the shady porch, and she would stroll with Roland through the orange groves, hand in hand, or sit at his feet while he played a guitar . . .

"Because you were not born to live like a peasant," Roland said. "You like your beautiful clothes and your jewels."

"Jewels!" Laura exclaimed. The diamonds! She had the diamonds! "Roland, there may be a way out for us after all!"

She broke away from him and began running back toward the house. She heard him calling after her, "Laura, where are you going? What's wrong now?" But she didn't stop.

CHAPTER THREE

"Laura, what are you doing?" Emma asked for the fourth time, following her sister as she sprinted up the back stairs to the old nursery. "Laura, please tell me what's going on."

"Not until we're safely shut away," Laura called over her shoulder. She was consumed by an irrational fear that Celia had somehow come upon the diamonds and that they would be gone.

"Come inside, quickly," Laura commanded, glancing back down the hall before she shut the door behind them. She looked around the room at all the dear old familiar objects: the big rocking horse, the two matching doll cradles, Emma's well worn, her own hardly touched, and the collection of dolls on the high shelf. In the middle was the most beautiful, ornately dressed china doll.

"She's still there where we put her," she said, breathing a sigh of relief.

"Who is?"

"The queen's doll, of course," Laura said. She reached up to take down the grandly dressed doll.

The head came off without much difficulty,

and Laura withdrew the little velvet bag in which her mother had placed the stones. "Here they are, Sissy," she said breathlessly, "the answer to my prayers."

"What are you talking about, Laura?" Emma begged. "Please explain what's going on and what you're doing with the diamonds."

Laura had tipped the sparkling necklace into her hands as she sat on a low nursery chair. She looked up, her eyes glowing. "I expect they've told you by now," she said.

"They told me that you are to marry Viscount Treadwick," Emma said, puzzled. "I didn't expect that the news would make you so happy. You're not going to give him the diamonds, are you?"

Laura shook her head impatiently. "You're such a ninny sometimes, Emma," she said. "Of course I'm not going to give Lord Treadwick the diamonds, nor am I going to marry him. I'd rather die than marry him."

"Then what?"

Laura looked steadily at her sister. "I'm going to run away," she said.

"Laura! Where would you go? What would you do?"

A slow smile spread across Laura's face. "I'm going to marry Roland and live in Italy or Spain," she said.

"Roland?" Emma looked horrified. "You're going to marry Roland? Laura, please be sensible. He's not the sort of man to marry."

"Because he's beneath us, you mean?" Laura asked scornfully.

"No, because I don't think he's completely trustworthy," Emma said. "He's dangerous, Laura."

"How would you know? What do you know about men?" Laura demanded, her cheeks flushing.

Emma's gray eyes were troubled. "I don't know much, it's true, but I have a bad feeling about this, Laura. I've heard rumors. Roland has fought duels over women before now. He had to get out of France in a hurry. He likes to live dangerously."

"I know that, Emma, but so do I," Laura said. "We're made for each other, Roland and I. And he adores me. We could have a good life together, if only we had the money." She let the diamonds spill through her fingers, one perfectly matched round stone after another and then the huge teardrop queen stone at the center, lying heavy in her hand. They caught a shaft of sunlight coming through the high dormer window and sent rainbow sparkles across the nursery walls.

"You're going to take the diamonds," Emma said flatly.

Laura looked at her sister's face, and her own expression softened. "Only if you say I may," she said. "Mama meant them for both of us, although I'm sure you won't need them. You'll be the good child and make a perfect marriage and live happily ever after."

Emma ran across to her sister and knelt beside her. "Take me with you, Laura," she whispered. "You promised you wouldn't leave me here alone with her."

"But Emma, dearest, if you come with me, you'll ruin your own chances of a good life," Laura said gently. "You'd be an outcast like us. No one of class would ever want to marry you. You're not like me, Emma. You couldn't be happy living on the fringe of society. You belong in polite drawing rooms." She took Emma's hands in hers. "I want you to be happy, Emma."

Emma's lip trembled. "I won't be happy stuck here alone with Stepmama," she said.

"She likes you better than me," Laura said. "She thinks you're the docile one. I'm sure she'll find you a delightful husband as soon as I'm out of the way. After all, she won't have to pay for two weddings, will she? She can go to town on yours."

"But what if I don't like the man she chooses?" Emma said. "I'll have nobody, Laura. You have Roland. I'll have nobody."

"Then you must have your own insurance," Laura decided. "Remember what mother said when we were little? She said the stones were our insurance, to give us power in our lives." She stood up and with a sharp tug she broke the gold chain that held the diamonds together. The central stone, an exquisite ten-carat beauty, fell to the floor. The two halves of the necklace hung limp in Laura's hands.

"What have you done, Laura?" Emma asked in horror. "You've ruined the necklace."

"They're just stones, Sissy," Laura said. "We'd have to break up the necklace before we could sell the stones anyway. We'd never be able to sell it whole—it would be recognized! As it is, I doubt that we'll be able to use the big stone. It would call too much attention to itself." She held out her right hand. "Here. Take your half. I'll feel better knowing that you have your way of escape if you should need it. Go on. Take it. And the center stone too!"

Haltingly, Emma reached out and took the string of liquid fire.

"Keep your half in the doll until it's needed," Laura said. "If you really can't stand it here any longer or they want you to marry a man you hate, then come out to join us on the Continent."

"You're not going right now, are you, Laura?" Emma asked, her voice breaking with emotion.

"As soon as Roland can make arrangements," Laura said. "Nobody must suspect a thing, Emma. If Celia gets a whiff of our plans, I'm doomed."

"I won't say a word, Sissy," Emma said. "I truly want you to be happy, and I really hope that Roland is the right husband for you. I hope he'll take care of you and cherish you the way you deserve."

"Emma, I'm not a porcelain vase. I don't need to be taken care of and cherished," Laura retorted, tossing back her head proudly. "I want excitement. I want to live. You say that Roland is dangerous and you're right, but that's what attracts me to him. There's nothing else I want more than to be with him. I'll be counting the hours until I can be in his arms, Emma. I must go and tell him right away so that he can start making plans for us." She grabbed her sister and spun her around. "Oh, Emma, I'm so excited. My life is about to begin!"

She danced ahead of Emma down the stairs and outside, to find Roland, who was up at the stables, about to mount his black mare.

"Oh, you're going for a ride, how splendid," Laura said. "I'll come with you." She signaled the groom. "Thompson, saddle up Blackbird for me immediately."

The groom bowed and went into the stable. Laura could feel Roland's inquiring eyes on her.

"Why the sudden urge to go riding?" he murmured.

"You'll see." She flashed him a mysterious smile, then swept past him as the groom appeared with her horse. A stable boy came running up to assist her onto the mounting block. She pushed his attentions aside, swung easily into the saddle, and they set off.

"You seem in a more cheerful state of mind than when I last left you," Roland said. "Has Lord Treadwick died in the meantime?"

"No, but I've found a solution to our problem," Laura said. "I'll tell you when we're safely away from here." They had reached a gravel drive between the trees. "Come on, let's gallop," she said. Without waiting for a reply, she spurred her horse forward. Gravel sprayed up from the flying hooves. Roland laughed and urged his horse after her. Side by side they galloped, until the gravel drive became a pathway between the trees. Abruptly Laura reined in her horse. "She seems to be running a little lame, Roland," she said. "Help me down so I can take a look at her feet."

He slid from his own mare, then came around to lift her from the saddle. His arms lingered on her body long after she had touched the ground.

"Which foot is it?" he asked.

"Foot? What foot?" Laura said innocently.

He laughed, his eyes flashing. "You little minx," he said. "There's nothing wrong with your horse's leg, is there?"

"Only if somebody comes past," Laura countered, wrapping her arms around his neck and laughing into his eyes. "I had to feel your arms around me again, Roland. And to tell you the news . . ."

"News, what news?"

"I've wonderful news—I've found a way that you and I can be married."

"Married? You and I?" She felt him tense as he held her.

"You do want to marry me, don't you?"

He ran his tongue around his lips. "Of course, if it were ever possible, but . . ."

"But now it is possible, Roland. I've just remembered a certain little legacy we can use. . . ."

He shook his head. "I don't think, my love, that a little legacy can keep you and me in the style of life we both like."

"You don't think so?" she asked. She put her hand inside her bodice and calmly drew out the velvet bag, shaking the diamonds into her hand. They caught a sunbeam shining through the beech leaves and shot fire around the clearing. She heard Roland gasp, and she laughed, deep in her throat. "I would have thought that stones like this would purchase quite a fine country house in Italy, with a maid and cook thrown in, and provide quite a good life for me and any man I chose to take with me. . . ."

He grabbed her wrist, holding her so tightly that she cried out in pain. "My God, Laura, where did you get them—they're magnificent!" Roland exclaimed. With his other hand he took the stones and held them up so that sunlight sparkled on them. "Your father would be in a rage if he found you had smuggled them out of the house to show me."

"My father knows nothing about them, and is to know nothing about them," Laura said proudly. "They are my legacy, from my mother, to use as I see fit. And I see fit to use them for my happiness." She took them back from him, put them into the pouch again, and deliberately stuffed the pouch back into her bodice, noting with delight his eyes on her. "So what do you say, my dearest?" she whispered, entwining her arms around his neck.

His arms slid around her waist. "I'd say that we could live very happily ever after," he said huskily. He bent his head and began nuzzling at the exposed white flesh of her neck. Laura gasped with pleasure and pressed against him. This was how she had imagined it in all of her fantasies. She had no clear idea of what came next, but her body knew. The ache for him was becoming overpowering. "Oh, Roland," she whispered, "take me now. Let's make love here on the grass."

"You're crazy, my sweet," he whispered. "This is neither the right time nor place. A stone's throw from your father's house with gamekeepers prowling around? No, my love, we must be patient."

"But I don't want to be patient," Laura said. "I want you to love me."

Roland laughed uneasily. "It's supposed to be the man who leads the woman astray, not the reverse," he said. "You're a fiery little thing. I can see that I'll have my hands full with you."

"But you won't be bored, will you, Roland?" she whispered, rubbing her body against his, like a cat.

"Definitely not bored," he whispered. The temptation was too much for him. He began kissing her again, his lips crushed against hers, his hands sliding down her body. A noise in the undergrowth made them jump apart hastily, fearful of being discovered, but it was only a cat, and they both laughed at their fear.

"Maybe you should give me the stones for safekeeping," he said with casual ease as he helped her remount. "Then I could go ahead and find us a house in Italy."

Laura looked down at his dark, handsome face. She put her hand to her bodice to take out the stones, then lowered it again. She found herself remembering what Emma had said, that he wasn't entirely trustworthy. She had denied it then, but now she had to admit she wasn't completely sure. She knew so little about him. Maybe he wasn't trustworthy, but that was part of his danger and excitement. "I'll keep the stones until we're married," she said calmly. She urged her horse forward, leaving him standing in the dappled shade, watching her with admiration on his face.

"You will tell me, won't you, Sissy?" Emma whispered as the two girls strolled beneath the spreading chestnut trees that dotted the Sutcliffe park. It was a hot, sultry August day, two weeks since Lord Treadwick's proposal, and the strain of continually acting the part of the new fiancée was beginning to tell on Laura. She had been so determined not to give herself away that she had endured long talks with Celia about her bridal gown and her trousseau and even an intimate dinner with Lord Treadwick, after which he had taken her out on the terrace and presented her with a magnificent string of pearls. He had insisted on fastening the pearls around her throat and it had required every effort of willpower not to shudder at the touch of those pudgy fingers lingering on her flesh.

"Tell you what?" Laura asked, twirling her parasol impatiently.

"When you plan to leave with Roland. I

don't want to wake up one morning and find you gone."

Laura took her sister's hand. "It might be better that way, dearest. Then you can answer with all honesty as they interrogate you—which they are bound to do."

"But I want to say good-bye," Emma said. "We may never see each other again."

"It probably won't be for a while. Roland has a friend in Italy right now. He's written to him but no answer yet. Roland wants to find us a suitable house before we leave. He thinks I won't be happy unless it's a lovely palazzo, although he's quite wrong. I'd be happy in a hovel with him. And I'd be happy to run away tomorrow. I hate all this waiting around and being pawed by Lord T." She looked up at Emma, a mischievous smile on her face. "But I suppose there is a good side to it. The longer I'm here, the more expensive presents old Treadwick might give me. The pearls were quite delightful. I must say he has good taste, for all his ugliness."

"He's not ugly, Sissy," Emma said. "He's just not another Roland."

Laura let her parasol fall to her feet. "There could never be another Roland, Emma," she said with an ecstatic sigh. "Oh, Emma, I can't tell you what it's like when I'm with him. We've only had the briefest moments together, but the way he kisses me. . . . I feel as if I'm on fire. I can't wait until I can belong to him body and soul."

"How will you take your things with you when you go?" Emma asked.

Laura sighed again. This time with frustration. "That's my biggest problem," she said. "I do love my dresses, and I can't see any way of taking even half of them with me. I can hardly slip out with more than one trunk."

"You could start carrying items down to Roland's cottage one at a time in your flower basket, and he could ship them down to London," Emma said.

Laura looked surprised. "Why Emma, I believe you could be as scheming and devious as me if you wanted to," she said, laughing. "But only small items. I couldn't take any of my ball gowns that way."

"Maybe I could send them to you after you've gone," Emma suggested.

Laura flung her arms around her sister. "Emma, you are the sweetest, dearest sister in the world," she said. "You're willing to risk so much for me."

"I'd do anything for your happiness," Emma said softly. "I know Mama wouldn't have wanted you to marry a man you didn't love."

Laura kissed her on the cheek. "Sweet Emma," she said. "I hope you fall madly in love one day and find someone as gorgeous and desirable as Roland."

Emma looked away, blushing. "I don't think someone like Roland would be right for me," she said. Then she looked up suddenly. "Did I hear Papa say that Lord Treadwick was coming this weekend?"

Laura wrinkled her nose. "He's been invited for three whole days. You must promise not to leave my side for one instant, Sissy. I don't want to find myself alone with him."

"I'm sure that's what he's coming for," Emma said with a knowing look.

"Then he'll go home disappointed." Laura tossed back her hair and put her parasol firmly over her shoulder again as she strode out across the grass so fast that Emma had to run to keep up with her.

From her bedroom in the East Wing, Laura saw Lord Treadwick's coach arrive. She watched him get out, portly and pompous, and she watched Celia and her father come down the steps to welcome him.

"Don't forget, Sissy," she said as she found Emma in her own room. "You promised you wouldn't leave me alone with him for a second."

"I'll do my best," Emma said. "I imagine they'll summon you down any second."

But half an hour passed and still nobody came for Laura.

"They're obviously thrashing out all the business details," Laura said, peering out the window at the rain that was just starting. "How many maids I get and how much clothing allowance. How terribly boring and what a waste of time. . . ."

The girls looked up as they heard heavy feet

coming down the hallway. That would be Funston the butler. Laura got up and sighed. "The lamb to the slaughter," she said, and made an attempt at a bright smile as she left Emma.

Lord Treadwick was sitting with Edward and Celia in the study as the butler ushered Laura in. He had a large whiskey in his hand and looked very genial. His face lit up as he saw Laura. She smiled politely at her fiancé. Now that she knew she didn't have to marry him, she decided that he wasn't such a bad old thing after all.

"We have been making plans, my dear," Edward said. "Do sit down."

Laura sat. Celia leaned across the table. "Lord Treadwick tells us that he does not want a long engagement, Laura, and we quite agree with him. You are ready for marriage and so is he. If we can get those wretched dressmakers to work nonstop, I think we can have your dress and train ready by the end of the month."

"The end of the month?" Laura stammered. Roland's friend would not have had time to find them a house by then. She wouldn't have time to smuggle out her clothes.

"I'm not getting any younger, Laura my dearest," Viscount Treadwick said, "and I'm growing impatient for you. Treadwick House awaits your pleasure. We'll be married from Treadwick church. I've already spoken to the vicar. Your sister and my young nieces will be your attendants. A simple wedding, but tasteful."

Laura kept the fixed smile on her face. Her lips

were pressed tightly together. She was scared that if she tried to speak, her voice would give her away.

"So you can start packing, Laura," Celia said, sounding triumphant.

"Packing?" Laura's voice shook.

"We leave for Treadwick with the viscount when he goes home on Tuesday. Since you are to be married from there, we'll have flowers and decorations to arrange, as well as fittings for the wedding dress."

As soon as she could, Laura sped up the stairs to find Emma.

"You have to help me, my sweet," she said. "They plan to send me to Treadwick Hall on Tuesday. That only gives me three days, Emma. You're more sensible than I—help me go through my clothes and decide which will be suitable for a simple life in Italy. And you're so good with your needle too—I want all my jewels sewn into the lining of my cloak. They'll be safer that way."

Emma glanced nervously toward her half-open door and hurried across to close it. She came up to Laura and put her hands on her sister's shoulders. "I'm frightened for you, Sissy. I wish you didn't have to go."

"I have no choice, dearest," Laura said. "Once I'm at Treadwick I'll be a prisoner. It's now or never. Promise you'll help me."

"I'd do anything for you," Emma said earnestly. "You're the only person in the world I truly care about, Laura. I don't know what I'll do without you, but I'll be very brave because I want you to be happy."

Impulsively Laura kissed her. "My darling sister. I love you too. I want you to be as happy as I'm going to be. As soon as we're settled, you can come and stay with us. Who knows, we might find you a handsome Italian count!"

Both girls wiped away tears as they laughed. Then Emma went up to Laura's boudoir to begin sewing while Laura went to find Roland. He was in the fencing room, and he looked up as her feet tapped across the polished wood floor.

"It's now or never, Roland," she whispered. "You must go to London right away and arrange for somewhere for us to hide until we can find a safe passage across the channel to France. And someone who will marry us without asking too many questions."

He looked at her warily. "All of this will take money, Laura."

She pressed one of the diamonds into his hand. "Take this," she whispered. "It should cover our immediate needs, don't you think?"

He stared at the glittering stone in his palm. "More than cover," he said. "And the rest of the stones?"

"I'll find a way to bring them with me safely. I'll be leaving on Monday night. You must arrange a place for us to meet and get a message to me."

He looked at her steadily. "At your service, my lady," he said.

"Not your lady much longer, Roland,"

Laura whispered. "Soon I will be your wife."

She reached up to brush his lips with a quick kiss. "Take care, my love," she whispered.

"You too," he said as she turned and ran from the room.

That night Roland slipped away under cover of darkness, leaving a note in his cottage that he had gone to visit a dying aunt in Ireland.

Back at Sutcliffe Hall, Laura played her part superbly all weekend. She went out riding with Viscount Treadwick. She sat next to him at a banquet in his honor. The gracious smile never left her face. She heard Viscount Treadwick tell Celia that he had had no idea he was getting such a little treasure for a wife, and she smiled secretly.

Then on Monday night Laura begged to spend the evening alone with her sister. "We're soon to be separated and it breaks my heart to know she'll be far away from me," she said.

"Nonsense, my dear," Viscount Treadwick said, patting her hand. "She'll be welcome to come and stay with us anytime. We'll have a suite of rooms kept at her disposal year-round."

"You're very kind," Laura murmured, "but it won't be the same. You see, since our mother died, we've had only each other."

"Then of course you must spend a quiet evening together," Viscount Treadwick said. "I mustn't be selfish about wanting your company every minute. Run along now, and my compliments to your sister."

Back in her chambers, Laura changed into drab traveling clothes.

"I do hope they have good dressmakers in Italy," she said to Emma, looking at the pitifully small traveling bag she was taking with her, containing only the essentials for her toilet and her plainest dresses and undergarments. "But it's two miles to the stagecoach stop, and that's all I can carry."

"I can always send you more, once you're settled," Emma said.

Laura put on her cloak. "You did a wonderful job with the lining," she said. "Nobody could ever tell . . ."

The two sisters stood facing each other.

"This is it, then," Laura said at last. "I must be on my way. If anyone asks you, I developed a bad headache and I went to my room to lie down."

Emma nodded solemnly, her eyes brimming with tears. "Good-bye, Laura, and God be with you."

"Good-bye my dearest, my precious sister," Laura said. "May God be with you too. Say a prayer for me every night, and I'll do the same for you."

They embraced for a last time; then Laura put up her hood, picked up the bag, and slipped down the back stairs, out into the chill, starlit night.

CHAPTER FOUR

"Roland, where are you taking me?" Laura whispered as they turned into a dark alleyway. It was late at night and this wasn't at all the London she knew. Her family's town house stood on a fine square with well-kept gardens in the middle and carriages passing. But when Roland had met her from the stagecoach at Charing Cross, he had taken her east, toward the slums that clustered around St. Paul's Cathedral. The streets had become narrower and dirtier. There were no carriages here. Instead, ragged children looked up from the gutter and men pushed handcarts laden with produce through the crowd, shouting in coarse, cockney accents and darting sharp, distrustful looks at Laura's fine clothes. She pulled her cloak around her, fighting to keep calm.

"Don't worry, my dearest. Trust me," Roland said, reaching back to take her hand. "There is an innkeeper I know at the Pig and Whistle on Cratchborne Lane. We'll be safely hidden there until we take our coach to Dover in the morning."

Laura looked around her and shuddered. "Just a little longer," she told herself. She would be brave. The next few days would be full of strange experiences, but she was a Sutcliffe, she could handle anything. And at the end of it all, she'd have the reward of eternal happiness with the man she adored.

Roland took her bag and set off, melting from the broad street to the maze of alleyways behind Covent Garden. They had passed the vegetable market with its smell of rotting vegetables underfoot and had then come to this dockside quarter where Roland had said they would be spending the night.

"How much farther? I'm so tired," Laura murmured.

He looked down at her, and the harsh lines melted from his face. "Almost there," he said gently, stroking her cheek. "I'm sorry to put you through this, but we have to be safely hidden before your father comes looking for us. This was the only place I knew. It's just at the end of this alleyway."

The alleyway smelled foul, and rain dripped from the rooftops above. As they passed, a window opened and something came splashing down, almost on their heads. Laura grabbed Roland's arm tightly.

"Cheer up, my love, here we are," Roland said, indicating a light ahead. "A good supper at the Pig and Whistle will soon put you to rights. And then a cozy room above, just big enough for two . . ."

"But we won't be married until tomorrow," Laura said. "What will the landlady think?"

Roland smiled. "I've registered us as Mr. and Mrs. Banks," he said easily. "I thought it a wise precaution if anybody comes looking for us."

Laura said nothing, fighting her disappointment and fear. She had been longing to find herself in Roland's arms, but she had never imagined it would be in a situation like this—a squalid little tavern on an alleyway that smelled of garbage and decay.

"Think of Italy," she told herself. She closed her eyes and recalled the house she had invented during the long coach ride. She must be brave until they were safely out of England.

The landlady gave her a funny look as she carried the bags up the stairs. "Not the sort of place you're used to, my pretty," she said, showing a mouth of blackened teeth.

"Oh, yes, we often stay in places like this as we travel back to our home on the Continent," Laura said. "My husband is a musician, and money is not always plentiful."

The old woman grinned to herself as she put the bags down. "There's pie and ale in the parlor, or would you rather I had something sent up to you?"

Roland looked at Laura's face and nodded. "That would be very acceptable," he said. "Here, take this for your trouble." He threw her a coin, and she bowed as she left. It was a cramped little room with a sloping ceiling, one small bed, and a rickety table. Laura suddenly felt that her legs wouldn't carry her any longer, and she sat down on the bed. It creaked in protest.

"I expect we'll be able to look back at this and laugh when we are living in our Italian castle," she said bravely, and managed a weak smile.

He nodded encouragingly. "We'll be safely across the channel by tomorrow night," he said. But he went across to the window and pulled back the blind, scanning the alley before letting it fall again. The landlady soon returned with a tray of steaming meat pie and two mugs of ale. Laura ate halfheartedly while Roland seemed to be enjoying every mouthful.

"An early night, I think," Roland said as the dinner tray was carried away. He saw Laura look at the bed with apprehension. "Don't worry, my sweet," he went on, before she could say anything, "I want your first experience with me to be one of ecstasy, and I hardly think that this is either the time or place. You will sleep quite safely in my arms."

"Oh, Roland," she said, going to lean her head against his chest. "Are we quite insane to be doing this?"

"Would you rather be in Lord Treadwick's arms tonight?" he asked playfully, nuzzling her cheek. "I'm sure he's a lusty lover. He'd approach the bed the way he does his hunting . . ."

Laura began to laugh, relaxing in his embrace. All the same, she could not bring herself to undress in this strange situation. She lay at the edge of the bed, conscious of Roland's body beside her, and prayed for sleep to come. At last she must have drifted off because she woke to hear someone moving in the room. She reached out her hand and felt an empty space where Roland had lain.

"Roland?" she called anxiously.

"Right here, my love. Go back to sleep. I was just looking for a powder for my headache," he said, and came back to bed. Laura closed her eyes but could not shake off the uneasy thoughts flying around inside her head. One of these thoughts whispered that Roland had been searching for the diamonds. Surely Roland would never . . . she told herself. But she wasn't completely sure. She had never been completely sure. As she had said to Emma, it had been this quality of danger that had attracted her to him in the first place. Back at Sutcliffe Hall it had seemed exciting, but now that he was all she had in the world she needed to know that she could rely on him to protect her. She felt him get back into bed beside her. He slipped an arm around her shoulders.

"Don't worry," he whispered.

She felt the warmth and comfort of his arm and tried to relax. She must put aside these childish worries. If Roland was going to be her husband, she had to trust him!

She had drifted into sleep again when she was woken by raised voices.

"They're not here, I tell you! I swear I've got

no one of that name here! No, you can't see for yourself! Be off before I call the nightwatch."

There was the sound of scuffling and curses, then heavy feet on the stairs, and the door flew open.

"Not here, you say!" the intruder said, bursting into the room. He held a lamp in one hand and he shone it on the bed. Laura recognized him. He was a servant from her father's London house. "They're up here, Jolly. Fetch the lads. Go tell the master!"

"Not so fast," Roland said. He leaped from the bed and snatched up his sword. "Laura, leave by the window. There is a way down from the back of the building. You know where to meet me in the morning. Stay hidden until then. Go, I tell you!" His voice rose as Laura hastily fastened her cape and took her bag.

"Don't go, Miss Laura. It will be the worse for you," the servant begged.

"One step nearer and I'll be obliged to run you through," Roland threatened.

The servant drew his own sword. "Put that down, Mr. Marshall. It won't do you no good to resist," he said. "My lads will be here with the master and the Bow Street Runners. You're in deep enough trouble already."

"And ready to face even deeper if you try to stop us," Roland said.

The man made a halfhearted lunge. It was clear he was no swordsman. He swung his blade wildly. Roland countered and the blade went deep into the other's chest. He gave a little sigh and fell to the floor. Laura had remained frozen, standing on the little area of flat roof outside the window, watching in horror as the scene unfolded. As the servant fell to the floor she screamed, "Roland, what have you done?"

Roland pulled out his blade. "Get going, foolish girl, or you'll be the death of both of us."

Laura plunged into darkness, feeling the parapet wall in her hands. She climbed down from one level to the next until she was able to jump from a shed roof to an alleyway. She had no idea where she was or where she should go. All she had to do was stay out of sight and out of danger until the morning. She crept past back doors and evil-smelling heaps of garbage. Dogs leaped, barking, from chains. At last she came to a street she recognized. She and Roland had come this way. Shops were still open, and the sound of singing came from an open tavern door. She pulled her hood over her face and tried to blend into the evening crowds. At a busy crossroads she stopped to watch an organ-grinder and his monkey. Children were laughing and everyone seemed happy. The organ-grinder had almost finished his performance when the sound of galloping hoofbeats made the crowd leap out of the way. A black wagon, pulled by four black horses, came thundering past. At the back was a barred window, and as Laura looked up at it, she saw Roland, holding on to the bars as he looked out in desperation.

"Please, where are the prisoners being taken?" she asked the man standing next to her.

"Eager to witness a hanging, are you, miss?" he said, laughing. "He'll be held in Newgate Jail until his trial. Then the execution will likely be on Ludgate Hill."

Laura swallowed hard. "Are all prisoners executed?"

"The lucky ones, miss. The lucky ones," the man said, and melted into the crowd.

Laura passed a long, terrible night, walking the streets of London. She was weak with fatigue and cold and half ready to go to her father's house and throw herself on his mercy. But she couldn't abandon Roland. In the morning she bought herself some breakfast with the last of the money she had taken with her and pawned her pearl necklace. The man at the pawnshop didn't even ask where she got it. He heard by her accent that she was a lady of quality and obviously assumed that, like many of her sisters, she had become pregnant and been cast from her family.

"That's all I can give you, miss," he said with genuine sympathy in his face. "Times is hard."

"That's all right," Laura answered, secure in the knowledge of the diamonds in her cloak lining. She'd have to do some research before she decided where to sell those for the best price. Roland would probably know. If only she could see him, talk to him. He must be feeling so desperate and hopeless, she thought. She imagined him shut in a cell with pickpockets, murderers, thieves. If only she could find a way to get him released. . . . She wondered if judges could be bought, and for how much.

As she moved through the city she was always conscious that her father's men would be out looking for her. She slipped into a second-hand store and bought herself the sort of clothes that would blend into this part of London. Then she took a room at a small, clean boardinghouse off the Strand and hung around the law courts at the Old Bailey, finding out as much as she could about how the trial system worked. She made friends with others who waited, hopelessly, for their loved ones to come to trial. One of them was an Irish nursemaid called Molly. Her sweetheart had been part of an uprising in County Cork.

"Likely he'll be sentenced to Botany Bay," the girl said, tears running down her cheeks. "They say 'tis a terrible place, and no returning. Ach, if only I could go with him to ease his burden there."

Laura looked at her in horrified admiration. To admit it was a terrible place with one breath and to want to go there with the next showed a fierce and loyal love. Did she feel that for Roland? Was she ready to die for him?

"Of course I am," she told herself. "It's my fault that he's in jail. I can't abandon him now, whatever happens next."

After that she made sure she spent all her time with Molly, gradually picking up her accent and her identity. An Irish nursemaid could hang around the law courts without suspicion. She didn't try to see Roland in jail because she was sure her family would be alerted to her visit, so she waited, one day of unreality merging into another, until she finally found out the date for Roland's trial.

"I wouldn't have too much hope, miss," Molly told her. "They usually hang for murder."

Laura swallowed hard but said nothing. What would she do if Roland were executed? Would she be prepared to crawl back home and beg for mercy? She didn't think so. But where else could she go? Only fallen women and governesses were alone in the world. She missed Emma so much at that moment. Emma would be able to comfort her. But Emma was out of reach, out of reach in Laura's former life at Sutcliffe Hall. . . .

Roland came to trial on a brilliant spring day of glass-blue sky and puffy white clouds. From her hiding place in the shadows, Laura watched the police wagon draw up. Roland looked thin and drawn, but the hollow cheeks only seemed to emphasize his beauty. She had to stop herself from running to him.

Laura slipped into the back of the courtroom at the last moment, her face and hair hidden under her hood. In the crowd she saw her father, sitting with his steward and servants, so she remained hidden, close to the front door. Witnesses were called.

The jury didn't take long to decide that Roland was not guilty of murder, but guilty of manslaughter. Laura let out her breath when she saw that the judge did not put on his black cap when he returned from his deliberations. The black cap was always worn to pronounce sentence of death.

"I agree with the members of the jury that you did not intend to take a life," he said. "Nevertheless, a life was taken while you were on the run from the law. You are not the sort of citizen we want back on our streets, corrupting young girls and using your sword to settle arguments. Therefore I am sentencing you to deportation to our colonies at Botany Bay in Australia for life. I hope that hard work and fresh air will make of you the sort of man God intended."

Time seemed to be frozen for Laura. The words *Botany Bay* echoed through her head. It was a terrible place, Molly had said. Nobody returned from it. As if she were watching something happening very far away, Laura saw the judge rise from his seat and depart. She watched the guards jerk Roland to his feet and begin to lead him from the courtroom. He seemed dazed, stumbling forward with a blank expression on his face. Laura could bear it no longer. She took the risk and ran up to him as he came out of the door.

"Roland, my love," she cried.

He turned dark, haunted eyes on her, eyes

that were full of despair. "Get away from here, Laura. Go back to your old life."

"Tell me what I can do to help you, Roland," she begged. "I'll do anything."

He shook his head sadly. "There's nothing more you can do for me," he said. "I'm doomed, Laura. Forget about me. Go home."

The crowd began to file out of the courtroom, talking and laughing as if they had just witnessed an entertainment. Laura glanced back, remembering that her father was in that courtroom. But she couldn't let Roland go.

"I love you," she called. She wanted to touch him one last time. But the guards pushed her aside as they led him out to a waiting wagon. The iron door slammed shut on him and he was gone. Laura stood in the doorway of the Old Bailey, staring down the street. Then she remembered what Molly had said.

"There *is* something I can do for you, Roland," she muttered. "I can follow you to Botany Bay."

CHAPTER FIVE

"My dearest sister,

By the time you read this letter, I will be far, far away from you. My heart breaks when I think, dearest Emma, that I may never see you again, but I am doing what my heart and duty dictate. Roland risked his life to save me and I cannot desert him in his hour of need. He is being sent to the colonies, dear Emma—banished as a convict to Botany Bay in distant Australia.

I shudder when I think of it, and yet I have made the decision to go with him! I don't want to go, believe me. My heart trembles when I think that I may never see England's green countryside, London's elegant streets, or your smiling face again, and yet I am prepared to risk all for the sake of the man I love.

The only free settlers who can secure a passage are healthy young men and young families, but they are allowed to take servants with them. That was my salvation, Emma. I overheard a young mother lamenting that the children's nursemaid could not be induced to follow them to Australia, so I stepped in to offer my services. Not as Laura Sutcliffe, of course. I am now Molly O'Brien, young Irish lass longing to join her Shamus who was deported in the uprising—don't laugh, Emma. I've been practicing and I'm rather good at it. Now all I have to do is convince Mrs. Catchpole that I can take care of her precious children. What can be hard about that? After all, I was a child myself once—and a naughty one too!

Please pray for me that good may come of this: that I may be allowed to marry my Roland and ease his burden of loneliness and despair.

God grant you a happy, tranquil life, Emma. May we meet again in this world or the next. Your ever-loving sister, Laura."

On October 12, 1808, His Majesty's ship, the transport *Norfork*, slipped from her berth at Tilbury docks and made her way slowly down the Thames estuary. The wharves and waterfront houses receded as the wind caught her sails and the mighty Thames opened into the English Channel. Laura stood on board, her cape wrapped around her for warmth, the diamonds still safely concealed in its lining, trying to take in every feature of the English countryside. It was a gray, cold day, and the trees and empty fields seemed to echo her despair.

"Say good-bye to England, Bobby," she whispered to the little boy at her side. "I doubt we'll ever see this shore again."

The *Norfolk* was a former slave ship, converted to transport convicts. There were only five other free settlers traveling with the Catchpoles, all young men who shared a cabin. The rest of the ship housed a hundred or more convicts. Laura wondered if, by some miracle, Roland might be on board. If so, it would be too good to be true. But she had heard that all the prisoners held with him in the holding hulks at Woolwich had already been shipped out. She tried not to think of those poor men, lying in irons down in the hold, but now and then cries and groans rose up through the open hatch and she imagined Roland down there. It was almost more than she could bear.

As the sea wind took the sails, the ship sprang to life, surging forward, creaking and groaning as she strained against the breeze.

"Don't worry, she's a fine, sturdy ship," said a voice behind her. Laura looked around to see one of the five young male passengers smiling at her. "The captain says she can take whatever the Atlantic wants to give her. We'll be in Australia before you can say Jack Robinson," he added in a broad West Country accent. He had the friendly, open face of a farm boy, with bright blue eyes and rosy cheeks, and he was looking at her with a hopeful smile.

Laura eyed him haughtily and opened her mouth to tell him not to speak to his betters, when she remembered. She was simple Molly, the nursemaid. These people were now her equals and her only companions. But she was still lady enough not to want to encourage an overfriendly farm boy. She nodded politely. "I think it's getting too chilly up on deck for the little one," she said, picking up Bobby. "Please excuse us if we go down below."

The next time the young man nodded when he passed her but didn't attempt to speak to her again. On the third day south they came to the Bay of Biscay, notorious for its sudden storms. The stiff breeze became a howling wind, and the little ship shuddered with each mountainous wave. Mrs. Catchpole became very seasick and demanded constant attention from Laura. Until that moment she had been fairly easy to please. Now it had finally dawned on the woman that she was being taken halfway around the world, far from everything she had known, and she began to take her fear out on Laura.

"Don't do that, stupid girl," she snapped. "Watch the child, not me." And then, two seconds later, "Where is the flannel I asked for to wipe my face? All you want to do is play with the children."

As the cabin became more foul-smelling they went up on deck. "Put Master Bobby's coat on, foolish girl," she snapped to Laura, thrusting a coat at her. "Not like that! Really, you are the most useless, no-good creature on God's earth." She lifted her hand to strike Laura when the young farmer intervened.

"Pardon me, ma'am, but anyone can see

the young lady is weak with seasickness herself. She's trying to do her job but she can hardly stand. Maybe I can help you with the little one. I've precious little else to do."

"Very kind of you, sir," Mrs. Catchpole said. "Go and lie down if you must, girl," she snapped to Laura. "But make sure you recover quickly. I didn't bring you to do all the work myself."

Laura escaped to the cabin, but after dinner that night she sought out the young man as he stood up on deck, watching the stars. "Thank you for what you did today," she said. "It was nice of you to stand up for me."

He looked at her solemnly. "I couldn't bear to hear that old cow, if you'll pardon the expression, talking to you that way."

"What is bringing you to Australia?" she asked him, smiling.

"Well, I heard there was land for the taking in Australia, as much land as a man could want, and I thought, why not? There weren't much for me in England," he continued. "I'm the fourth son and never likely to get a farm of my own."

"You're very brave," Laura said, looking at him with frank admiration. She'd always taken the farmhands on the Sutcliffe estate for granted, as much part of it as the cows and sheep. She hadn't ever thought that they might have feelings like her own and she was ashamed of her narrow, snobbish upbringing.

"No," he said, "I'm very proud. I don't like

the thought of working another man's land all my life. I want to be my own master and to make my mark on the world."

"But won't it be very lonely?" Laura asked.

"At first, I suppose," he said. "But I thought, if I succeed, then I'll come home and look for a bride—or maybe find myself a bride in the colony. There are more free settlers coming all the time. It will be a grand place to live one day, you'll see."

"I hope you're right," Laura said. "From what I've heard, it is only one step better than hell."

"For the convicts, I daresay," he said. "I don't suppose they're enjoying the voyage too much either, poor devils, chained down below while we're up here, enjoying the fresh night air."

Laura shivered. "It must be terrible for them," she said, her thoughts going to Roland. "Don't they ever let them up on deck?"

"When we're safely far from land," he said. "They'll start bringing them up, a few at a time, to scrub the decks, if they behave themselves."

Laura drew her cloak around her, imagining Roland in chains, scrubbing a deck. "I should go back to the cabin to see if Mrs. Catchpole needs me," she said. "But thank you again, Mr.—er?"

"Farnworth, Jack Farnworth," he said. He held out his hand to her.

"I'm—Molly O'Brien," she said, wanting to tell him her real name but hesitating at the last second. She felt very much in need of a friend right now, someone she could really talk to, and she sensed that Jack Farnworth would be kind and sympathetic. But she couldn't afford to make the slightest slip. If anyone on board found out who she really was, she'd be shipped home from the nearest port. She had to keep up the pretense until they reached Australia.

"Pleased to meet you, Molly," he said. His hand was firm and warm as he shook hers.

After that they met frequently up on deck. They could hardly fail to meet—the deck area for the free settlers and crew was a small square forward of the mainsail, and the cabins were so small and foul-smelling that almost every second possible was spent in the open air.

As the days passed, they crossed the South Atlantic into warmer climates, and the ship flew before the wind to Rio. Convicts were brought up on deck, and Laura looked at them with uneasy interest, hoping and yet not hoping to see Roland among them. They were nothing more than ragged sacks of bones with hollow eyes and shaggy beards. Round their ankles were great bands of iron that clanked as they shuffled. They stood blinking in the sunlight as if they had forgotten that a real world existed. Laura wondered if Roland now looked like this.

In Rio the passengers were allowed ashore, and Jack bought a parrot, which delighted the children. Laura bought a bright cotton skirt, which was more suitable than her heavy English clothing. She put it on and twirled to the music of a guitar player. Jack stepped forward and began to dance with her, spinning her around while the onlookers clapped and shouted encouragement. Suddenly she was conscious of his hand around her waist. "I'm getting giddy," she said, feeling her cheeks hot with confusion. She felt guilty that she was enjoying herself, dancing with another man while Roland was suffering. But she couldn't shake off her delight at going ashore and seeing the bright tropical colors.

Everyone was in good spirits as they set sail again. There was fresh fruit and fresh meat, so different from the boring diet of salt pork and suet puddings the ship's cook usually served. But just out of Rio, the festive air quickly ended when one of the convicts tried to escape. He dived over the side with his leg irons still attached and would have drowned if two sailors hadn't rescued him. As a punishment he was given forty lashes. Laura kept the children below, but his screams echoed throughout the whole ship. When they went up on deck again, they could see his blood and flesh still spattered across the deck, although other convicts were scrubbing hard to clean it up.

Laura felt her stomach heave as she remembered the awful screams. She put her hand to her mouth and looked away.

"He was foolish to try and escape, poor beggar," Jack said, coming up to her and placing a comforting arm on hers. "Nobody can swim far in irons like those."

"Poor man," Laura said.

"He's probably used to lashings if he's a convict," Jack said with a sigh. "Most of them are hardened criminals, you know. In and out of jail most of their lives."

"That's not true," Laura burst out. "Some of them were innocent—fine men robbed of their freedom by bad luck."

He looked at her with interest. "You sound as if you have some personal knowledge," he said.

Laura nodded. "My fiancé has been shipped to Botany Bay," she said. "I'm going to join him."

"Ah," he said, nodding as he digested this. "I thought there had to be a good reason for a young lady like you going there. He's a lucky fellow to have such a devoted sweetheart."

Laura looked away. Tears were stinging in her eyes. "I just pray he's still alive," she said.

From Rio the ship picked up the southern trade winds to South Africa, and they took on supplies at Cape Town. No convict tried to escape this time, and they set sail again, knowing that there would be no port until they docked in Sydney Cove, more than six thousand miles away. The journey became one of terrible monotony, and Laura began to look forward to her talks with Jack Farnworth.

As they stood together on deck, staring out at the waves and sky, Jack would tell Laura his plans for the future. He'd start by growing vegetables for the colony from the seeds he had brought with him. If that went well, he'd send for a ram and a couple of breeding ewes. He knew a lot about sheep, and he'd heard that Australia had wide-open spaces suitable for grazing. He had drawn up plans for his farm, and he showed Laura his little book with its neat drawings and calculations.

Laura admired the way he could look at the clouds and tell what the weather was going to be, and she loved his self-sufficiency. If he needed something, he made it for himself. She told herself that he was the sort of person who was more likely to survive in the colony than either she or Roland. She worried about Roland a lot. When she tried to picture his face, it was blurred and indistinct, like a fading dream. This terrified her. "I'm going to be with him again soon. Everything's going to be all right," she reminded herself.

At last they reached Australian waters, and everyone on board was excited about journey's end. Convicts were brought up to scrub the decks. Sailors and soldiers mended their uniforms. Spare time was used by the travelers for leaning out over the rail, straining for another glimpse of the barren, rocky shore.

"Almost there now," Jack said to Laura. "This time tomorrow you'll be with your sweetheart and I'll be striking out to claim my own piece of land."

Laura nodded. She didn't want to speak in case her voice gave away her doubts and fears. Roland, she told herself. Roland was all that mattered. She'd heard that they let convicts marry and start little farms of their own after good behavior. Surely Roland had behaved perfectly. Soon she'd be in his arms and everything would be all right.

"I don't like the look of those clouds," Jack said. "If this were the Northern Hemisphere, we'd be in for a bad storm, but since these are coming from the south. . . ." He hadn't stopped to think that southerly winds came straight from the Antarctic snows. The southerly burst on them with a vengeance, snapping the main mast like a match and tossing sailors into the boiling sea. The captain tried to find a sheltered bay, but the sky and land had melted into solid sheets of rain. Laura pulled the children close to her, but Mrs. Catchpole snatched them away. "If I'm going to die, my children will die with me," she screamed hysterically.

As the clouds shifted, a rocky coastline could be seen not too far away. The ocean around them was studded with jagged rocks, and the *Norfolk* was being swept onto them. It hit with a judder that threw people to the deck. Water poured in and over everything.

The message to abandon ship spread like wildfire. The convicts struggled up on deck, eyes wide with panic as they realized that they had irons around their ankles.

"Quick, get the key!" Laura begged the officer in charge of them. "They'll all drown."

"I'm not waiting around to release a load of

scum like them," the man said, pushing Laura aside as he made for the longboat. Mrs. Catchpole had already been helped in by her husband and had her children on her knee. Laura refused to get on board, searching frantically for someone who would have a key to release the poor convicts from certain death.

"Molly, come on! The boat is ready to cast off," Jack yelled, grabbing her arm. "We've got to leave now if we're to have a chance."

"But these poor men . . ." Laura looked at the hopeless faces.

"There's nothing we can do for them. Come on!" He was wearing his thick tweed jacket and carrying his bundle containing his precious seeds. He took her hand and almost dragged her down the deck. As they reached the longboat, two sailors jumped in and launched it into the waves. "No, wait for us!" Jack yelled. His voice was lost in the howl of the wind. Waves washed over the deck as Jack held Laura tightly. "We have to get off before she breaks up completely," he said, looking around. The ocean was already full of driftwood. A spar from the mast came floating past. Jack grabbed Laura. "Take off your cloak. It will drag you down!" he yelled.

Laura hesitated. She wasn't yet ready to abandon the diamonds in the lining. "Jump, now!" he said. Laura gasped as she plunged into the icy water. She came up, spluttering, feeling the weight of her cloak dragging her down again. The mast was bobbing far ahead of her. She tried to swim, but the waters sucked at her clothing and she couldn't free her arms. Ahead she could see that Jack had already reached the spar. He looked back. "Molly, where are you?" he screamed. Already he seemed so far away, and the cold had numbed her. "You go on," she called.

"Don't be stupid!" He threw aside his bundle and swam back for her, strong strokes cutting through the water. In seconds he was at her side, dragging her patiently toward the spar. "Now hold on and don't let go until I say so," he commanded.

As Jack made for the shore, they could hear the cries of the convicts as their irons dragged them down. "There's nothing we could have done!" Jack shouted. "Even if we'd found a key, those irons are rusted shut. Try to swim. We're not far."

They scraped against jagged rocks. Laura swallowed mouthfuls of salt water. Her hands were raw, but Jack kept encouraging her and she held on. At last Laura felt her feet kicking against solid rock. They came into shallow water and staggered over a rocky shelf before collapsing among the first shrubs, where they lay panting and exhausted, trying to catch their breath.

"I wish I could build a fire for us, but I had to leave my tinderbox in my bundle," Jack said. "You're one big shiver." He rubbed her arms and legs, then wrapped her in a tight embrace.

"You saved my life," she murmured. "You left your precious seeds behind to save me."

"Nothing could be more precious to me than you are," he said.

They stared at each other in wonder, both just realizing what he had said.

"I mean it, Molly," he went on, boldly. "I'd willingly die for you. I can tell you that now, just in case we never make it to Sydney town. I know you love another, but I've loved you since the first day I set eyes on you, and if I die now with you beside me, I'll die content."

"Oh, Jack," she whispered. She laid her cold cheek against his chest. He didn't evoke the wild shivers of passion that raced through her body when Roland touched her, but she felt his warmth and strength creating a quiet glow. He had the will enough for both of them. He had got them to shore and she knew that his strength would keep her going. She closed her eyes and drifted to sleep in his arms.

Laura opened her eyes to see the cold light of morning on a desolate landscape—scrub and stunted eucalyptus trees stretched down to a rocky shore. For a moment she wondered where she was, but her stiff neck and damp clothing brought back the events of the past night and she sat up, looking around in alarm for Jack, frightened that he had gone off without her. Then she saw him, walking down on the shore, striding out purposefully among the debris. She got stiffly to her feet and went to join him.

"No sign of any other survivors, I'm afraid,"

he said, looking back at her tenderly. The ocean was calm now, and the *Norfolk* couldn't be seen, except for the driftwood and various household objects that littered the beach. Jack rummaged among them and dragged the most useful items up into a pile. "We'll come back for these if we get a chance," he said.

"What are we going to do?" Laura asked, shivering as much with fear as with cold.

"Walk, of course," Jack said. "Nobody's likely to come looking for us. We know that Sydney is north, so we'll walk north along the seashore. That way we'll see a ship if one comes."

"Maybe the longboat made it safely to shore and they're already sending out a rescue party for us," Laura said. Jack shook his head. "Likely as not they all drowned, poor devils," he said with a sigh. "I don't see any signs of a fire. Looks like we're on our own now, my dear." Laura looked out at the calm ocean, thinking of little Bobby and Sallie and their mother and blinking back tears.

They started walking. It was hard going, sometimes over jagged rocks, sometimes over tiring sand dunes. They never stopped until nightfall. Jack usually succeeded in making a fire and they sat beside it, talking. By the second night Laura found she could no longer lie to Jack and told him her true story. He was very quiet and reserved when she had finished. "What's wrong?" she asked.

"I'd rather not have known. A farm boy like

me could imagine himself in love with Molly from Ireland, but never with a fine English lady. You're too far above me, Laura."

"Nonsense," Laura said. "We're all equals here, remember. There's no above and below."

"I suppose it makes no difference, really," he said, staring past the flames into the blackness of the night. "You're betrothed to another man and you'll be with him again soon."

"Only thanks to you," she said. "I'd have died without you, Jack. You've given me another chance at life." She leaned toward him and kissed him gently on the cheek.

Ten days later, they stood on a sandy hillside and looked down at the jumble of shacks around Sydney Harbour. Jack and Laura faced each other awkwardly. "Well, I'll be off," Jack said, trying to sound casual. "I've got business to arrange and I know you're anxious to find your sweetheart again. I wish you the best of luck, Molly-Laura." He held out his hand to her. Laura took it. There were so many things she wanted to say to him. Instead, she acted like the lady she was brought up to be. She shook hands and smiled politely. "All the luck in the world to you too, Jack Farnworth," she said. Then she hurried on her way without looking back.

Laura picked her way through the mud to the new sandstone convict barracks. Horrible-looking unkempt men working in chain gangs leered at her as she made her way across the sopping ground. At last a helpful overseer took her to the barracks commander.

"Marshall?" he asked, looking to his overseer for help. "Marshall? Wasn't he the one?"

"I think so, sir. Let me check the records," the man said, thumbing through a thick book. He looked up and nodded. "Roland Marshall. That was him all right."

Laura could hardly make her tongue obey her. "Has something happened to him?"

"He bolted, miss," the overseer said.

"Bolted?"

"Took off, vamoosed," the overseer went on.

"He ran away?" Laura asked. A voice inside her head was whispering that Roland was free. "You didn't catch him?"

"No need, miss," the overseer said. "They never survive long in the bush. If the natives don't spear 'em, they usually come crawling back and take their beating. If they don't show up within a month, we reckon they're lost and died of starvation."

"And Roland?"

"He's been gone two months, miss. I wouldn't hold out any hope that he's still alive."

"Oh," she said, feeling faint. "Oh, I see."

She staggered back through the mud to the government buildings and sat on a sandstone bluff, overlooking the harbor. She tried to put her thoughts in order, but her brain was numb with grief. She had made herself focus on Roland for so long that it was impossible to plan out a future without him.

She was still sitting there, watching the sun set across distant hills, when Jack came up the hill toward her. "There you are! I had to find you and tell you the news," he yelled. "I got it. Best bit of land you could ever imagine: right on the Hawksbury River, as many acres as I want. And they can loan me oxen to plow." He saw her face. "Is it bad news?"

"He ran away," she said. "Presumed dead."

"Oh, I see," Jack said. He stared out across the harbor. "I'm very sorry, my dear. It must be a terrible shock to you, having come so far. . . ." She nodded, biting back tears. "So will you go back home again?"

"Another voyage like that? Not in a hurry," she said. "And what would I do back home? When I left, I left for good. I have no one back there, Jack."

"So what will you do?"

She looked up at him, noting every feature of that pleasant, hopeful face. It was the sort of face that would always be honest and never let anyone down—the right sort of face for this country. She knew that she didn't feel passion for him, not the way she had for Roland, but Jack made her feel warm and secure, and right now that was what she needed most. She gazed at him steadily. "I've no experience of farming," she said, "but I think I could learn to milk a cow and use a hoe as well as any young wife."

"What are you saying?" he asked cautiously.

"That your farm will be a lot of work for one person, and lonely too."

His face lit up. "Are you saying you'll marry me?"

"If you'll have me."

Tears sprang to his eyes. "Never in my wildest dreams would I ever have dared to ask," he said. "You've made me the happiest man in the Southern Hemisphere, Miss Molly-Laura, and I promise you, I'll be the best husband a woman ever had."

"There's something else you should know," Laura said. She led him to a sheltered spot under a big eucalyptus tree. "I brought these with me. I want you to have them to start your farm." She handed him the pouch containing the diamonds. Jack's eyes opened wide, but then he handed them back to her.

"I'm honored," he said, "but you keep them for a rainy day. The life I make for us is going to be made by honest hard work. That's just the sort of man I am. Take me or leave me."

"Then I take you the way you are, Jack dearest," Laura said. She slipped her arms around him and nestled her head against his chest.

The next morning they were married by the chaplain and set off with an ox wagon piled high for the lush land beside the Hawksbury where they were to start a new life together.

CHAPTER SIX

"And did Laura ever come back to England?" the present-day Laura asked her grandmother.

It was late afternoon, and the two of them were sitting in the shade of a giant chestnut tree on the grounds of Treadwick Hall.

Helen Sutcliffe shook her head. "She never saw her family again, but she lived a long and happy life with Jack Farnworth."

"So how do you know all this?" Laura asked. For a while she had been completely caught up in the first Laura's story, but now she was suspicious again, wondering if her grandmother had just made up this tale as a warning to her. Maybe it was all part of the family plot to convince her that Brian was wrong for her and could only lead her into trouble. But she'd never known that her grandmother could be so creative in her storytelling.

Helen Sutcliffe answered her inquiring gaze. "You ask me how I know?" she said. "I know because it's my family history."

"But if she never came back to England, how

does anyone know what happened in Australia between her and Jack Farnworth?" Laura insisted.

"She remained close to her sister for the rest of her life," Helen said. "They wrote long letters to each other, and Emma kept a diary. I've read them all."

"You've read the letters?" Laura asked excitedly. It was suddenly very important to her to see proof that this was not just a fairy story. She still hadn't gotten over the shock of seeing her portrait on the wall, and she felt strangely bonded to the first Laura, almost as if she had been reincarnated. Now she wanted to touch something that the first Laura had written, to feel it in her hands . . .

"And the diary," Helen said.

"You have them?"

"No, but I read them when I was a child and lived here at Treadwick. They were in a chest up in the attic. My sister and I used to sit up there for hours and read aloud from Emma's diary. It made our great-great-great-grandmother seem very real to us, as if she were still there."

Laura stirred as a tree root dug into her back. Out beyond the canopy of leaves she could see the fine outline of Treadwick Hall. Another busload of tourists had arrived, and the sound of voices drifted across the peaceful meadow. "What I don't understand," Laura said, "is how you could ever give up a lovely place like this. What made you sell it?"

Helen snorted. "I didn't sell it. I was just a

87

child when we moved out, and my parents didn't want to sell. They loved this place, but unfortunately, like so many of our ancestors, they were not very prudent with money. They lost a fortune in the great stock-market crash of 1929 and then, when my grandfather died, they had no money to pay the death taxes. So they had to sell and move into a little cottage instead. The shock killed my mother, and my father was never the same man. I was too young to realize what I was giving up. I didn't really miss Treadwick until much later. . . ."

"But didn't you take the diary and letters with you when you moved out?" Laura insisted.

"We didn't think about it at the time," Helen said. "We left behind all the furnishings. What use was all that enormous furniture to us in a two-bedroom cottage?"

Laura got to her knees, shading her eyes to get a better look at Treadwick Hall. "Do you think it's possible that there might still be stuff in the attic?" she asked. "The letters might still be there?"

"I doubt it, dear," Grandma Helen said. "It was all so long ago."

All the way back to London on the train, Laura was very silent. *"I have to see for myself if those letters are still there."* She knew the first Laura wouldn't have let a little thing like trespassing stand in her way. If Roland had been up in that attic, she'd have climbed up the ivy to reach him.

When they got back to their hotel she found a postcard from Brian waiting for her.

"Hope you're not dying of boredom. I've got my international hostel card and I'm ready to split. Must think of a way to get you out of the old bag's clutches. Stay alert, I'll be in touch. Love ya. Brian."

She read each word over and over, running her fingers down the card and lingering on "I'll be in touch." The thought that he would soon be on the same continent as her, and that he'd be coming to rescue her, sent shivers up and down her spine. She hadn't realized just how much she had been waiting for this card and how she longed to be held and kissed by him.

She thought about him that night as she lay in bed beneath the heavy eiderdown in the old-fashioned hotel room, listening to the muted roar of the London traffic as it sped along the Bayswater Road, past Hyde Park. The hotel was described by Grandmama as "respectable," but Laura thought it was only one step better than a dump. Even Motel 6 had better beds and showers! She turned over restlessly, hearing the bedsprings creak, and lay on her back, staring up at the high ceiling. She tried to remember every detail of her time with Brian, of the way his lips tasted and the way he looked at her that made her melt inside. But there was something else that was bothering her. Something that didn't quite make sense. Something to do with the visit to Treadwick. Suddenly she knew what it was.

"Grandma, are you still awake?" she whispered.

"I am now," Grandma Helen said, turning over and making her ancient bed creak.

"I was just thinking," Laura said. "We were at Treadwick Hall today, right?"

"Right."

"But Laura didn't marry Viscount Treadwick. She was a Sutcliffe. How come our ancestors lived at Treadwick Hall?"

"Ah," Grandma said. "I've told you Laura's story. Tomorrow I'll tell you Emma's."

CHAPTER SEVEN

SUTCLIFFE HOUSE, LONDON. MAY 11, 1809

"Dear Diary:

I miss Laura so much. Not a word from her since she left England. I don't know if she is alive or dead. I only pray that she is happily reunited with her Roland by now and that they will build themselves a fine life in the colonies.

Life without her here seems bleak and dreary. I am forbidden to mention her name. Her things have been removed to the attic, and it is as if she never existed. The portrait of her, painted in anticipation of her wedding, was not even unwrapped but was taken straight to the attic. I would dearly love to have it in my room to remind me of her, but Celia would not allow it.

Most of the time she tries to be nice to me, thinking that I lack Laura's spunk and can easily be won over to her side, but I cannot bring myself to love her. Lord Treadwick has finally forgiven our family for the insult to his honor and has invited us for the weekend. I shall be interested to see the splendors of Treadwick Hall for myself."

August 8, 1809

"Dear Diary:

I have heard from Laura. A letter was delivered to the groom's cottage, as we had arranged. She is alive! She is well and she is happy! Most amazing of all, she is married but not to Roland. Her husband is a farmer named Jack Farnworth and they are hewing a farm of their own from the virgin forest. I don't know whether to be happy or sad for her that Roland died. I know how much he meant to her, but I never could trust him and I think he would have made her unhappy before too long. Therefore I must be happy and hope that she is too. She speaks very highly of her new husband, but he does not sound like the sort of man that my sister would have fallen in love with. At least she has someone to provide and to protect her. At least she has someone. . . .

Lord Treadwick has invited us to his castle in Scotland for the shooting. Celia is anxious I should go too, although I hate to see poor little birds so senselessly slaughtered."

September 12, 1809

"Dear Diary:

Lord Treadwick has asked Papa for my hand. I wish Sissy were here. I have nobody to talk this over with. Celia says it is an important match and I'll be one of the richest women in England. I have no wish to be rich. I know that Treadwick Hall is a beautiful house, and Lord Treadwick is not at all unpleasant to me. But he's old, dear diary, and I don't love him. I wish I had Laura's fire and bravery so that I could defy father and state my own wishes. The trouble is, dear diary, that I don't know my own wishes. I have met no man who inspires in me the sort of passion that Roland inspired in Laura. I wish that just once in my life I had known that sort of love."

Emma sat in the shade of a broad horse chestnut tree, her back against the solid trunk, her diary on her knees. She often came here, away from Celia's prying eyes. Out in the Sutcliffe park she felt at peace and closer to Laura. She imagined Laura looking out across all that wasteland and thinking about her, and her heart felt so heavy and lonely that she sighed. She looked up as a shadow fell across her book. She closed it hastily and peered up into the sunlight. The figured outlined in harsh silhouette was a strange man. He was bareheaded, and his dark hair was held in place with a black bow at the back of his neck.

"Your pardon, miss, but I disturbed your dreamings, I fear," he said in a soft voice. "Pray, do not be alarmed."

Emma's face resembled Laura's as she gave him her haughtiest stare. "Indeed, I am not alarmed, sir, since I sit in my own garden and it is you who are the intruder. Perhaps you did not realize you were trespassing. . . ."

Far from blushing or looking embarrassed, the young man smiled. "Hardly trespassing, since I was bidden to the house by Mrs. Sutcliffe."

Emma took in his fresh, youthful face, his well-worn coat, and the fact that he had come on foot. A boy summoned to run errands for Celia, or maybe a young journeyman carpenter. "Then you'll find the servants and tradesmen entrance round at the back," she said.

"I was about to say that I was bidden to the house for tea, Miss Sutcliffe," the man said. "Allow me to introduce myself. I am Thomas Conway, newly arrived as curate of St. George's church in the village."

Emma's fair skin flushed scarlet. "Oh, Reverend Conway, pray forgive my rudeness," she said, scrambling to her feet. "My stepmother did mention something about a clergyman coming to tea, but I expected someone a little . . . older."

He grinned. "I was warned at the seminary that my boyish looks would be a hindrance in my profession," he said. "I assure you I am older and wiser than my appearance." He tried to maintain a solemn face as he said this, but his mouth quivered and, as Emma regarded him quizzically, they both burst out laughing.

As she made to rise to her feet, he held out his hand to assist her, and she blushed as she nodded politely. "Come in to tea, please, Reverend Conway. I must say you are a big improvement on the last curate, who was at least a hundred and nodded off to sleep during dinner." Emma was amazed at her own boldness. It had been only to Laura that she spoke with such frankness.

"And you, Miss Sutcliffe, are a big improvement on the usual ladies who entertain poor curates at afternoon tea," he said, smiling shyly at her.

"And might one ask if there is a Mrs. Conway?" Emma asked, again surprised to hear herself say the words.

Thomas Conway smiled ruefully. "My stipend is barely enough to keep a church mouse alive, let alone a wife and children," he said. "I don't think I'll be able to think of marriage until I've a parish of my own—and that seems unlikely, as I have no family connections high in the church. No, Miss Sutcliffe, I fear I am doomed to live a solitary life."

"I too live a solitary life here at Sutcliffe, Mr. Conway," Emma said, conveniently ignoring the fact that this solitary life was soon to come to an end when her marriage to Lord Treadwick went through. "I hope that you will be persuaded to visit Sutcliffe House very often. You must tell me what kind of books you like to read and what sort of music you play."

As they crossed the lawns together, Emma couldn't believe the way she was talking to this young man. She had always been rather tongue-tied around men, leaving the talking to Laura. But knowing that Thomas Conway was a clergyman and not a potential suitor made her relax with him. She knew that Celia could not disapprove of her talking to him unchaperoned, and she liked the way his blue eyes twinkled when he smiled.

Celia greeted him cordially in the salon. "I see you have already met my daughter Emma," she said. "And I feel that your arrival is at a very opportune moment. As you have probably heard, Emma is soon to marry Viscount Treadwick. I'd like it very much if you could instruct her on the church's teaching regarding the role of a good wife."

"I'd be happy to, Mrs. Sutcliffe," Thomas said. Emma noticed that he didn't take his eyes from her face as he spoke. She was amazed at the great surge of joy she felt that she would have a reason to spend a lot of time with Thomas Conway.

They met most afternoons after that, strolling in the grounds when the weather was fine or sitting in the library when it was not. Thomas told her about his days as a student at Oxford University. Emma looked at him with astonished delight when he recounted some of the pranks he had taken part in. "And to think that you were a divinity student, Mr. Conway!" she teased.

Thomas had the grace to blush. "I always felt that God has a sense of humor, Miss Sutcliffe," he said. "Otherwise why would he have created man?"

"You believe that man is such an amusing creature?" she asked.

"A tragicomic creature, Miss Sutcliffe, destined to blunder through the beautiful world God has given him."

She thought for a moment and then she nodded. "Maybe you're right, although I fear that life as I have witnessed it has more tragedy than comedy."

He looked at her with deep, solemn eyes. "That is not right for a young girl about to embark on a lifetime of adventure," he said. "You're to be married soon. Doesn't that prospect fill you with joy?"

Emma looked away, a picture of Lord Treadwick springing into her mind, pompous, pleased with himself, laughing loudly as he swaggered home from the hunt. How could she be joyful about the prospect of being married to a man like that? And yet weren't all men like Lord Treadwick—all men except for Thomas Conway, that is?

Summer mellowed into autumn, and the leaves began to turn golden on the chestnut trees that lined the drive.

One afternoon Emma walked with Thomas Conway through the dying petals of the rose garden. "I must say, Mr. Conway, that you are neglecting your duty," she began, trying to keep the conversation on a light level and not let him know the turmoil that was going on inside her.

"How is that, Miss Sutcliffe?" he asked, his open face showing dismay.

"You were commissioned by my stepmother to instruct me in the art of being a good wife, and I fear you have neglected that topic in our discussions so far."

He turned to look at her steadily. "There is no need for instruction, Miss Sutcliffe."

"Oh, but there is," Emma said. "I am very perplexed, Mr. Conway. Am I really to obey my husband in all things? Did God really put us women here to be subject to men all our lives? It doesn't make sense to me that he gave us good brains but allowed us to be little more than servants and lapdogs."

"The teaching of the church is very simple in the matter," Thomas said quietly. "Our Lord constantly compared his own relationship to the church with that of a bride and bridegroom. Is that not self-explanatory? It is all a question of love. As Saint Paul says in Corinthians: Love is not haughty or proud. Love does not seek to dominate. If a man and woman are united as true partners, like Our Lord and his church, then they share all things, they are equals in all things, and their only concern is to make the other happy." He had spoken eloquently, spreading his hands as if he were preaching. Then he lowered his gaze and added, "At least, that is how I see it."

Emma felt a great lump in her throat. "And if love is not present?" she whispered.

"There should be no marriage without love," he said quietly.

"Then what should I do, Thomas?" Emma blurted out, unaware that she had used his first name. She grabbed his sleeve, her eyes pleading. "I am to marry a man I don't love. My father tells me that this is the way of things at our level of society, but I find it very hard to accept."

Thomas nodded. "I'm afraid it does seem to be so among the noble houses. Marriage has long been a tool of power and connections." He gazed at her tenderly. "Maybe love will come later, when you know your husband better."

"I don't think so." Emma shuddered. "He's almost twice my age and fat and pompous. He likes hunting and shooting—all the sorts of things I dislike."

"Have you told your parents how you feel?" Thomas asked her gently.

Emma sighed. "It would be no use," she said. "Laura begged not to marry him. They didn't listen to her."

"Laura?"

"My sister. She was betrothed to the viscount before me. She ran away to marry the man she loved. I must never speak of her now."

Thomas nodded with understanding. "It must be very hard for you to be separated from your only sister in this way."

"I have nobody," Emma said, then turned to him. "I had nobody until you came. You don't know what a comfort you've been to me, Thomas. You are the first man I could ever talk to—really talk to, I mean, not silly, polite, drawing-room chatter."

They walked on. The first dead leaves crunched beneath their feet. "I only wish . . ." he began. Emma looked up.

"I only wish . . . that things could have been

different," he said wistfully. "If I were a man of property, I know what I would say to you now. . . ."

She waited for him to go on. She knew that he would have asked her to marry him, and suddenly she realized that *this* was the sort of relationship he had been talking about: two equals, sharing feelings and quiet, warm love. She pressed her lips together, afraid that she might cry. They walked back to the house in silence, side by side.

All winter long her unspoken love for Thomas grew stronger, and then Celia announced that she and Emma would be going to Treadwick to plan the wedding from there.

"So soon?" Emma gasped.

"You don't sound like the eager young bride," Celia said, looking at her sharply.

"It's just that . . . I think I'd now prefer a summer wedding," Emma stammered, blushing under Celia's piercing gaze.

"You know your fiancé doesn't want to wait any longer. He's not getting any younger, Emma. He wants an heir."

Emma tried to hide the shudder that went through her body at the thought of Lord Treadwick's embraces. She thought of Thomas's smooth, youthful cheeks and Lord Treadwick's red, podgy face. Of Thomas's slim, artistic hands and the way he held her hand tenderly when he said good-bye. There was nothing gentle or tender about the viscount.

"Mama," she mumbled, hating to address her stepmother the way she required, "if I didn't love Lord Treadwick, would there still be time to call off the marriage?"

"If you didn't love him?" Celia said scornfully. "How can you love him? You hardly know him. Love will come later, child. Let's have no more of such nonsense."

"But if I fell in love with another man . . ." Emma began.

"Another man? What other man?" Celia demanded.

"Nobody. There's no one. I was just supposing," Emma said hastily, blushing under Celia's sharp stare.

A few days later, she looked out of her window to see Thomas running across the meadow to the house. He was bareheaded and his jacket flew open as he ran. She slipped out of the back door and met him in the copse next to Roland's former cottage. "Why, Thomas, what is it?" she asked. His face was flushed and his eyes were haunted.

"I'm being sent away from here, Emma," he panted. "The carriage is waiting, but I had to say good-bye to you. I couldn't just leave without seeing you once more."

"I don't understand," Emma said.

"Oh, I understand perfectly," Thomas said. "Your stepmother knows the archbishop. She's had me transferred to a parish on the Yorkshire Moors—about as far from anywhere as I could be. The old vicar has died, and I'm to leave today. They even sent a carriage for me."

"But why, Thomas?"

"She must have found out about us," he said.

"But there's nothing to find out," Emma said. "We have behaved as good friends, no more."

"Maybe love can't stay hidden," Thomas said. "It must be very obvious that we love each other. Perhaps she sees me as an obstacle to your marriage to Treadwick."

Emma cursed herself when she remembered her conversation with her stepmother the week before. She put her hand on his sleeve. "Oh, Thomas, what are we going to do?"

Thomas looked at her with hopeless eyes. "There's nothing we can do. I have to obey my bishop and you have to obey your family. You know I want to marry you more than anything in the world, Emma, but it's not possible. I have no money to support a wife. I'll never have money . . ." He looked away as tears began to flow down his cheeks. "But I want you to know this, Emma. No man could ever love you the way I love you. Farewell, my dearest."

"Oh, Thomas," she cried. She threw herself into his arms. They kissed with abandon, their arms locked around each other in a desperate embrace. Then he broke away from her and ran back across the meadow. Emma watched him go until he was lost among the trees. There was a physical pain around her heart as if it had broken at that moment and could never be mended.

CHAPTER EIGHT

Emma Sutcliffe walked down the aisle at Treadwick church on her father's arm. It was a blustery March day, and outside the bare trees were swaying in a wild dance, their branches tapping against the church windows. She took her place beside D'Arcy, Fourth Viscount of Treadwick, and the ceremony began. Like a puppet she answered when she was spoken to, and put out her finger for the ring. It was as if the real Emma had slipped away from the ceremony, leaving only a hollow shell that looked like her. Afterward she danced and smiled and played the hostess, and that night she closed her eyes and turned her head away as the viscount made love to her.

It was another blustery day, almost a year later, as Emma sat in her sitting room, staring hopelessly out the window at Treadwick. The viscount was out hunting again with his friends. All winter long he had filled the house with noisy acquaintances who drank, gambled, and above all rode with the hounds. At the end of every day they'd come home, muddy, sweaty, smelling of beer, and often streaked with blood. Emma shuddered as she thought of it. She had begun a letter to Laura but could find nothing to say that didn't betray her misery. She knew that Laura had a fine baby girl called Katherine and sounded happy and contented with her Jack.

She was about to turn away from the window when she saw a horseman coming up the drive. He reminded her so much of Thomas that her heart lurched. The rain-spattered window made it hard to see him clearly, but she heard the hoofbeats on gravel and then the sound of knocking on the big front door. Emma seated herself in her favorite chair and waited.

The butler appeared immediately. "A gentleman to see you, milady," he said. "He says he is an old friend from the far north. Shall I show him in?"

Emma could hardly speak with anticipation. She nodded and held her breath until the visitor was shown into the room.

"Thomas!" she exclaimed, holding out her hands to him. "I can't believe it's you. How good of you to call on me. Are you still up in your parish on the Yorkshire Moors?"

"Yes. Yes, I still have the same parish," he said hesitantly. "It's a good living. Good honest farm folk. . . ."

"Unlike the corrupt upper classes you had to deal with at Sutcliffe," she said, her nervousness in his presence making her resort to light humor.

He managed a smile. "You're looking well, Emma," he said softly. "Is married life suiting you after all?"

She looked away, into the fire. "I am . . . well provided for. Any luxury I desire . . ." she said, but couldn't finish the sentence.

He took her hands, his eyes gazing at her hungrily. "There hasn't been a minute I've not thought of you, Emma," he said. He went over and closed the door behind them. "Your husband is away?"

"Out hunting, as usual," she said. "He won't be back until dark."

She saw Thomas's eyes light up.

"Did you have business in the neighborhood, Thomas?" she asked, trying to stay calm and composed. Her heart was hammering so hard that she was sure he must hear it. To know that he was so close and yet unobtainable was the most exquisite torture.

"I came only to see you," he said simply.

"You came all this way just to see me. That was good of you," she stammered, "but was it wise? Are we not putting each other through renewed suffering?"

He shook his head. "I hope not. I hope that I might have found a way to put an end to both our misery."

"What are you saying, Thomas?" she asked uneasily.

He knelt at her feet. "My love, a miracle has

happened—at least, I look upon it as a miracle: I've come into money!"

"Thomas! That's wonderful," Emma managed to say. Feeling his hands warm in hers had made it hard to think. "But I thought you had no relatives."

"Not a relative, Emma. A dear old lady parishioner died and left me her house and an income of a thousand a year. I'm a man of property, Emma. Oh, I know it's not property like Treadwick Hall, but it's a good solid Yorkshire home. We could be happy there, you and I."

Emma looked at him in amazement. "But Thomas, I'm married to another man. I should have thought you, a clergyman, would realize that marriage is a sacred bond."

"But do you love him?"

"You know I don't, but that's not the point."

"Of course it's the point," Thomas said impatiently. "If there is no love, there is no sacrament, no sacred bond blessed in heaven. It's a marriage of convenience, Emma, a linking of property, not of souls." He grasped her hands more tightly. "I might be able to get your marriage annulled, Emma. I could prove you were forced into it against your will . . . but even if I couldn't, I'd willingly give up my parish to be with you. Who cares if we are legally married? We'd be united in God's eyes, I know we would . . ." He took her hands again. "We could slip away together, Emma, right now, and go to my house in Yorkshire. We'd be happy the rest of our days. Won't you come?"

Emma looked into the fire. A tear ran down her cheek. Thomas wiped it away gently with his finger. "Don't you love me anymore, my darling?" he whispered.

Another teardrop followed, splashing down onto her silk dress. "I'll always love you," she said, "but you don't understand. I can't come with you now, or ever, Thomas. It's too late." She got to her feet. Thomas looked at her, taking in the shape of her dress, her rounded figure. He stepped back.

"You're going to have a child!" he said.

She nodded, her face a picture of misery. "In three more months, Thomas. So now you see why I can't leave. My child will be the heir to Treadwick. I can't rob him of that, can I?"

There were tears in his own eyes as he looked at her with tender pity. "Forgive me, Emma," Thomas said. "I've only upset you by coming here. I had hoped . . . I had dreamed that this might be our miracle, but it wasn't to be."

She went over to him, putting her hand gently on his shoulder. "You must go now, Thomas. Go back and get on with your life. Find a wonderful wife for yourself, a wife who can make you happy."

"You know I could never be truly happy without you," he said, "but I see now that our happiness was never meant to be. I wish you well, my love. I won't trouble you again."

He backed to the door as he spoke, then opened it quickly and was gone. Emma reached out her hand as if she wanted to draw him back, then let it sink hopelessly to her side.

She was still sitting staring at the fire when she heard the sound of loud voices down below, then the stomp of boots up the stairs. Her door burst open and her husband stood there, his hunting clothes spattered and muddy, his face beet-red, his eyes bloodshot and blazing. His whip was still in his hand. "What's this I hear, madam?" he demanded. "You've taken to entertaining gentlemen callers while my back is turned?"

He strode over to her and dragged her to her feet.

"Let me go, D'Arcy, you're hurting me," she protested.

"Not until I get the truth out of you," he shouted. His breath in her face was heavy with alcohol fumes and his speech was slurred. "Who was the young rascal you admitted to your boudoir when I was away? Eh?"

"You're being ridiculous, D'Arcy," Emma said. "An old friend stopped by to visit on his way back up north. He was here all of two minutes."

"Old friend, eh? Not that simpering parson you used to moon over, the one we had to get rid of once before?"

"He's gone now, what does it matter," She said in a tired voice. "He'll be back in Yorkshire by now."

"That's neither here nor there," D'Arcy blustered. "I don't allow my wife to have gentleman callers when I'm not around, is that clear, madam?" He dug his fingers deep into her arms as he shook her like a rag doll.

"D'Arcy, remember my condition!"

"You better remember it yourself, madam!" he screamed, "and remember that I'll whip you within an inch of your life if I find you with another man again. Is that clear?"

"Get your hands off me!" she screamed. "You're hurting me!"

"I'm your husband," he leered. "I can put my hands on you whenever I want. You are only here for my pleasure . . . and speaking of pleasure . . ." His eyes strayed to the open bedroom door.

"Go away and leave me alone!" she shouted. "I don't want you anywhere near me." She struggled to free herself from his grip.

He started laughing. "That's just fine. I love a good struggle. Makes it all the sweeter."

Emma was no longer frightened, she was angry. Cold anger such as she had never felt before surged through her. "I mean it, D'Arcy, take your hands off me now!" she said. She gave him a mighty push, catching him by surprise and off-balance. If he hadn't been so drunk no harm would have been done, but he bumped into the sofa, tripped and fell heavily, striking his head against the side of the marble fireplace.

"D'Arcy?" Emma whispered as he lay still on the floor. A trickle of blood ran from his forehead across the white marble.

CHAPTER NINE

ENGLAND. THE PRESENT

Laura stood in St. George's churchyard, Tread-wick, and looked down at the grave. It was a plain marble slab, not the ornate cherub she would have expected for Viscount Treadwick. The inscription read: D'ARCY, FOURTH VISCOUNT TREADWICK, JULY 18, 1774–MARCH 2, 1810.

So he had died from the fall.

Underneath was added in a different script, AND HIS WIFE, EMMA, VISCOUNTESS TREADWICK, OCTOBER 14, 1789–FEBRUARY 28, 1852.

She had not remarried in all that time, Laura thought. Forty years alone and she had not remarried. She had not had someone sent to find Thomas, to tell him that she was now free. Why? They could have been so happy together and yet she chose to live out her life alone and be buried in Treadwick churchyard next to her disgusting husband.

"Stupid," Laura said angrily to the over-grown gravestones.

There was so much that she still wanted to know. Her grandmother had had to move from

Treadwick before she had a chance to read all of Emma's diaries. She knew the story in detail only up to when Emma gave birth to a son. His grave was there, next to his parents'. ROBERT, FIFTH VISCOUNT TREADWICK, APRIL 11, 1810–NOVEMBER 12, 1879, and then a whole line of Treadwick graves, ending with Edward, who died in 1930. He must have been Grandma Helen's grandfather. Sad that he had no son and there were no Treadwicks today. Only the Sutcliffe name had gone on, and that didn't make sense either, because Grandpa Jimmy had been a Sutcliffe and Grandma Helen had married him. Laura was still not at all sure where she belonged in this story, and she was very anxious to find out. Had Emma been content to stay alone at Treadwick and raise her son? And what of the first Laura, in far-off Australia? Did she really live a long and happy life with Jack or did she get bored with his simple farm ways and long for the elegance of her former life at Sutcliffe House? And what happened to the diamonds? Did Laura's family in Australia ever sell them? Why didn't Emma use them to run away with Thomas? So many questions she needed to have answered.

Laura gazed across the meadows to the distant outline of Treadwick Hall. She had come here alone this time, without her grandmother's knowledge. London was sweltering in an unusual August heat wave, and Grandmama Helen was feeling the heat. "You go out without me today. I'll just sit in the lounge and read," she said to Laura. "Kew Gardens should be nice, or maybe a trip down the river . . ."

Laura had agreed that either would be fine. She didn't let her face betray that she had no intention of going to either Kew Gardens or the river. The moment she had heard that Grandmama was staying in the hotel room, she had made up her mind to go through with her plan. She caught the first train down to Treadwick, determined to get answers.

Laura left the churchyard and took the footpath across the meadow to the house. There were cows grazing, and they looked up in a bored way as Laura walked past. Wildflowers were blooming in riots of yellow and white: Buttercups and Queen Anne's lace were underfoot and wild roses covered the hedgerow, filling the air with a sweet, heady scent that gave the scene an unreal quality. Brian had given her some pot to try at a party, and she had felt the same way after she smoked it: as if she weren't really there. She thought about Brian and wondered where his travels had taken him, but even he seemed as remote and unreal as Thomas Conway.

Just as Laura got to Treadwick Hall another large crowd arrived to tour the mansion. They milled around outside, laughing loudly and licking bright Popsicles, wearing colorful T-shirts and looking so completely out of place that Laura felt insulted for her ancestors. She hoped the girl at the desk wouldn't recognize her and she didn't. She merely handed her a ticket and said, looking bored, that the next tour began in ten minutes at the bottom of the staircase.

As she waited in the coolness of the echoing entrance hall, Laura noticed a young man come in and start walking around on his own. He looked different from the average tourist because he was dressed in an old tweed jacket, even on this sweltering day, and the camera he carried around his neck was a big, professional-looking one. "Must be from the press," Laura decided. She wondered if there was a celebrity here, and then she let her mind slip into a daydream in which he had been sent to report on the return of Laura Sutcliffe to claim her inheritance.

"Over here, ladies and gents!" The clipped voice of the guide brought her down to reality with a bump. She was just another tourist here. Nobody special at all. She joined the crowd and endured the droning on of the guide through all the main rooms, then followed the group upstairs, her excitement growing. She listened impatiently while the guide went into his spiel about the Treadwick ghost who had often been heard moaning down this very hallway. "Some say it was Lord D'Arcy Treadwick, who met a violent death . . ." the guide intoned. The other tourists looked around uneasily. Laura smiled with her insider's knowledge. From what she knew of Lord D'Arcy, he wouldn't be likely to moan. He'd be the sort of ghost who roared down hallways, blowing off the pictures!

All along the main gallery she kept looking

for a place to slip away and hide until the tour had gone. Her moment came when a child tripped over the rug and started crying. Everyone looked, and Laura darted into a side passageway, moving silently through the shadows until she came to another stairway at the back of the house. This was obviously the servants' staircase: It was narrow and uncarpeted. Laura stood there, listening and alert, her heart beating so loudly that she was sure it must be heard all over the house. Then, after a few minutes, when she was certain she hadn't been missed and the only sound was that of a grandfather clock tocking on the floor below, she began to creep up the stairs. She was glad she had worn sneakers, because the slightest sound echoed from the bare stone floor.

Above was another floor. At last, at the far end of the hall she came to a twisty narrow stone stair in the wall that led upward. Round and round she went, praying that the door at the top would not be locked. The handle was stiff, but finally she gave it a good shove and felt the door creak as it moved. Obviously nobody had been up here for a long time. A good sign. Maybe nothing had been touched since Grandmama had been a child here.

Light came from a high casement window as Laura pushed open the door. Dust motes danced in the sunlight, and the whole place had a sleepy, musty feeling to it. Now that she was actually here, she hesitated to go in. Laura couldn't help remembering what the guide had said about the ghost. She would have said that she didn't believe in ghosts before, but now, with the dust sheets stirring in an unseen draft, she wasn't so sure. She realized how far she was from anybody—that nobody would hear her if she screamed.

"This is my house. I belong here. I'm a Treadwick too," she said out loud, and it seemed as if the dust sheets suddenly stood still.

There was so much stuff! Laura went through pile after pile of old books, cane chairs with no seats, badminton rackets with broken strings, old croquet sets, and at last she found a small trunk. Inside it were letters, tied in neat bundles with pink ribbon. Laura's heart started racing as she read, "My dearest Sissy:"

She threw the dust sheet off an old armchair and sat in the sunlight to read.

CHAPTER TEN

AUSTRALIA. 1814

"My dearest Sissy:

The whole colony is in a state of turmoil. We have a brazen outlaw gang in our midst, making day-to-day living very uneasy for us settlers, who live far from an army post. It's supposedly led by a nebulous character known as Johnny Flash. Of course, you know how rumors fly and exaggerate with every telling in an isolated place like this, but this outlaw seems to delight in making a fool of the authorities and carrying off daring raids from under the very noses of the most prosperous settlers. So far nobody has come close to catching him. They say he has a camp the size of a small town in the deepest forest—women too. One of the latest rumors is that he kidnapped a servant girl from a nearby township and rode off with her with half the town in pursuit.

It's strange, dearest Emma, but our lives here are often so monotonous that one longs for excitement. Now we have our excitement but not in a way I would have wished. We had a sheep stolen last night, and Jack is never without his gun. But we are pitifully undermanned if it came to a real attack. Several settlers have been murdered trying to protect their property. I'd be willing to do my share, and I can handle a rifle as well as any man, but Jack wants me home to protect Katherine. It's hard to keep little Katie safely indoors. She loves to follow her father around the farm and is even more horribly independent than I was at the same age—and more hardheaded too! Be grateful your son took after you in nature. Imagine if you'd had another Laura to contend with. . . ."

Laura broke off from her writing and looked up as Jack came into the room. The candlelight flickered as he closed the door firmly behind him.

"Any news?" she asked, seeing his worried face.

"I'm leaving Amos and a gun up with the sheep in the top pasture tonight," Jack Farnworth said.

"Jack, do you think that's wise?" Laura asked.

Jack shrugged. "I can't risk losing any more animals," he said.

"But if this outlaw, this Johnny Flash, is really in the neighborhood and helping himself to our sheep, won't Amos be in terrible danger? I'd rather risk losing more sheep than put Amos's life in jeopardy."

"Amos can handle himself," Jack said. "He did a stint in the army back in England before he got into that stupid brawl and was shipped out to Australia."

"And you don't think he'd be tempted to join the outlaws?" Laura asked. "I suppose being a bushranger does have a certain excitement."

Jack put another log on the fire. "Sometimes I wonder if this Johnny Flash even exists," he said. "So many rumors, but who has actually come face-to-face with him?"

"Nobody, and lived to tell the tale," Laura said. "But somebody has to have been responsible for those murdered settlers and for the gold that was stolen from the stagecoach. And what about your sheep?"

"I know," Jack said, "and I intend to take the threat seriously enough. We'll bar all the doors and windows tonight, and I'll stay up with the rifle. And make sure the little one keeps close to you," he added, glancing across at the sleeping child who curled with her doll on the trundle bed in the corner. "You know how bold she is. She'd go with any stranger."

Laura's heart lurched as she looked at her daughter. "Surely he wouldn't sink so low as to kidnap children?"

"If he thought we could pay him the ransom? We've done too well, my love. We've become prosperous landowners. Just the type that Johnny Flash likes to hit."

"Only because we worked hard for everything we have, Jack," Laura said. "We both worked far too hard. . . ."

She looked away from him. "I know," he said. "Don't remind me. If I'd taken better care of you, if I'd stopped you from working yourself into exhaustion, our boy wouldn't have been stillborn. Do you think I don't dwell on it every single day?"

"Some things just aren't meant to be," Laura said gently. "Maybe we could have done nothing to prevent it. And we have Katherine. We can be thankful for that. She's as lively as any boy."

"Just like you, my love," Jack said. "Another willful redhead. Afraid of nothing. Breaks every rule she can get away with. I think she's going to give us trouble when she grows up." But he smiled fondly, then went over to ruffle the sleeping child's flame-red hair.

Laura looked at them both tenderly. In the five years she had been with Jack her life had completely changed. Now when she looked back on Laura Sutcliffe, the English lady who went to balls and parties and clapped her hands for servants to attend her, it was hard to believe she had ever existed. She remained in Laura's memory like a character in a book. Even the Sutcliffe diamonds, buried in the dirt floor behind the fireplace when Jack built the house, had become mythical objects in her mind. The only thing that was still very real to her was her sister, Emma. She grieved for Emma all the time: Her letters sounded so sad and lonely. Even after the death of her husband and the birth of her son, she wrote only of the weather and how many teeth the boy now had. Nothing that was close to her heart at all, so that Laura couldn't guess how she was feeling. She had written, urging Emma to find a new husband, but

Emma had replied primly that her life was now devoted to her son. It was in one of her later letters that she confided in Laura that the Reverend Thomas Conway had married a Yorkshire girl and now had a son of his own.

"Poor Emma," she thought. "I have Katherine and Jack. Two people who love me and need me." She looked across from the sleeping child to Jack's sturdy body, his weatherbeaten face. Not the sort of man she would have looked at twice back in England, but the right sort of man for these rugged conditions. He had conquered the bush and built them a fine farm and a good, solid house. He promised he would replace it with a mansion just as good as Sutcliffe House when he had upgraded the quality of his merino herd and his wool was shipped to England. Laura was sure he'd manage it. He was the most hardworking man she had ever known.

When she first told Jack she'd marry him, she thought that meant she'd given up the fiery passion she'd felt with Roland, and in a way she'd been right. But she and Jack shared a different kind of love, fierce and passionate in its own way, and even in the midst of their difficult life—maybe because their life was so difficult—it grew with each passing day.

Still . . . Roland . . . Her gaze moved to the flickering logs in the fireplace, and as she watched the flames dancing, she remembered his touch. Pure fire, she thought, an unbeckoned tingle moving down her spine. Then, coming to her senses, she wondered how she would have survived here if she had married him. Poor Roland would have had no skills to tame the bush. In spite of being only a fencing master, he had been born with his aristocratic mother's love of the good things of life. He belonged in the elegant drawing rooms they had left, not in this untamed country where a bushfire or a snakebite could snatch away all that a person had worked for.

She knew that, all things considered, it was better that Roland had died and Jack had lived. She had something very special with Jack, and the fire with Roland surely would have faded. And she had Katherine, her feisty little pride and joy. She worried about Katherine, though, Katherine who was afraid of nothing and curious and bold.

The dogs growled, and Laura was immediately alert. Jack took his rifle from the wall. "I think I'll go check on the horses," he said. "Those bushrangers would do anything to get their hands on a good horse."

"Take care," she called as he opened the door, letting in the night sounds of the bush, the rustle of eucalyptus leaves, and the soft bleating of the lambs.

A little later he was back. "All quiet," he said. "Probably just some wallabies. You go to sleep. I'll sit up tonight."

Laura lay down, glancing across at Katherine, curled in a tight ball in her trundle bed. The last thing she saw before she fell asleep was Jack's profile in the firelight, sitting with his rifle on his knees, listening and waiting.

The next morning she woke to sunlight streaming in and the wild laughter of the kookaburra in the forest. She reached out her arm and touched only a cold sheet. She sat up. "Jack? Katie?"

The trundle bed was empty. The door was open and the house in silence. In panic she jumped out of bed and ran across the room. Jack's coat was gone from the peg, and so was Katie's shawl. Jack's horse was missing, but she saw that the bridle and saddle were also gone. This reassured her a little. Jack must have had reason to go out early and he must have taken Katie with him. After all, kidnappers would not have stopped to take her shawl with them.

At any other time she would not have been worried. Jack often made early-morning rounds of his stock and fields. Katie sometimes rode along on his saddle. She must just think of this as an ordinary morning and try to shake off the pit of fear she felt deep in her stomach. She busied herself with her usual chores. She collected eggs and milked the cow and put the coffeepot on. She had just started baking bread when she heard the jingle of harness. Relieved, she rushed out.

"There you are, you rascals," she said. "Slipping off without telling me!"

She stopped. Jack was with Amos, not Katherine.

"I left at first light to see that Amos was all right, but he'd had no problems bigger than mosquitoes," Jack called, waving to her as he rode up to the house.

Laura intercepted him. "Where's Katie?"

"Katie?"

"Didn't she go with you?"

"She was asleep when I left." Alarmed, he sprang down from the saddle. "Are you sure she's not hiding, playing one of her silly games?"

"She's nowhere, Jack, and she took her shawl."

They stared at each other in horror.

Jack slid from his saddle. "See to the horses, Amos, and then come and help us look."

"Don't worry, boss," Amos said, skillfully gathering up the reins and leading the horses away. "You know what a little devil she is. Remember that time she hid in the henhouse and said she was pretending to be a hen?"

They rushed to the henhouse, but she wasn't there. They tried the stable and barn, calling her name all the time.

"What's the betting she went after me to the top pasture," Jack said. He tried to give Laura a reassuring smile. "You stay here and keep calling her. Amos and I will head back up in that direction and then over to the Murphys'. She always has a good time over there. Maybe she decided she wanted to visit. I bet we'll find her, footsore and sitting by the track."

"Let me come with you. I can't just stay here," Laura begged, grabbing his sleeve.

"And what if she comes home to an empty house?" Jack said. "If we get to the Murphys' and we haven't found her, we'll alert the neighbors and start an organized hunt. She's only a baby. She can't have gone far."

Laura shuddered, thinking of the trackless bush around them, of the snakes and funnel-web spiders and gorges and ravines where a child might fall and never be found.

"She can't have gone far," Laura echoed.

Jack bent to kiss her forehead. "Try not to worry too much, my love. Wherever she is, I'll wager she'll be home when she's hungry." He gave her a smile, but Laura could see the panic in his eyes. "He thinks she's been kidnapped too," she thought.

The moment the men had ridden off, she started a systematic search of the property, checking and rechecking all of Katie's favorite places: the pond where the ducks lived, the field where the wallabies often played at night, the big sunflowers in the vegetable garden. She walked up and down the track, looking for footprints from a small shoe, but the ground was baked hard and dry, and Katie was so very light.

The day dragged on and on. When the sun hung like a red ball over the eucalyptus trees, she started mechanically preparing a meal. Jack had had no real food since last night. He'd be starving. So would Katie, Laura told herself, and she might have a search party of neighbors to feed. She began preparing vegetables for a stew. As she worked, she glanced up, out the window. A movement in the meadow beyond the vegetable garden made her start. She ran outside, but it was only wallabies.

"Shoo," she cried, running toward them and driving them away. No sort of fence could keep them out of the vegetables. Suddenly she stopped, imagining that she heard a voice calling her name. She peered into the twilight among the gum trees. It almost seemed as if a figure was standing there. She went closer and closer.

"Mummy, over here!" a small voice called.

Laura picked up her skirts and ran like a mad thing. "Katie! My baby! It's you! It's really you!"

The little girl was standing solemnly at the edge of the trees. "The nice man brought me back," she said.

Laura started as a tall figure stepped out from the shadows. It was a man, tall, slim, dressed all in black and wearing a black mask.

"Johnny Flash!" Laura gasped. Her anger made her forget her fear. "You were trying to kidnap my baby!"

"On the contrary, madam," he said in a deep, voice, muffled by the black mask, "I had a little business to attend to in this part of the woods and I found her, lost and crying, among the trees."

"He brought me home, Mummy," Katherine said. "He gave me some of his lunch."

"That's very kind of you, sir," Laura said. She felt a shiver going up and down her spine, but somehow she wasn't afraid. "And quite the opposite of your reputation."

"I might resort to stealing corn or sheep or even gold," he said, "but I don't stoop to stealing children."

"Then why didn't you just let her run home from here?" Laura asked, puzzled. "Why wait around and risk possible capture?"

"Because I heard who her mother was," the outlaw said in his deep, cultured voice, "and I had to see if it was true."

"If what was true?" Laura was trembling now.

"That I once knew her, once loved her."

Slowly he removed the mask. "Roland!" she whispered. Somehow she had known it from the moment he spoke to her. "It's really you. They said you had died in the bush."

He smiled that lazy, smoldering smile that she so well remembered. "Contrary to popular belief, it is very possible to survive in the bush. I made friends with some natives. They fed me and showed me how they survive. We were doing pretty well until a party of soldiers slaughtered them all. After that I was alone and I took to raiding homesteads for my food. It's a very easy way to make a living—all those unguarded sheep and crops, and the army is more than useless."

"I can't believe it's you," Laura said. She was still trembling and, in spite of herself, she could feel the old magnetism flowing between them as if she were being physically pulled toward him.

"Do you know him, Mummy?" Katherine

asked, tugging impatiently at her skirt.

"Mummy and he were friends, long ago," Laura said, not taking her eyes off his face for a second.

Roland was looking at her in a way that made her insides flip-flop. "And I must say that motherhood really suits you, Laura. You look quite radiant."

"I'm very happy, thank you," she managed to say. "Jack is a good husband. He's built up all this single-handed."

"With the help of a few diamonds, I don't doubt," Roland said mockingly.

"Oh, no, he wouldn't touch my diamonds," Laura said proudly. "They are still mine to pass on as my legacy."

"A noble farmer," Roland said. "You've done well for yourself, Laura. Far better than if you'd married a common convict like me."

Laura looked up uneasily. It was dark now. "You must go," she said, "or you'll risk being found here. My husband and the neighbors are out combing the woods, looking for Katie. There's a reward for your capture."

He laughed. "It's nice to know I'm finally worth something, isn't it?"

Katherine tugged at her skirt again. "I want to go home now, Mummy," she said. "I'm tired."

"All right, darling." Laura bent to scoop up her daughter. "Your mummy and daddy have been very worried about you. You were naughty to run away."

"I saw Daddy go and I wanted to go with him," Katie said. "He didn't hear me when I called."

"You're very naughty, Katie," Laura said, "but we're so glad to have you back." She looked up and caught Roland's expression of wistful longing. "I should get her back home," she said unsteadily. "And you should get away from here before they come back."

He nodded. "Good luck to you, Laura."

"And you, Roland."

"Put your hands up and don't move!" said a commanding voice.

There was a rustling among the trees, and Jack came crashing through the brush, his rifle aimed at Roland's back. "This way, boys, we've got him!" he yelled. "You dirty scoundrel. If you've harmed my wife and child I'll kill you myself."

"Just a minute, Jack," Laura said, stepping close to Roland. "This man found Katie lost in the woods and brought her back to us. We should thank him, not wave guns at him."

Jack eyed the outlaw skeptically and kept the rifle aimed. "For all we know he tried to kidnap her, then thought better of it," he said. "You can't trust him, Laura. Even if he's innocent this time, he's an outlaw, there's a price on his head, and I aim to turn him in."

More feet came crashing through the bushes, and the men stood around, eyeing Johnny with suspicion mixed with admiration. More guns were aimed at him. Laura tried to protest, grabbing her husband's arm, but he brushed her aside. "Laura, get the child back to the house at once, do you hear me!" he commanded. "It's not safe for her out here. The rest of his gang may be close by."

One of the men ran to get rope from a saddle, and they quickly bound the outlaw's hands behind his back as Laura dragged a reluctant Katherine away. The child was crying loudly. "Why are they hurting that nice man, Mummy? He gave me food and carried me when I was tired. They aren't going to put him in jail, are they?"

Laura said nothing. She knew that if Roland were taken to Windsor, the nearest town, he wouldn't be put in jail. He would hang. But she didn't know how she could help him. He was, without doubt, an outlaw, and some of the terrible legends about him had to be true, but he was also Roland, the man she had risked everything for once. . . .

The men soon followed with the outlaw and pushed him into the stable, putting the big bar across the door, even though he was trussed up like a chicken.

Back at the house, Laura set about mechanically serving food to the search party, her ear tuned to everything they said. The men sat around the kitchen fire, eating and boasting about their capture, discussing how they would divide the reward money. At last Laura could stand it no longer. She slipped out unnoticed into the darkness and ran across to the stable.

Roland was sitting in the straw and managed to scramble to his feet when she arrived. "You have to get out of here, quickly," she whispered. "They'll take you to Windsor in the morning."

"I can hardly run away tied up like this," he said. Laura produced a kitchen knife and cut through his bonds. "Go. Now," she commanded.

He didn't go but stood there looking at her. "Come with me," he said quietly.

"What?"

"I want you to come with me," he said again. "We belong together, you and I. We're two of a kind." He took her in his arms, crushing her against him. She tried to resist him but couldn't. She could feel his heart pounding through the thin black shirt.

"I belong to Jack now," she said, barely getting the words out. Roland's nearness was making her feel dizzy and light-headed.

"He doesn't love you the way I loved you, Laura. Tell me he sets you on fire the way I did . . . the way I'm doing now . . ." He lowered his lips to her face, kissing at random her eyes, her cheeks, before fastening onto her own warm lips. Laura gave a shuddering sigh of desire as his hands ran down her body. Her body ached from the years of wanting him.

"You still want me, don't you?" he murmured huskily.

"You know I do." It was impossible to fight it. She tried to think of Jack and Katie, but their faces were blurred by her haze of desire for him.

"Then come," he whispered, his lips nuzzling at her white neck. "I've a camp in the forest where no one will ever find us. We can be there by daybreak."

The mention of his camp brought her back to reality. This was Johnny Flash, the man who rode off with servant girls across his saddle. "From what I hear, you have convict girls there to keep you company."

"Maybe we do," he said. "But none of them means anything to me. There's always been just one woman for me, Laura. You know that."

His lips began to kiss their way down her neck. "Just say you'll come, my darling," he whispered.

Laura shuddered at his touch. "This is madness. I must be mad to even think of this. I have my home, my family . . . my little Katie."

"Not mad, fulfilling your destiny, Laura. You'll be with me, where you belong, where you can be happy." His hands continued to caress her as he talked. "We'll take the child with us, if she means so much to you. We'll make a good life, my darling. New settlers are arriving all the time. The place is opening up. We'll slip away and set up a business where nobody will recognize us—down in Victoria maybe. What do you say—your diamonds and my gold? We'll be rich!"

"My diamonds are hidden. I can't get at them now."

"Tell me where they are and I'll come back for them later."

"No, Roland," Laura said. The diamonds had brought a note of sanity to her. She was remembering that night at the inn when she had awoke to find him looking for something among her things. The old feeling of distrust returned. "I can't come with you. It's no good."

"Yes, you can. Come on, give me your hand. We'll slip away now. You want to, Laura. I know you want to."

Laura shook her head. She didn't know what she wanted anymore. "My daughter," she said. "I can't go back in there to get her and I'm not leaving without her."

"We'll come back for her, when it's safe."

"I can't leave her, Roland. She's the thing I love most in the world."

"You love me too."

"She needs me."

Laura pushed away from him. "Please go, before they come looking for you."

"I'll come back for you then," he whispered. "I'll come back for you and Katie. When all this fuss has died down. You get the diamonds and we'll just slip away together."

"I don't know," Laura said, shaking her head hopelessly, brushing at her tears. "I can't just leave Jack and everything he's built here."

"Of course you can," Roland said. "This kind of life is not for you. Look at your hands . . ." he took them in his, running his fingers over her calloused, chapped skin. "Your hands weren't meant to be rough and raw like this. You have a lady's hands. I want to make you a lady again, Laura. I want to make a better future for Katherine . . . and for any children we might have." He pulled her back into his arms. "Promise me you'll be waiting for my return, Laura."

Laura couldn't speak. She held him tightly in her arms, committing to memory the feel and smell of him, the way his hair curled at the back of his neck. She ran her hands over his head and face. "I love you, Roland," she whispered, "but this can never be. Please go now and be safe."

"I'll be back, Laura," he said, giving her one last kiss. "I swear I'll be back for you."

He ran out into the night, across the meadow like a black shadow, then was swallowed up into the trees. The next morning when Laura went out to get the eggs, she came running in to report that the stable door was open and the prisoner gone. Soldiers were called in to search the neighborhood for him, but he wasn't found.

A few weeks later Jack took Laura and Katherine into town for the day. When they came home at sunset, the first thing they noticed was the house door, swinging on its hinge. Jack leaped from the buggy. "Someone's been here!" he yelled. Laura went to follow him. "Stay in the buggy and don't move until we tell you," she commanded the child.

As she reached the open door, she gasped. Every drawer was opened, its contents spilled out onto the floor. Everything was upside down.

"Has anything been taken?" she asked in a shaken voice.

"Some ammunition, that's all," Jack said, looking around worriedly. "If it was that outlaw fellow, he didn't even touch my watch."

"I know what he came for," Laura wanted to say. "He came for me and my diamonds." And she wondered which of them had drawn him back more strongly. She couldn't help noting that he had been prepared to take the diamonds without her, and she was both glad and sorry that, for once, she hadn't been home alone.

For the next weeks she was constantly alert as she walked through the fields, but Johnny Flash never showed up again. Soon after, they heard that his camp had been ambushed by government troops and that all the outlaws had died in a hail of bullets. Laura received the news dry-eyed, but late at night she went outside, standing in the cool darkness under the still-unfamiliar stars. She wanted to cry for him, but instead she felt as if a great weight had lifted. Now she would never have to make that terrible choice again. The rest of her life would be safe with Jack and Katie where she belonged. And she tried not to think what it might have been like if she had gone with Roland.

CHAPTER ELEVEN

KATHERINE FARNWORTH, AUSTRALIA. 1830

A plume of yellow dust flew up behind the pounding hooves as a young girl rode along the bush track between the tall, gray eucalyptus trees. Her flame-red hair streamed out behind her and blended so well with the chestnut coloring of the horse that the pair of them looked like a creature from ancient mythology, half woman, half beast.

At the top of the ridge she reined in suddenly, bringing the horse to a halt. She paused to look over the valley that spread below her, open grassland dotted with stately, ghostly gum trees. This was all her father's land now, and the thousands of white dots on the landscape were his sheep—the biggest herd in New South Wales. Among the trees on a bluff above the river, a fine new house was taking shape with a graceful veranda and white columns at the front. Her father said it was going to be as good as any European mansion and that her mother could entertain the king if he came this way.

Katherine Farnworth smiled with pride. It was good to be the daughter of such a prosperous landowner. All the boys in the neighborhood wanted to marry her. As the only child, she would inherit all this one day. Her parents had made it clear to her that her future husband would have to run the property so she had better choose wisely. Katherine sighed impatiently as she thought of it. She didn't want to choose wisely when it came to a husband. She wanted to be swept off her feet with love. Wisdom and running a farm had nothing to do with it! None of the boys she had met had impressed her at all. They were all so slow, so backward, interested only in their little world of New South Wales. Katherine knew that a big, wonderful world existed far away from here. Her parents had both come from that world, where there were dances and parties and where ladies wore velvet and jewels and were presented to royalty.

The other day she had overheard her father saying that if wool prices kept up, he might take them all to England next year. Her mother had seemed very reluctant even to talk about it, but Katherine had thought about nothing else since. She desperately wanted to go to Europe, to see England and France and the sort of society her mother had told her about. It almost seemed like a fairy tale. Katherine could hardly believe that her mother had really met the French queen when she was a little girl.

She was on her way now to pick up the mail. She hoped that there would be another letter from her Aunt Emma. She loved to get those letters as much as her mother did—full of details of a life that was so different from theirs. She knew that her aunt Emma was Lady Treadwick and lived in a mansion with hundreds of servants. She never even had to brush her own hair, Katherine's mother had told her. That sounded intriguing to Katherine, who had helped with all the chores since early childhood. Equally intriguing, her cousin Robert was already Lord Treadwick, even though he was only twenty—a year younger than Katherine herself. *Maybe he is handsome,* Katherine thought. She wondered if cousins were allowed to marry. Being Lady Treadwick wouldn't be half bad, although she wasn't sure that she could ever stay away from Australia forever. She had grown up with freedom and wide-open spaces. It might be fun to sample elegant English life, but would she want to put up with all those rules of polite behavior forever? Her mother said that ladies in England had to wear corsets all the time and could only ride sidesaddle. Katherine thought that was a lot of nonsense. She herself hardly ever wore shoes and put up her hair only on special occasions. The rest of the time it flew wild behind her, as it did today.

The horse stirred impatiently as she stared out over her father's land. She loved this view, where the Hawksbury River and its valley merged with layer after layer of blue hills beyond.

Ever since she had been allowed to ride alone she had come up here, gazing out over the horizon and thinking about things.

She was still lost in thought when she heard the jingle of harness and the pounding of hooves. Before she could even gather in the reins, a coach-and-four came flying around the bend in the track, its horses flecked with foam and going at full gallop. The air was suddenly full of shouts and yellow dust. Katherine tried to swing her horse out of the path of the thundering vehicle, but her terrified mount started fighting for his head, dancing uneasily. He had never seen anything like this swaying monster bearing down on him. He reared in alarm and Katherine, to her intense annoyance, fell off.

The driver of the stagecoach brought his horses to a halt and jumped down from his seat as Katherine was picking herself up from the dust.

"I'm so sorry. Are you all right?" he called.

"Of course I'm all right," Katherine said, furious at having made such a spectacle of herself in front of strangers. They'd think she didn't know how to ride. "If you hadn't been driving so recklessly fast, it would never have happened. What are you doing on my father's land, anyway?"

He pushed his hat back on his head. "Roads are public property, miss. This is now an official stagecoach route, courtesy of the government of New South Wales, and I'm the official stagecoach driver." He raised his hat to her. "Tip McNally at your service."

She saw his face clearly for the first time. It was a very handsome face: dark eyes, ridiculously long lashes for a man, and lots of black curls escaping from under his hat. He was tall and slim, with a sort of elegance she hadn't seen in the local boys. He was young too—about her own age.

"Katherine Farnworth," she said. The way he was staring at her with obvious appreciation made her voice take on the superior tone her mother used when dealing with what she considered to be lesser people. "My father owns all this land around here. Those were all his sheep you passed, and that's our new house being built on the bluff."

He looked impressed. "Very fine, I'm sure," he said. He walked across to her horse, which was now grazing contentedly beside the track. "Let me help you back into the saddle."

"I can manage alone, thank you," she said stiffly. "I've been riding since I was three. Amber doesn't usually startle so easily. I wouldn't have fallen off if I'd been paying attention. I had my mind on other things, you see, and your coach came upon us way too fast." She put a foot into the stirrup and swung herself easily into the saddle. "In fact," she continued, now that she had the advantage of looking down on him, "in fact, I think I'll write to your employer and let him know that you were driving at a dangerous speed. We don't want to risk any more accidents on our property."

A slow grin spread across his handsome face. "You're looking at him," he said.

"What are you talking about?"

"My employer. That would be me. You see, I'm

Tip McNally and this is McNally's Stage Line. No doubt you've heard of us. We're spreading across the whole of New South Wales. Maybe we'll branch down to Victoria soon, if things keep going well. If I can keep up what my father started. . . ." His voice dropped and he looked suddenly young and vulnerable. "He died in a coach accident last year. So now I own it and I run it."

For the first time in her life, Katherine was at a loss for words. She felt a blush spreading all over her fair skin.

One of the passengers poked his head out of the carriage window. "Come on, driver, let's get going," he called. "We were making good time until this. I've an appointment in Paramatta I don't want to miss."

"Right you are, mate," Tip said.

Katherine noted the easy way he spoke, as if the pompous elderly man was his equal, and she thought how he must have despised her haughty attitude.

"Watch out for us next time," Tip said to Katherine. "We'll be coming through here every Tuesday from now on. Windsor to Paramatta and on to Sydney. I usually drive this route myself, seeing as it's the most traveled. Maybe I'll have the opportunity of driving you to Sydney one day."

"We go to Sydney in my father's carriage," she said, still uneasy with the frankness of his gaze, "but I'll certainly be more alert when I go to collect the mail on Tuesdays."

"You're going to collect your mail?" he asked.

"I always do on Tuesdays and Fridays at the post office in Windsor."

He looked very pleased with himself, which annoyed Katherine. "No need from now on. We've got the contract to deliver mail, starting next month. All you have to do is put up a box by the road and I'll drop it off to you, just like in the cities. In fact, Australia will soon be considered as civilized as Europe."

Katherine gave him a superior smile. "Then I take it you've never been to Europe, Mr. McNally," she said. "My mother experienced true civilization as a child, and I'd say we still had a long way to go."

His eyes still held hers, challenging. "My father also mixed with the cream of English society, Miss Farnworth, so I have some idea of the definition of true civilization—although I'd say that Australia had surpassed England in some important ways."

"Such as?"

"All that ridiculous preoccupation with class distinction for one," he said. "Why should a man be better than another man because he was born to a certain family? I say let your works prove who you are. I think that Tip McNally is as good as any man in Australia right now!"

"Driver, get going, or I'll demand a refund for half my ticket!" the man yelled from the carriage. Tip shot Katherine an embarrassed grin. "Maybe we'll continue this conversation next time, in less hurried circumstances," he said. He ran back to the coach and swung himself up onto the driver's seat. With a crack of the whip and a great "Huuup!" the horses moved off. Katherine watched until all that remained was a fine golden dust in the clear air.

There was definitely something about Tip McNally, she thought as she rode on to Windsor. Other boys she had met had been tongue-tied by her beauty. They had constantly praised her and couldn't do enough for her, hanging around and gazing at her with puppy dog eyes until she couldn't stand them another minute. She had liked Tip's challenging stare. It made her feel alive and excited. She would make sure that she just happened to be around to pick up the mail in the future when the coach came through.

A week later she was rewarded by the coach's coming to a thundering halt at the track leading to her house. Katherine swung her horse around and urged him into a trot, pretending that she hadn't been waiting at all and now had a mission in another direction.

"Miss Katherine," she heard Tip's voice calling. "Mail for you, delivered hot from the boat."

Katherine turned her horse.

"A letter from Lady Treadwick," Tip said, handing her a letter decorated with an impressive seal. "My, we do hobnob with the best, don't we?"

"She's my aunt," Katherine said, tossing back her hair proudly. "We might be going to visit her soon."

"You're going to England?"

"Next year, maybe, my father says."

"I'd love to see England," Tip said. "I'd like to see the place my father came from and all the big houses he talked about."

"Your father was also from the English nobility?"

"Something like that," he said airily. "He had enough fancy tales, but it was hard to pin him down exactly. He had certainly rubbed elbows with the gentry and he talked like a gentleman. He used to try and make me speak like that, but it sounded all wrong to me."

"What made him come out here?" she asked in surprise.

"What do you think? He was shipped out as a convict like most other people."

"Oh, I see," she said. She tried to control her natural curiosity but couldn't. "What did he do?"

"Killed a man in a duel over a woman." Tip said, sounding fairly proud of this. "They say he was one of the best swordsmen in Europe. He was pretty handy with a pistol too, but I wish I could have seen him in action with a sword."

"And your mother?"

"She was a convict too, but I know nothing about her. She died when I was born," Tip said. "My father raised me. We lived out in the bush when I was very little. My father escaped, you see. He said he couldn't stand being a convict for a moment more. It must have been horrible for someone like him, not used to doing hard manual work. He was hunted for a while, as an outlaw. They sent soldiers after him and they thought they'd got him, but they'd only wounded him and he managed to get away. He escaped with me down to Victoria. Nobody bothered us there and after a few years he started a stage line. Then, a couple of years ago, we moved back up here."

"But your father died?"

He nodded. "Ironic, isn't it? He survived the convict ship, he survived living in the bush and being hunted as an outlaw. Then, when he was finally earning an honest living, a wheel came off and the coach went down a ravine," Tip said. "It was the only accident the stage line has ever had, and he had to be driving the coach himself. I miss him. He was a good father. You'd have liked him."

"So you're all alone now?" Katherine asked.

"I'm used to being alone," he said. "My father went off a lot and left me when he had to. I'm used to fending for myself."

"That's good," Katherine said. "Most men want a woman to look after them."

"Not me," Tip said. "When I take a wife, it will be for other things. I'll want her to share my life, not look after me."

Katherine nodded approvingly. "I'm glad to hear that."

"Anyone would think I was asking you to marry me," Tip said, teasing her with his eyes.

"You'd be wasting your time, then," Katherine retorted. "I'm going to Europe to meet far finer boys than you."

"And far stuffier," he said, laughing as he drove on. "Any girl who married me would never be bored. That I'd guarantee," he called. It was with a curious gaze that Katherine watched Tip McNally disappear as his coach flew down the track.

CHAPTER TWELVE

"So tell us about this young man," Laura said at supper one night.

"Which young man?" Katherine asked innocently. She hadn't mentioned Tip to her parents, knowing how overprotective they were.

"You know very well," Laura said. "The one you meet each time you collect the mail. The young coach driver."

"His name's Tip. Tip McNally," Laura said.

"As in McNally's Stage Line?" Jack looked up with interest.

"That's right. He owns it, now that his father's dead."

Jack nodded. "I've heard good things about them. They're doing a great service, linking all the small communities as far as the Blue Mountains."

"And soon to go farther still," Katherine said. "He's starting a service to Bathurst in one direction and up to Newcastle in the other. He even plans to reach down to Victoria one day."

"An ambitious young man." Laura gave Jack the sort of speculative glance parents give each other. "Maybe we should invite him to luncheon the next time he's free."

"Oh, yes, Mother." Katherine flung her arms around Laura's neck. "You'd really like him. He's very handsome, and he's from a good family too!"

"McNally—that would have to be Irish," Jack said. "Was his father one of the Irish rebels shipped out here?"

"Oh, no," Katherine said. "He was an English gentleman. He came from a great house like Treadwick."

Laura gave Jack an amused glance. "I think that sounds like a touch of the blarney, Katherine. He'd hardly be an English gentleman with a very Irish name like McNally."

"But that's not their real name. His father had to change his name when he managed to escape from the convict settlement."

"He managed to escape?" Laura's voice was sharp.

"Yes, he went and hid out in the bush," Katherine said. "He had to live like an outlaw until he got away down to Victoria. Doesn't that sound romantic—just like Robin Hood."

"Very romantic," Laura said, "but not the sort of boy I'd want my daughter mixing with."

"I don't understand you, Mother." Katherine was close to tears. "Tip's a nice boy. He's hardworking and ambitious. A few seconds ago you were all for inviting him to lunch. Now you're about to condemn him without even meeting him, just because of his father. I bet if you'd been convicts you'd have tried to run away too, especially if you were falsely imprisoned in the first place."

Jack went over and put a comforting hand on Katherine's shoulder. "Don't upset yourself, child," he said. "It seems to me that she's right, Laura. We can't judge the young man without a fair trial. We should have him over and meet him."

Laura nodded. "I suppose I am overreacting," she said. "There are plenty of good people in this colony who started off as convicts. Very well, Katherine, invite him to lunch."

Katherine danced across to kiss each parent in turn. "Thank you, thank you," she said. "I know you'll like him when you meet him."

Tip came to lunch the next Sunday. As he climbed down from his horse Katherine saw that he was dressed in his Sunday best. In his long black coat and frilled white shirt he looked like a true gentleman, and Katherine heard her mother's intake of breath.

"Doesn't he look handsome, Mother?" she whispered, but Laura's face was frozen. "What was his father's name before he changed it?" she demanded.

"He didn't tell me," Katherine said. "You can ask him yourself if it's important."

"No, it can't be," Laura muttered as Katherine ran forward to meet Tip.

She noted her mother's coldness all through lunch, although Tip behaved with perfect manners and got along well with her father. Laura, meanwhile, bombarded him with unnecessary questions. "And you say your father started the stage line down in Victoria?" she asked.

"Yes, ma'am."

"And still operates down there?"

"Unfortunately no. He was killed a while back. A wheel came off the coach he was driving."

"Oh, I see," Laura said, and was unnaturally silent for the rest of the meal.

"The boy's got a good head on his shoulders," Jack said as they all stood on the porch, watching Tip ride away. "Ambitious but practical. I like that."

"There's something about him I don't trust," Laura said. "That look he has. It reminds me of someone. He'll only bring her grief, Jack."

"How can you say that, my dear?" Jack asked, giving Laura an amused glance. "What did he possibly do to upset you?"

"It's just a feeling I have," Laura replied, looking away from him. She had never told him the truth about Johnny Flash, believing him to have died in the ambush. Tip was so like Roland in manner that there could be little doubt who his father was. To know that he had lived through the shootout and had fathered a son and started a respectable business had thrown Laura off guard.

Having been lukewarm about the trip to Europe before, Laura was now the one who revived the subject. "You wait until you meet European boys," she kept saying to Katherine. "You wait until you've danced with a young Frenchman or gone out hunting with a young

English aristocrat. You can't know your own mind until you've seen the best."

She started looking into booking a passage on a ship, but Jack was now reluctant. "I don't know that I can leave the ranch for so long, Laura," he said. "Nobody around here knows sheep like I do. The whole herd could be wiped out while we're away."

"But I want her to go, Jack," Laura said. "I see danger ahead if we don't send her to Europe."

"Then you take her and I'll stay here," he said.

Katherine was still excited about going to England, but not as much as before.

When Katherine came home one afternoon after seeing Tip, she flung herself onto the sofa and sighed.

"What's wrong, darling?" Laura asked.

"Would it be too terrible if we didn't go to Europe after all?" Katherine asked. "I mean, do you really want to go very badly?"

Laura eyed her daughter suspiciously. "But you were looking forward to it, Katie."

"I don't want to leave Tip," she blurted out. "I think I'm falling in love with him, Mother."

"How can you know anything about love until you've experienced life a little?" Laura said sharply. "When you've had a chance to meet the cream of English society, then you'll know your own mind. We'll leave as planned and let's have no more silly arguments about it."

But then the whole matter was decided for them. Jack came down with a fever and was so ill that the doctors despaired of his life for a time. Laura and Katherine tended him night and day, sponging down his sweating face and feeding him cool drinks. When the fever finally broke, it left him weak and with bad lungs. There was no question of going to Europe.

Katherine rode up to the ridge, waiting for Tip to come through with the coach.

"Any news?" he asked as he reined in the horses.

"The fever has broken."

"Thank God."

"But he's very weak, Tip. The doctor says he mustn't undertake any strenuous work for six months or more. We're having to hire an overseer."

He climbed down from the driver's seat. "Ten-minute rest stop, ladies and gentlemen. Need to spell the horses after that last climb on a hot day." He took her arm, and they walked a little way into the bush, away from the track. "So you won't be going to Europe as you planned?" he said.

Katherine shook her head. "We can't leave Father now."

Tip's face lit up. "That's good news for me," he said. "I didn't want to let you out of my sight. I was scared silly you'd meet a sophisticated European man and like him better."

"I was scared you'd find another girl you liked better than me."

"Silly, as if I would," he said. He took her into his arms. "There's only ever been one girl for me, Katie," he said. "From the moment I first set eyes on you I wanted you."

He took her chin into his hand and brought her lips to his. Katherine responded to the warmth of his kiss, running her fingers through his tangled curls and pressing her body close against him.

"Let's get married, Katie," he whispered. "We belong together, you and I."

"Oh, yes, Tip, yes," she whispered.

"I'll even take you to Europe if you want," he said, gazing at her adoringly. "We'll have a great life together. I'll build you a house even bigger than your father's."

"Oh, Tip," she said, laughing.

"You don't believe me?" he demanded. "I swear to you, Katie Farnworth. We're going to be rich someday, not just comfortable but rich—stinking rich. You'll be decked out in diamonds and dripping with jewels."

Katherine watched as he walked back to the coach. She liked his swaggering walk. She liked his big dreams, even if they were just that. He was exciting, and he made her feel as if she were on fire. She knew she'd never be bored with him. As the stage drove off again, Katherine rushed down to tell her parents the news. She couldn't understand why her mother wasn't more excited. "I still can't understand why you don't like him," she snapped.

"You're so young. You don't know your own mind yet."

"You were only nineteen when you left England to follow the man you loved," Katie said. "That's the same age as I am now."

"And maybe I made the wrong decision," Laura said steadily. "Luckily for me, I met your father and that was a good decision, but I could have made a big mistake."

"How could Tip be a mistake?" Katherine demanded. "He owns a whole stage line. He's going to be very rich one day. And I'm going to inherit all this."

"Your father would like you to marry someone who could take over the running of the farm," Laura said.

"Fiddlesticks. Marry a farm boy! Not me," Katherine exclaimed fiercely. "I love Tip and I'm going to marry him, whether you let me or not."

"You won't be twenty-one for two more years, and until then your father and I say who you can marry!" Laura shouted back. "And it won't be Tip McNally if we have our way!"

"I think you're being hateful," Katherine said.

Laura begged Jack to speak to her, but he was still tired and weak. "It's no use fighting with her, my love. She's as headstrong as you are and it seems that she's made up her mind," he said. "Just get them to agree on a long engagement and tell him he has to provide her with a house before we'll let her go."

"But you don't understand, Jack," Laura insisted. "He'll make her unhappy, I know he will."

"You're right. I don't understand," he said, looking at her curiously.

Laura realized then that she couldn't tell him. If she told him that Tip was Roland's—Johnny Flash's—son, she'd have to admit to her encounter with Roland, and that would only give him extra worries, which would be bad for his health. But she knew that she didn't trust the boy any more than she had trusted his father.

Katherine chafed at the conditions, but Tip seemed to accept them. "Although I don't know how long it will take me to get a fine enough house built," he said as they sat together on a rocky outcrop overlooking the valley. "When do you inherit your legacy?"

"My what?"

"The famous diamonds," he said.

"What diamonds?" Katherine asked.

"You mean you don't know about them? The Sutcliffe diamonds your mother brought out to Australia?"

"I've never even heard of them," Katherine said.

"Then I suppose they must have been used to build up the farm," he said, "although I heard that your father wouldn't touch them and kept them hidden safely away for your legacy."

"How did you hear this?" she asked, suddenly angry that he seemed to know family secrets about which she knew nothing.

"I have my sources," he said mysteriously. "I know a lot of things I'll tell you one day. Things that would surprise you!"

"Tell me now," she said, laughing and fling-

154

ing herself onto him. "I'll make you tell me!"

Playfully he wrestled her until their fighting turned into kissing.

"This long engagement is driving me mad, Katie," he whispered huskily as he gazed down at her body, pinned beneath him.

"Then let's not wait," she said. "Let's run away to Sydney and get married now, Tip."

"We're both underage, Katie."

"How are they to know that?" she said excitedly. "How many people in this colony have no birth certificate? We'll give fictitious names and ages. We'll be wed before they can find us and stop us!" Excitedly she dragged him to his feet. "You do want me right now, don't you, Tip?" she whispered. "And I'm not going to your bed until I'm your wife . . . so what's your choice?"

"But what about a proper ceremony, Katie? Don't you want one of those big, fancy weddings like other rich girls?"

"I want you, Tip," she said, "and I'm afraid my mother will try and come between us if we don't act soon. I don't know what she's got against you, but she's set against our marriage."

Tip laughed. "I'll tell you the story someday," he said. "Then you'll understand. In the meantime, if you're really set on this, let's go then. I'll get my horse and you get yours. We'll be the one couple who rode up to get married on horseback!"

Laura and Jack were frantic with worry when the two young people rode up next day, laughing.

"How could you do this to us?" Laura demanded. "Where have you been? What possessed you to go off without telling us? I told you he was nothing but trouble."

"It's all right, Mother, you don't have to worry," Katherine said as Tip slid from his saddle, then lowered her to the ground. "We've just been to Sydney and got married."

"You can't. You're underage, both of you. We'll have it annulled," Jack stormed.

"We gave fictitious names and ages," Katherine said triumphantly. "But we're married just the same. You're too late, Mother. But I'd like you to wish us well and give us your blessing."

"I suppose we have no choice," Laura looked across at her husband, "although I still mean what I said before—you're not moving from this house until Tip can provide you with a nice home of your own."

"You could give us the diamonds as a wedding present," Katherine said, sliding her arms around her mother's neck. "After all, they're going to come to me someday, aren't they?"

"How did you hear about the diamonds?" Laura demanded.

"Common knowledge," Katherine said lightly.

Laura said no more but that night she whispered to Jack, "He's only married her to get his hands on them."

"How can you say that, my dear? He seems fond enough of her."

"He may be fond of her, but you can be sure

that the diamonds were always a factor. He'd always planned to finance all his big plans with Katie's diamonds. Well, now she'll see him in his true light—he'll have to work for success like everyone else. Make sure they're well hidden so that Katherine gets them only when we're both dead."

"I'll build them into the new fireplace," Jack said. "That way they can search all they want."

It was Saturday night, and Tip would be coming over very soon. Katherine put on her bonnet and started walking up the path to meet him. Everything seemed to have gone wrong since they got married. She had pictured them together in a little love nest, and here she still was, living under her parents' authority, treated like a little girl, while she hardly saw Tip. And he seemed to have changed too. He had been furious when he heard that she'd not get the diamonds until her parents died.

"They have all they want. How can they be so selfish?" he snapped. "You'd think they didn't care a hoot about you, making you suffer like this."

He'd asked her a lot of questions about where the diamonds were kept and what they looked like, but Katherine had no answers for him.

"Why, Tip," she'd said jokingly, "I think you're more interested in those diamonds than you are in me. We only have an hour together and all you've done is talk about the silly diamonds."

Then she saw that he wasn't laughing. A voice whispered in her head that maybe her mother had been right after all. Had Tip been more interested in her assets than he was in her? She'd dismissed the thought instantly. When they were together she was sure that he loved her. She was in ecstasy in his arms. She shivered with desire now at the thought of his touch. A week was so long to be away from him. She hoped he'd be in a good mood when he arrived. He'd been so grouchy, so preoccupied since they married. She'd just have to find a way to bring back the old, fun-loving Tip!

At the mailbox she draped herself across a stone and waited, playing a siren luring a poor sailor to his death. She imagined how his eyes would light up when he saw her. He'd jump from his horse, laughing, to sweep her up in his arms and cover her with kisses. After a while she got tired of posing. The sun began to set. She heard her mother calling and went in for supper, and still Tip didn't come.

"He probably had a little delay on the last stage run," Jack soothed his daughter. "One of his passengers kept him waiting, no doubt."

"Not as long as this," Katherine said.

About ten o'clock they finally heard hoofbeats coming up the path. Katherine grabbed her shawl and ran out. "About time too," she said, but her heart sank when she saw it wasn't Tip but Ken Murphy from the neighboring ranch.

"I came right over as soon as I heard the news," he said, sliding from his saddle. "I figured that you might not have heard yet."

"What news?" Katherine demanded, feeling suddenly cold.

"There was an accident with the stagecoach," Ken Murphy said. "It went around a bend too fast, coming down Bellbird Hill. It went over the side and into the river. There weren't any survivors. I'm sorry, Miss Farnworth, I mean Mrs. McNally. My ma says if there's anything she can do . . ."

Katherine was still standing there, just staring, as her parents led her back into the house. "He was trying to cut time off the Lithgow run," Katherine said, as if she were speaking to herself. "He wanted to get business from that new stage company operating out of Bathurst. He took too many risks. . . ."

She allowed herself to be led inside, given hot milk, and put to bed, where she lay staring at the ceiling.

"Maybe it's all for the best," Laura whispered to Jack outside her door. "I always said he'd bring her grief, didn't I?"

"I hate to see her like this," Jack said. "If only there was something we could do."

The days went by, and still Katherine wouldn't speak or move. Jack went to the inquest in town and rode back with a solemn face. He took Laura aside before he went into the house. "I think there's something you should know," he said in a low voice. "It seems that your suspicions were right. Young Tip wasn't all aboveboard after all. He was using his stage line to smuggle goods stolen from the army. He had a load of stolen rum on board

159

when the coach went over the cliff. The authorities were after him—that's why he was going so fast."

Laura sighed. "I always knew there was bad blood there," she said. "He had that look, Jack."

Jack nodded. "It might be better if none of this gets to Katie at the moment. I worry about her, Laura. Maybe you and she can go to Europe after all. That might bring her back to life again. . . ."

But Katherine listened without interest while Laura suggested a trip to Europe.

"How can I go to Europe when Tip's grave is here?" she said after a long silence.

"You've had a terrible shock, my darling, but believe me, it's not the end of the world," Laura said gently. She attempted to hug her daughter. Katherine didn't respond. "You'll go on missing him for a while, but you will get over him, my sweet."

Katherine shook her head, her eyes bright with tears. "I don't think I ever will," she said. "You see, I'm going to have his baby. That bad blood you were talking about is going to show up in your grandson."

"My dearest sister, most beloved Emma:

It is with heavy heart that I put pen to paper to tell you of our great loss: Our lovely, lively Katherine, our bright, beautiful Katie, died last week giving birth to a son. It was a terrible shock to both Jack and me. The doctor said it was quite unanticipated: She seemed to be rallying nicely after a long and difficult labor. But as night came, she just slipped away from us and seemed almost happy to go.

She was a mere shadow of her former self since the tragic death of her young husband, and we think that she actually wanted to be with him. We pray that she is happily reunited with him in heaven, but, oh, what a huge emptiness she leaves behind in our lives. As you know from my letters, she was our joy, Emma. If only Roland Marshall and his son had never existed she would be here with us now. But I can't curse poor Roland in my misery. He did not have the life he deserved any more than I did or you did. You also have known tragedy, Emma, and have borne your sufferings like the noble lady you are. At least I have known the love of a good man, and at least you have a raised a fine young man to take over his father's estates. If only we weren't so far apart, Emma. I long for a hug from the dearest person to me in the world.

Now I shall put all my energy into raising Katherine's son. He is a handsome little chap—dark-eyed like his father and grandfather, and he seems very alert and lively already. Since his parents were married under a false name, we are registering him as Farnworth, and Jack will raise him to take over the estate. We will sell the stage line. It brought only grief.

I will write more when my thoughts are less jumbled. Your devoted sister, Laura."

CHAPTER THIRTEEN

Margaret Treadwick, England. 1850

"My dearest sister:

How I wish you could see the English spring this year! The woods are carpeted with bluebells, and the apple trees in the orchard are a froth of pink blossoms. There was a nightingale singing last night across the lake. I stood at my open window and listened to him for quite half an hour. You must forgive my lapse into poetry, but springtime always brings out a strange longing in me—a longing for what might have been, I suppose.

As I look out of my window, I can see young Margaret getting ready for her afternoon ride. She reminds me a lot of you, dear Laura, when you were her age—but not as headstrong. I rejoice to say that she takes after her father not one bit. Her sweet temper comes entirely from me and her mother, who is also a sweet creature—far too good for Robert. The latter has become even more pompous recently. Reminds me of his father in every way, in spite of all my efforts to turn him into a sensitive young man. I think he was born pompous. Remember when he was a little boy and he wouldn't sleep until I'd straightened every crease out of his sheet?

We had a wonderful ball here last week, to introduce Margaret to local society. She's only seventeen, but she's already attracting the attention of many eligible young men. I must say she looked radiant in her crinoline—like some exotic flower."

Emma paused in her writing as hoofbeats clattered into the yard. She watched the young groom, Peter, help Margaret into her saddle. She couldn't help noticing how gently he handled her—as if she were made of precious porcelain—and how his hand lingered on Margaret's waist far longer than necessary.

"Mother! I want a word with you!" Without waiting for permission, Robert burst into Emma's sitting room. "Ah, good, there you are," he said.

"Where did you think I'd be?" she asked dryly. "I've been here every afternoon since you were born."

He closed the door behind him and came over to her. "I wanted to tell you the news," he said, looking very pleased with himself. "You'll never guess who I lunched with today." He didn't wait for her to guess but went on, "Reggie Haverford. The duke of Haverford, Mother! And it seems he was very taken with young Margaret at her ball last week. He thinks she'll make a fine match for his son, Crispin."

"Crispin Haverford?" Emma said in horror. "Wasn't he the young man who looks as if he's got no eyebrows? And he stutters and his teeth stick out?"

"And he'll be a duke someday," Robert said. "I admit his behavior is awkward, Mother, but he'll grow out of it. He's only nineteen, after all."

"And what does Margaret think about this idea?" Emma asked. She listened as the hoof-beats died into the distance.

"Margaret? I haven't discussed it with her yet, but what she thinks doesn't really matter. It's up to her mother and me to find her the most suitable husband. What can a girl of her age know about selecting a mate?"

"I let you choose your own wife," Emma reminded him.

"Ah, yes, but that was only because you didn't know any better," Robert said, patting her hand. "You always were too much of a softie, Mama. Young Francis will inherit all this someday, but I must make a good match for Margaret. It wouldn't hurt to link two such great families as ours. She'll get used to the idea in time."

He started for the door again.

"Watch how you put it to her, Robert," Emma said. "Try to be tactful and understanding. You know how you bluster when you can't get your own way."

"I do not!" he began, then cleared his

throat and closed the door behind him.

Emma waited tensely for Margaret to come back. She heard the returning hoofbeats and almost immediately the sound of light feet across the parquet floor to her room. "Grandmama, may I come in?" a small voice whispered. Margaret's elfin face peeped around the door, and then she ran across to her grandmother, flinging her arms around the old woman.

"Grandmama, the most amazing thing!" she said breathlessly.

"Have you spoken to your father?" Emma asked. The child did not sound as upset as she would have expected.

"Not since breakfast," Margaret said. "I've been out riding with Peter, and you won't believe what happened. My horse bolted with me!"

"Child, that's terrible. Were you riding Blackbriar again? That horse is too strong for you."

"But it wasn't terrible at all," Margaret said. She still sounded breathless, and her eyes were very bright. "It turned out just wonderfully. We were going down Emmett's Lane, and someone was shooting in the woods. Blackbriar just took off with me and I couldn't control him, but Peter was marvelous. He galloped alongside me and brought Blackbriar to a halt. Just before we would have plunged into Halton Pond too." She looked at her grandmother with glowing eyes. "He saved my life, Grandmama. He is so wonderful." She knelt beside the old woman and rested her head in her grandmother's lap.

"He's a very nice young boy," Emma said cautiously. "We're lucky to have such good servants here. I must get your father to thank him."

"Oh, no, Grandmama, it's more than that," Margaret said, lifting her head to look at the old woman's face. "I think I love him, Grandmama. Really, truly love him. Oh, why does he have to be only a groom? I could be so happy with him. He's the nicest person I've ever met."

Emma put out her hand to touch her granddaughter's hair. "Before you go on, child, I think you should speak with your father," she said. "He has some important news for you."

"Bad news?" Margaret asked, her eyes growing fearful.

"You'll probably see it as bad news."

"Can't you tell me then? I'd rather you told me than Papa. He always shouts so."

"Very well, I'll tell you," Emma said, "although you mustn't give me away when your father tells you later. He wants you to marry Crispin Haverford."

Margaret looked up, half laughing. "You're joking. He's hideous. He's repulsive. Surely Papa couldn't really be serious . . ." The smile faded. "He is serious? I can't believe it. Granny, I can't marry him. I could never marry him. I'd rather kill myself!"

"Gently, child," Emma said, stroking Margaret's white arm. "You know what your father's like when he gets an idea into his head. We'll have to find a way of talking him out of it."

166

Margaret's arms tightened around the old woman. "Promise me I won't have to marry anybody I don't like, Grandmama! I'd just die if I had to marry someone as repulsive as Crispin."

"I'll do what I can, sweet one."

"No, promise me!" Margaret begged. "You're my only hope, Grandmama. Mother wants me to be happy, but she can't stand up to Father when he's in one of his moods. You and Peter are the only ones I can trust. Why can't any of the boys I'm supposed to marry be more like Peter?"

She gave a long, heavy sigh. Emma turned away to stare out the window.

"It's no use, darling," she said. "We live in a ridiculous society. Marriage between people of different classes is just not allowed. You'll have to face the fact that maybe you won't love your husband. But I promise you I'll do what I can to make sure it isn't that awful Crispin person."

Margaret got slowly to her feet. "Thank you, Granny," she said. "I do love you so much."

Emma watched her walk from the room. "Poor child," she thought. "I know just how she feels. If only there were something I could do. . . ."

Down in the stables, Peter Pratt was rubbing down the two horses and putting on their blankets. A shadow blocked the doorway. He looked up to see Margaret standing there, her face deathly white.

"Miss Maggie, what is it?" he asked, coming across to her.

"Oh, Peter, terrible news," she whispered. "I had to see you right away. I've been talking to my father. He's told me I've got to marry the duke of Haverford's son."

"What, young Crispin? The one who fell off his horse into that ditch at the New Year's hunt?" Peter said incredulously. "He can't be serious."

"But he is, Peter," Margaret said. "He said that Crispin is going to be a duke someday and it doesn't matter what he looks like." She grabbed Peter's arm. "You know what he's like when he gets his mind set on something. Grandmama has promised she'll do what she can to talk him out of it, but I don't think she'll be able to this time . . . You should have seen his face and the way he shouted at me . . . Oh, Peter, I'm so miserable I could die."

His arms came around her. "There, there, little one," he said. "Don't cry. Maybe it won't happen. Maybe when he sees how unhappy you are, he'll change his mind."

Margaret nestled her head against his chest, hardly conscious of what she was doing, but feeling the security of his arms around her. "He won't. I know he won't. He wants to be related to a duke. That's all he cares about, Peter. What am I going to do?"

Peter's jaw was clenched. "I just wish there were something I could do, Margaret," he said. "You know I'd do anything in the world for you. I'd marry you myself tomorrow if I were a duke or a lord like your father. But I'm not. I'm only the groom, and I'll never be anything better."

She looked up into his face. "You're better than any of them, Peter. You saved my life today. You've been my only friend. If only I could marry you!"

"And where would we go?" he said in a choked voice. "There's no place in England that would hire me if I ran off with Lord Treadwick's daughter. No door would be open to us, my sweet."

"Then maybe we'll have to leave England. My great-aunt Laura ran away to Australia with the man she loved."

"I don't want you to have to live like a peasant," he said firmly. "You were born to be a lady. You deserve to be treated like one."

"My father's not treating me like a lady," Margaret said bitterly. "He's treating me as if I were a slave at auction, sold to the highest bidder."

Peter stroked back her hair. "Let me think on this awhile. There has to be some way out for us. Be patient and I give you my word that I won't let you marry Lord Haverford's son."

"Oh, Peter," she whispered. "I knew you wouldn't let me down." She raised her face to him and touched her lips to his in a delicate kiss. Then, with a little sigh, he kissed her passionately. When they broke apart they gazed at each other in wonder.

"You'd best go now," Peter said, "before you get us both into big trouble."

*   *   *

A few weeks later Margaret tiptoed into her grandmother's room. Emma had already gone to bed and sat up in alarm at the sight of a shadowy figure.

"I have to talk to you," Margaret whispered, putting her fingers to her lips. "It's very, very secret."

Emma sat up. "You're going to run away?"

"How did you guess?"

"Because your father shows no sign of changing his mind about Crispin, and you love another man."

"I have no alternative, Grandmama," Margaret said, sitting beside her grandmother on the big satin quilt.

Emma considered this, then nodded. "I'm afraid your father is being impossible," she said. "I've tried talking to him, believe me, child. But he's turned out a domineering bully like your grandfather, in spite of all my efforts."

Margaret gently touched her grandmother's arm. "I know you've tried, Grandmama, and thank you for that."

"I only wish there were another way of securing your happiness," Emma said. "Running away with a groom . . ."

"I love Peter and I want to be with him more than anything in the world," Margaret interrupted.

"So when and where are you going?"

"Not for a while," Margaret said. "Peter has heard about the gold being found in California. He's taking the next ship to America, and when he's made his fortune in gold, he's going to send for me!"

Emma shook her head violently. "No, he's not."

"But Granny, I thought you were on my side!" Margaret exclaimed.

"I am. Believe me, I am. But it's a bad idea to have him go ahead and you to follow later. What if your father speeds up the wedding? What if something happens to your Peter?"

"But we have no choice." Margaret looked at her hopelessly. "We don't have enough money to pay for two of us to get out to California. Peter doesn't want me to have to live like a peasant. He wants to bring me out in style."

"And if he doesn't succeed at finding this gold? What then?"

"I don't know." Margaret sighed. "He will succeed. He's got to succeed."

Emma patted her hand. "Bring him to me, tomorrow," she said. "I want to talk to him."

Next morning the young pair slipped up the servants' staircase and into Emma's parlor.

"Sit down, both of you, and listen to me," she said. "Many years ago I loved a young man. He was a good, upstanding young man who had only one fault. He was poor. He couldn't afford to take a wife. I had no money of my own and I was a good child, always willing to please my parents. I married the man they wanted me to marry and I've regretted it ever since. Now I have a chance to make things right for you. I don't want you to make the same mistake I made. I want you to be happy together. That's why I'm giving you this." She handed Margaret a small velvet pouch. Margaret opened it, and sparkling diamonds fell into her hand. She looked up in wonder.

"Those are the Sutcliffe diamonds," Emma said. "My sister took half the necklace to Australia. I had the other half. I could have used them to run away to be with the man I loved, but I was too weak. I want you two to be strong, because even with these diamonds you are going to encounter many hardships. You are going to a rough, primitive country, but I want you to be together. If you have each other, nothing else will really matter."

Margaret looked from the stones in her hand to her grandmother's face. "But I can't take the family jewels," she said.

"They are not the family jewels, they are my jewels," Emma said. "Nobody else knows about them. I never showed them to my husband or son. They are very valuable. They should be enough to see you through the worst days."

"But what about you, Grandmama? What if you should need them?"

Emma smiled. "I'm keeping one stone for myself. The queen stone from the center will stay here with me. I don't think you'd be able to sell it because it is unique, and I wouldn't want you to run afoul of the law because it was thought that you stole it. I'll never use it, though. I'm old and

I've nothing to look forward to." She reached out her hand toward Margaret. "Your happiness is the only thing important to me now. Now pack your most useful clothes and go. Go as soon as possible, before your father suspects anything."

Margaret clutched the old woman's hand. "I'll never see you again," she said, tears welling in her eyes.

Emma nodded. "I'll be happy if you are happy," she said. "I told my sister the same thing when she went away all those years ago. And she was happy. She married a good man—a man who sounds a lot like your Peter—and he looked after her well, all his life." She turned her face away, to the dying embers of the fire. "Not all of us are destined to know happiness," she said, "but I wish it for you with all my heart."

The young girl kissed the paper-thin, wrinkled cheek. "I love you so much, Grandmama," she said. "I'll never be able to thank you for what you've done for me. I'll write and give you all our news."

"And I promise I'll take the best care of her, Lady Treadwick," Peter added, coming to put his hands protectively on Margaret's shoulders.

Emma smiled. "I'm sure you will, Peter," she said. "That's why I'm entrusting her to you. God be with you both."

It was only after they had left the room that she lay back and let the tears flow freely. After Thomas, she thought that she'd never love again, but she had come to adore this bright, beautiful child who was going half a world away.

173

CHAPTER FOURTEEN

FORT LARAMIE, OREGON TRAIL, AMERICA.
JULY 1850

"Dearest Grandmama,

By the time this reaches you, we will be in California, if we do not succumb by the wayside like so many poor unfortunates along this trail. Granny, if I had known what terrible hardships lay ahead for me, I think I might have preferred to stay in England, even if it meant marrying Crispin Haverford. Please don't misunderstand me: I love Peter with all my heart, and he is the dearest, sweetest husband a girl could ever want. It's just that I had never imagined, in my wildest dreams, how awful the conditions here would be, and I still don't know if I will be strong enough for the worst part that lies ahead.

When we chose to come overland, instead of risking the lengthy sea passage around Cape Horn, we thought we were choosing the safer, easier route. But we were wrong, Grandmama. This route is anything but safe, as the pathetic grave markers every mile of the way attest. Cholera sweeps through the camps and wagon trains. Even before we started out from Independence,

Missouri, there was a terrible epidemic of cholera, and the stench of death was everywhere. We hoped things would get better when we were out in the fresh air of the prairie, and to a certain extent they have. Nobody has died of cholera from among our small group of wagons, but there are still enough hazards to make us say our prayers earnestly every night. Yesterday a small child fell off the back of the Johannsons' wagon and rolled under the wheels. He was killed instantly. This is our second loss of a child: The Harzmann's little daughter Gretel wandered away into the tall prairie grass while we were making camp and, try as we might, we never found her. We suspect that maybe a coyote or wolf took her. Mrs. Harzmann goes about her daily chores and doesn't show her grief. How strong these women must be. I could hardly stop weeping for days and I scarcely knew the child.

There is also the ever-present threat of wild Indians lurking to attack us. We have met returning travelers who have told us frightening tales of Indian attacks and how they scalp all their victims. Pray God we don't meet such an end. We did see Indians once, when we were still crossing the open prairie: They rode past us, in pursuit of buffalo, not even casting a look in our direction. I thought they looked very fine, with their long black hair streaming out behind them!

Now we have left the endless waving grass for a more barren, rocky country as we ascend the Great Divide. Water and grazing for the animals have become more scarce, as many parties have gone before us this year and the only grazing has been used up. We have had to cross some mighty rivers, sealing the bottom of the wagon with tar and floating it across on ropes. The poor animals have to make their own way across, protesting wildly. Some get swept away in the current, and we hear their cries as they are carried downstream.

But what terrifies me most, dearest Granny, is the loneliness and immensity of this land. In England I believe that one is never more than a day's ride from a friendly village. Here it is many weeks' travel between the pathetic outposts they call forts. When we leave one, we know that there is nobody to come to our aid, whatever befalls us. We are entirely on our own.

Thank God that Peter was not brought up to be a lord's son like my brother, Francis, or we would never have survived. His skills and common sense have been much appreciated by the other travelers. He knows more about horses and other animals than most. It is he who manages to fix broken wagon wheels, or even stitch up broken harnesses. Beside him, I feel like a ninny. I have learned to do a few little things—like make bread in a pan over a fire and even roast a buffalo steak. But the other women are so handy at all sorts of household tasks. Why, oh why, did I waste all those years learning French and piano and embroidery when I could have been learning how to make a stew or mend torn clothing? I see how very false and shallow our life was. At least out here we know we're living, every moment of every day.

As we lie beside our campfire at night and I gaze up at a sky ablaze with stars like a magic temple, I think of you and of home and already they seem like a pleasant dream that fades upon waking. The thought of my whole life ahead in this strange, hostile land makes me want to pull the covers over my head. Then my dear Peter sees me awake and takes me in his strong, comforting arms and I really believe everything will be all right.

God bless you, Granny. I can't thank you enough for your kindness to us. Without you we would never have managed to escape. I hope Father has found it in his heart to forgive me just a little by now. Your loving grand-daughter, Margaret."

"It's no use, Peter," Margaret said helplessly, "I can't go on."

After the heat of the desert they had reached the summit of the Sierras only to be trapped by an early snowstorm. The past month had been like a walking, waking hell. Margaret staggered through the snow, dizzy with fatigue, her skirts feeling as if they were full of lead. She couldn't feel her feet in her thin leather shoes. All she could think of was sleep: a warm bed, a roaring fire, and blissful sleep.

Peter caught her as she stumbled. "Not

much farther now," he said, wrapping his arms around her.

"It's no use," she whispered. "I can't walk another step. You go on. Just leave me here to sleep."

"Don't be silly," he said, kissing her cold lips. "You haven't come this far to give up at the last minute. We're already in California. Can't you see the trail's starting to go down? What's the betting we see smoke from the first houses tomorrow?"

Margaret swayed in his arms, her face deathly white. Alarmed, he caught her up and carried her to the wagon. "This won't do," he said, placing her tenderly among the quilts and rubbing her cold limbs to restore life to them. "I can't have my best girl getting sick on me now. I thought you were a strong little thing. Remember how you always liked to beat me when we raced our horses back home?"

Margaret smiled weakly.

"So come on, where's your fighting stamina now? Weren't all those Treadwick ancestors famous for fighting battles? Now take this blanket and wrap it around you and take my arm. You'll just get colder if you sit still in the wagon."

"I'll try, Peter," she whispered. "It's just that I'm not feeling myself. I keep feeling so sick and faint."

"I'll get Mrs. Harzmann to have a look at you when we stop tonight," Peter said. "Maybe she can make you one of her famous remedies."

Step by step they walked through the snow. In the deepest parts, Peter forged ahead to make a path for her. Then gradually they noticed that the snow was getting less and less until it was a mere sprinkling. They had started to come down from the mountains.

That night at camp, Mrs. Harzmann talked to Margaret. When she got up to leave she was smiling.

"Is there anything you can do to help her?" Peter asked worriedly. "It's not the cholera, is it?"

Mrs. Harzmann's grin broadened. "There's nothing I can do for seven months or so," she said. "But call me then if you need me. I've delivered a few babies in my time."

Peter looked from her face to Margaret's in wonder. "A baby?" he whispered. "We're going to have a baby?"

Margaret nodded, her eyes shining. They were in California and they were going to have a baby. Surely now everything was going to be fine after all.

Three days later they came down from the mountains into Hangtown. This was where the trail officially ended. The party broke up, each family heading for a different area of the gold fields. Margaret tried not to cry when she said good-bye to Mrs. Harzmann and watched their wagon roll south down toward Angels Camp and other German settlers.

She stood holding Peter's hand in the middle of the main street, looking around her in dismay. For weeks she had been fantasizing about journey's end, about a real town with cozy cabins and smoke rising from friendly chimneys. But of all the things they had seen so far, this was the worst: The town contained only two or three real buildings. The others were all made of canvas and scraps, strung out along a main street that was a sea of mud and piled with every kind of garbage—open sardine cans, beer bottles, old boots, broken harnesses. It looked awful and smelled worse. As they watched, a man ran out of the saloon, slithering his way across the street. There was a shout, and another man ran after him, raised a gun, and fired. The first man sprawled facedown in the mud. Margaret started to go to him, but Peter's strong hand held her back.

"This is their kind of law," he whispered. "We can't make enemies or get involved."

Margaret shuddered as she watched a group of men come out of the saloon and haul away the dead man, dragging him along like an animal carcass.

Margaret slipped her hand into Peter's. She didn't want him to know how scared she was feeling right now. No home and only the vaguest idea of how to go about finding gold in this lawless land!

After having a hot meal at the ramshackle hotel, she and Peter went to the store to get supplies, and they were shocked by the price of everything: Flour cost thirty-five dollars a barrel. A shovel was twenty dollars, a tent seventy-five dollars. Even potatoes were a dollar each.

"This is crazy," Margaret said. "Everything costs more than most people can earn in a year!"

Peter nodded in agreement.

Margaret tugged on his sleeve. "We'll starve if we don't use the diamonds."

Peter looked anguished, but then nodded and fished for the pouch he carried around his neck. He cleared his throat and walked up to the storekeeper. "I need to know how much you'll give me for this," he said, holding out the sparkling stone. The storekeeper glanced at it, then spat onto the floor. "Two forms of currency here," he said. "Gold or goods. That ain't no use to man or beast."

"Then how am I going to pay for my supplies?" Peter asked.

"Likely you could trade that down in San Francisco, where they got fancy jewelry stores, so I hear," the man said.

Peter and Margaret glanced at each other. After such a long journey they had no wish to head away from the gold again.

"I have two oxen left," Peter said. "Can I trade those?"

The man nodded. "If they're only good for meat, I can't give you much for them," he said, "but if they've still got some work in them, I'll give you more."

He came to look at the oxen and they struck a bargain. "Good luck to you, Mr.—"

"Sutcliffe," Margaret said quickly. Peter looked at her strangely.

They left the store with a pan and shovel and basic food supplies.

"Why did you say our name was Sutcliffe?" Peter asked. "Wasn't plain old Pratt good enough for you?"

"In case my father sends someone looking for us," Margaret said. "I hear that nobody uses their right name out here. Sutcliffe is my middle name. It was the first thing that came into my head."

Peter laughed. "Very well, then we'll be the Sutcliffes."

They had the oxen take the wagon down to find a campsite, close to the river, and then Peter led them away.

"I'll build us a cabin just as soon as I find some gold," Peter said, "but right now we'll have to make do with the old wagon. We'll make it as snug as we can."

Margaret remembered how cold they had been in the snowstorm and didn't think that the wagon could possibly be snug enough, but she nodded and gave him a reassuring smile. "I'll come with you to help choose a site to start digging," she said.

"Come on then," he said. "Maybe you'll bring me luck."

They set off down the riverbank. It was very pretty, shaded with oak and pine trees, and the water bubbled over rocks. All along came the sound of picks and shovels and the rough voices of men.

"It doesn't look like they've left much space for us," Margaret said.

"I'm sure we'll find the perfect spot, my love," Peter said. "I'll start digging and up will come a big lump of gold." Margaret smiled at him. She hoped this was true, for his sake. He wanted so much to make things right for her.

"Here we are," he said. "It doesn't seem like anybody's working this bit!" He ran forward with his shovel and pan and started to take off his boots.

"Raise your hands, stranger," said a threatening voice behind them. A lean dark man came through the trees, his rifle raised at them. "You're lucky I didn't shoot first and ask questions afterward," he said, "but you're trespassing on my stretch of river."

"I'm sorry, sir, but it didn't seem to be occupied," Peter said, inching his way up the bank with his hands held high. "We just arrived here."

The man lowered his rifle. "Newcomers, eh?" He spat. "See that shovel against the tree? If you see any tools it means the stretch is taken."

"I won't be likely to forget in a hurry," Peter said with a nervous laugh. "Maybe you could suggest a part of the river that's not so crowded."

"It's all crowded now, boy," the man said. "Too many people here and all the easy gold's gone. Only the big fellas with the machines are getting gold out now. You're wasting your time. I'd go home if I were you."

"Thanks, but I still plan to try my luck," Peter said. They walked on until Margaret cried out, "Look, Peter, gold for the taking. Just lying there."

She went running down to the water's edge, bending to scoop up golden flakes with her hands. Other miners had heard her shouting and came hurrying to see. When they saw her they burst out laughing. "That ain't gold, lady, that's fool's gold," one of them said. "Only a worthless mineral. If it floats, it ain't gold. Gold's heavy."

They walked back to their campsite, depressed.

"I've made up my mind," Peter said one day. They'd had a week of torrential rains and still no luck in finding an ounce of gold. "I'm going down to San Francisco to trade in those diamonds. I can't take you with me in your condition, but I'm going to put you in the hotel until I get back."

"I'll stay here," Margaret said firmly. "If we look like we've abandoned our site, anybody could help themselves to our things."

"I'd rather you were in the hotel."

She faced him with the Sutcliffe stubbornness. "We don't have the money for hotels," she said. "I'll be fine here. I'll wrap myself up snugly and try to keep the stove going."

"I don't like leaving you," Peter said, "but I'll be back within a week, God willing."

Margaret watched him walk away, not knowing if she'd ever see him again. After a month went by with no sign of Peter returning, Margaret had to consider what she should do next. The baby would be born before long, and she didn't think she could go through that alone, in a place like this. Often when she lay alone, wrapped in quilts, she thought of her feather bed at Treadwick, of the food that always appeared on the table at meals and the servants who whisked away dirty dishes. She'd taken it all for granted. She longed so much to go home now, to be with her mother and grandmother, safe and secure. But she had no way of going anywhere. Peter was gone with the diamonds. She wondered if he had been robbed and killed for them. This was a lawless country, after all. She couldn't bear to think of life without him. She knew that soon she'd have to write home and hope that her family would send her enough for the fare back on a ship. Grandmama would send her the money, she knew that, if Grandmama was still alive. . . . She tried to be very brave and not cry, but at night the tears came anyway. Only the healthy baby kicking inside her kept her going from day to day.

At last the day came when she could put off writing home for help no longer. She forced herself to get out pen and paper and sat on an old tree stump, trying to compose the letter in her head. Suddenly she heard a shout on the hill above. She looked up and there was Peter, running down the slope, waving his arms like a madman. He swept her up into his arms, weeping and laughing and covering her with kisses.

"They wouldn't let me back," he kept on saying. "I've been worried sick about you."

"What happened?"

"The whole valley flooded and there was no way up from Sacramento for a month. I was stuck in Sacramento, which is a filthy, stinking hole, not able to send you any kind of message because there was a flood between us. But I'm here now, my love, and you're well and our little one is flourishing." The words poured out in a torrent as he almost crushed her in his embrace.

"And you traded the diamonds for money?" she asked.

A big grin spread across his face. "Better than that, my love. I've got a whole wagon full of supplies with me: shovels, jackets, boots, everything a miner could need. We're going to set up shop and make a fortune!"

"Dearest Grandmama,
I hope this letter reaches you safely. I am finally able to report that all is going well with us. Our beautiful little son, James Peter, was born last March. He is registered as James Peter Sutcliffe, so there are now Sutcliffes in America, carrying on the line for you, Granny.

Peter decided to be a storekeeper instead of a gold digger, and it has really paid off. From that first wagon load he has now built a fine store. I don't think we'll be here much longer, though. When the gold finally peters out, as seems likely, we'll take our profits and open a store down in San Francisco. And do you know the first thing that Peter says he'll do when we go to San Francisco? Retrieve our diamonds. They are in a pawnshop, waiting to be bought back.

We've come through some hardships, Granny, but it looks like everything is going well for us now. I do wish you could see our chubby little one, babbling to himself as he lies under the oak trees. We feel truly blessed. I love you, Granny. I'll never forget what you did for me. You gave me a chance at life. Thank you. Your loving grand-daughter, Margaret."

Emma wiped her eyes and tucked the letter back into her desk. She must not keep rereading it like this. It always made her cry. She was so happy to know that all was well, but California was so far away. She'd never see her lovely Margaret again now, nor chubby James Peter.

The days at Treadwick seemed to drag on and on for her now, and she felt her loneliness hang over her like a shroud. When the rain peppered the windows and the trees danced in a winter wind, she closed her eyes and tried to picture the warm California sunshine.

She was supposed to go and stay with old Lady Hartford up at Hartford Manor in Norfolk. She knew the change of air would do her good, but she wasn't sure she felt strong enough to go. Once she was there, though,

Lady Hartford welcomed her warmly and installed her in a comfortable suite with a roaring fire. Emma made polite conversation at lunch, but during the afternoon the chest pains began. By nightfall they had grown so severe that the doctor was summoned. "Shall I send for the clergyman?" he asked her gently.

"Is it time for that?" Emma whispered.

"It may be," he said. "Your heart is very weak."

"Very well, then."

She lay back, her eyes closed. It was hard to breathe, as if someone were sitting on her chest. She opened her eyes when she heard a voice calling her name gently. Then she was sure that she had died, because Thomas was standing there: older, grayer, but still very recognizably Thomas.

"Is it really you?" she whispered.

He nodded. "And it's really you, Emma."

"How did you find me?"

He smiled and took her hand. "I'm the vicar of this parish now. I've had the job for a couple of years."

"And I was imagining you still in Yorkshire."

He smiled. "I left Yorkshire some ten years back. When my wife died."

"Oh."

"And your husband?"

"He died the year we were married, Thomas. That very day you came to the house. A tragic accident."

"You've been a widow all these years?"

"All these years."

"You never wanted to marry again?"

She smiled weakly and covered his hand with her cold, white one. "There was only ever one man for me, Thomas. No one could have measured up to you."

"I've never stopped thinking of you, Emma," he whispered. "But I thought your husband still lived. I heard people talk of Lord Treadwick and I assumed . . ."

"My son," she said. "My son is Lord Treadwick."

He took both her hands in his. "So many years we wasted, Emma. So many years when we could have known happiness. She was a good woman, my wife, but I never loved her . . . not like I could have loved you."

Tears ran silently down both their cheeks. He wiped hers away gently with his hand. "But now, dearest, you must get well again for me. We could still have the best part of our lives ahead, Emma. Our golden years together. What do you say?"

The tears continued to flow unchecked down her cheeks. "If only you weren't too late, Thomas," she said. "If only you hadn't come too late."

"No, Emma. Not too late. You'll recover," he pleaded.

She shook her head. "I have one request, Thomas. Stay with me until the end. I want to die looking at your face . . . at the only face I really loved. . . ."

CHAPTER FIFTEEN

ENGLAND. THE PRESENT

A fat tear splashed down onto the book in Laura's hand. It had been Emma's diary, but the last few lines were in a different hand.

"Lady Treadwick passed away yesterday while visiting her friend in Norfolk. The Reverend Thomas Conway was with her when she died, and afterward her face was so peaceful and lovely that all the servants cried . . ."

Laura put her hand up to wipe her cheek. It was so sad! So unnecessary and so sad. Poor Emma and Thomas had had to live all their lives apart when they truly loved each other. "If Grandma was trying to teach me that it doesn't pay to fall in love with a man her family disapproves of, then I don't believe her," Laura thought. "Emma did what she was told and married the man her family picked for her, and look what happened to her—only unhappiness all her life!"

She moved stiffly, realizing how long she must have been sitting curled up in the chair. Then she noticed something else—the shaft of sunlight was no longer coming in through the window. Laura jumped up—she must have been up here for hours!

"I'd better get out of here before I'm shut in for the night," she thought. She didn't relish the idea of being alone in that great house with a ghostly ancestor and no light. Besides, Grandma would be frantic with worry if she didn't show up at the hotel.

She looked longingly at the letters and diaries as she returned them to the trunk. She would dearly have loved to take them with her, but she could hardly be seen dragging a trunk out of the building. Instead, she slipped Emma's diary into her purse. She'd get Grandma to write to the owners and ask for the rest later. Surely they couldn't refuse. They couldn't claim to own her family letters, could they?

The staircase was dark as she made her way down. The upstairs halls were also gloomy, and it was hard to see what lay at either end. Strange portraits stared down at her, and it was horribly quiet. Surely everyone hadn't gone for the night . . . surely they didn't lock the doors, turn off the lights, and go.

She made her way down the main staircase, trying not to wonder how on earth she was going to get out when she got to the bottom. She convinced herself that there would have to be janitors or security guards still hanging around and she'd only have to yell to be rescued. Which made her realize that she'd have to think up a good story as to why she got left behind. She was still trying to come up with something halfway believable when she stepped down from the stairs and crossed the black-and-white marble floor of the entrance hall.

She had only taken two steps when a loud clanging almost made her jump out of her skin. Alarm bells were ringing everywhere. Before she could decide what to do next, the front door opened and security guards came running in. The sound was so overpowering that Laura couldn't say anything as she was grabbed and dragged outside.

"Go and call the police, Fred," one of the guards said.

"No, wait a minute, I can explain," Laura began, but nobody seemed to be listening to her as she was half carried across the gravel courtyard.

They took her to the little building that housed the ticket booth. There was an office in the back, and Fred went straight to the phone. Several tourist stragglers came up to see what all the noise was about, and soon quite a crowd had gathered.

"You don't have to call the police," Laura said. She was now beginning to feel more angry than scared. "I wasn't doing anything. I was on a tour and I got left behind."

"Oh, yeah?" the guard said, smirking at her. "The last tour finished an hour ago. And we always do a thorough inspection before we lock up. We've had a few attempted burglaries lately."

"I wasn't trying to steal anything," Laura said angrily. "Now let me go."

"If you weren't stealing you were still trespassing and that's a criminal offense," the guard said. "It's not up to me. I've got my orders and I'm to call the police."

"This is stupid!" Laura said. "This used to be my family home. My ancestors lived in this house, and I wanted to hang around a little longer than the rest, just to get the feel of the place. What's so wrong with that?"

"Nothing, I suppose," the guard said, "except you should have come out when the last call was made. You're supposed to stay with your tour. Now your guide will be in trouble too."

"Excuse me a minute." A young man pushed his way through the crowd. Laura remembered seeing him earlier. He was the one dressed in a tweed jacket with the big camera—the one she thought had to be a reporter. "I couldn't help overhearing," he said. "You said this used to be your family home?"

He had a pleasant, very English-looking face with light brown hair flopping boyishly forward across his forehead and clear blue eyes. He didn't look much older than Laura. She smiled at him hopefully, realizing she might need an ally at the moment. "That's right," she said. "My grandmother was born here. I wanted to see the house she'd told me about."

"I see," he said. As she spoke he had taken a pad from his pocket, on which he was already

193

scribbling, reporter-style. "And your name is?"

"Laura Sutcliffe," she said.

"Sutcliffe? Weren't the Treadwicks associated with the Sutcliffes once?"

"Emma Treadwick was a Sutcliffe before she married," Laura said, "although my Sutcliffe name started when Margaret Treadwick ran away to America and had to change her name." She was amazed at the ring of pride in her own voice, almost as if the first Laura were speaking.

"Interesting," he said. Laura noticed the way his blue eyes actually lit up when he said this. "I think I might have a story here," he said.

"Just a moment, sir," one of the guards interrupted. "We've just apprehended this young lady. We're supposed to call the police . . ."

"It won't take a moment," the reporter said. "This is all so interesting. I might want to put it in the newspaper." Laura thought he made it sound as if he was straight from the *Times*. He held out his hand to her. "I'm Simon Davies. I've just started this job as reporter on the local paper in Cirencester. All they let me do is boring things like weddings, so I come to places like this on my days off, hoping for a scoop. I think I may have found my first one."

"You sure have, if they still hang people in England for trespassing," Laura said, giving him a friendly grin.

"Oh, no, they usually only put them in the stocks or the ducking stool," he said. "At the most, fifty lashes."

They stood smiling at each other.

"So, can I talk to you sometime about your family connection? It might make a good story," Simon said.

"Sure. But right now we're waiting for the police to arrive and drag me away in chains," she said.

"I'll have a word if you like," Simon said.

"Would you? Thanks," Laura said. She was feeling better by the minute.

Just then the police arrived in an ancient squad car.

"What have we got, Harry?" the constable called as he got out.

"Young girl here, trespassing, possible burglary," Harry replied. "She set off the alarm in the hall. Don't know if she was going in or out."

The policeman looked Laura over. "Let's have a look in your purse, love," he said.

"That's ridiculous. I didn't steal anything," Laura began, but the policeman had opened the purse.

"So what's this?" he asked, pulling out the old leather-bound diary. He opened it. "Emma Treadwick, 1808," he read. "Didn't steal anything, eh? You better come down to the station with me in the car."

"Look, I can explain," Laura said. "This really belongs to me . . ."

"Oh, yeah?" The policeman looked at her coldly.

"Yes. Emma was my ancestor. It means nothing to the people who own this house now."

"You Yanks are all the same," the policeman said. "Come over here with fancy ideas about looking for your ancestors. And always in stately homes too. You don't find nobody looking for ancestors in slums."

"Just a minute, sergeant," Simon said. "I think this case is different. Her grandmother was born in the house."

"I don't care if Prince Charles is her brother," the policeman said. "She was caught in the house, and she's got something what don't belong to her, and that's trespassing and stealing, and I have to take her down to the station and book her. She can do her explaining to the magistrate. Maybe he'll be more understanding."

Laura shot Simon a worried look. "How long do you think this will take?" she asked. "My grandmother is up in London."

"Really? Your grandmother is here too? Super. Maybe I can interview both of you," Simon said. "If you give me her phone number, I'll call her for you and let her know what's happened."

"Would you really? Thanks a lot," Laura said. "I hope she's not going to be too angry."

"That you got yourself arrested?"

"That I snuck down here without telling her. She's very big on law and order and all that stuff." Laura made a nervous grimace. She could just see Grandmama giving her a long lecture and then condemning her to a solid week of art galleries as punishment.

"I expect she'll be worried," Simon said. He handed her his pad, and she scribbled down her name and phone number.

"I'll call her right away," Simon said, "and then I'll catch up with you at the police station, just in case you need any help."

Laura gave him a weak smile, wishing he could ride along with her in the police car. She'd never ridden in a police car before or been to a police station. She had a feeling that Brian would think this was a big joke—something to boast to his friends about later, but she couldn't help feeling scared. Did they put you in a cell, fingerprint you, frisk you? What if they kept her overnight in a cell full of criminals? She let herself be helped into the backseat and was very glad that the man didn't try to put handcuffs on her—also that there was no siren as they drove away. She looked back at Simon and saw him give a friendly wave.

He was waiting for her on the bench outside the police station when she finally emerged, just as the village clock was striking six.

"Obviously not a day for forty lashes," he said, eyeing her with a boyish grin. "And here I was waiting for your screams, ready to dash in and rescue you."

"The worst I had to endure was a cup of ter-

197

rible strong tea," Laura said. "They were actually very nice to me."

"Ah, yes, well, we British are a civilized lot," Simon said. "I called your grandma, by the way, and I reassured her she didn't have to come down here, and you were okay."

"Thank you, Simon," Laura said. "I would have hated making that call. She would probably have freaked out before I got finished."

"She did freak out slightly at the mention of the words *arrest* and *police station*," Simon said. "But I assured her it was only a small crime."

They looked at each other and laughed. "Where to now?" he said.

"I suppose I should catch the next train back to London," Laura said, half regretting now that she had to leave.

"I'll drive you to the station," he said, "and then maybe we could arrange for me to come up to London and meet with you both later this week?"

"I have to come down here for my court appearance," Laura said. "I'm to face the magistrate on Thursday."

He took her arm. "Come on, the car's over here."

He opened the door and helped her in. At home Laura would have been furious if anybody tried such antifeminist stuff on her, but here it seemed sort of sweet. At the station they found that the next train was almost an hour away, so they went to the nearest café and sat drinking watery coffee and talking.

"You look very young to be a journalist," Laura said. "Are you already done with college?"

Simon played with the sugar wrapper. "I couldn't go to university," he said. "I wanted to, but my folks couldn't afford it. My dad was laid off a couple of years ago and hasn't got another job yet. So I had to settle for second best. I've got this sort of apprentice reporter job with a tiny newspaper, and I go to classes at night. It's hard work, but I'm determined to make it, however long it takes."

"That's amazing," Laura said. "Exactly the same thing is happening to me. I can't go away to school either because my father lost his job . . . and my older sister is already at Berkeley. She's got an IQ of about five hundred and loves studying, so it makes sense to let her stay there." She was amazed at hearing herself admit this. "I'll probably have to do what you're doing—work my way through school. Although in my case I don't have any idea what I want to do with my life yet."

Simon nodded as if he understood. He picked up his coffee cup and took a big gulp. "I'm dying of curiosity," he said. "How come you start off as owning Treadwick Hall and end up with a father out of work like mine?"

"It's a very long story." Laura toyed with her spoon, drawing lines on the white cloth. "You'd better wait until my grandmother can tell you. I'm still too confused. The family went in different directions, you see. The first Laura

199

went to Australia, and Margaret went to California, and yet we all got mixed up again later in a way that I don't understand yet. And I don't think that any of the branches have wound up rich, in spite of the diamonds . . ."

"Diamonds? What diamonds?" Simon was looking at her with keen interest.

"The Sutcliffe diamonds. We got them from Queen Marie Antoinette of France, and then the necklace got broken into three parts, but I haven't found out what happened to them. We sure don't own ours anymore or we'd have used them by now."

Simon looked at her, his eyes sparkling with interest. "Are you sure you're not making this up?" he said. "You're not trying to pull my leg because I'm just a new reporter, are you?"

"Of course not," Laura said. "I'm dying to find out more about them for myself."

"This is incredible," Simon said. "You don't think they're still hidden in Treadwick Hall, do you? What a scoop that would be if I was with you when you found them again."

"It would only be the big stone," Laura said, "and I don't think it can still be there or they would have used it instead of having to sell up and move."

Simon nodded. "You're right," he said. "But there's no harm in looking, is there?"

"That's what I was doing today, and I got myself arrested," Laura said with an embarrassed grin.

"Then maybe we should contact the owners. I could do that for you. If they thought there was going to be a story about Treadwick in the newspaper, they might see it as good publicity. These old houses need all the publicity they can get to keep going."

"Wow, I wonder if that would really work." Laura looked at him excitedly. "That would be terrific, Simon. There's all sorts of junk up in that attic, and who knows how many other rooms have got important clues in them?"

"I'll get onto them right away." Simon got out his notebook and began scribbling.

"Good luck," Laura said. "They're on a yacht in the Caribbean, according to the girl at the ticket booth."

His boyish face fell for a moment, and then he looked up again with a grin. "No problem. I'll just get the next flight out to Trinidad, charter a fast speedboat . . ." He saw Laura's face. "Don't laugh," he said. "I might be the sort of reporter who does that someday. And I will get in touch with them somehow. They must have an agent here—someone who represents them and who can call them in emergencies."

A hoot from a passing train made Laura jump. "That wasn't my train, was it?"

"No, that's only the local," Simon said, peering out the window.

"I should get back to the station," Laura said, getting to her feet. "I've really enjoyed talking to you, Simon."

"Me too. I'm still thanking my lucky stars that I went to Treadwick today. I must have a real newsman's nose after all! And I'll see you again on Thursday—and then if you're in jail down here, I can visit you every day . . . Hey, just kidding. The very worst would be a small fine. But you'll probably get off free because you're a foreigner and don't know any better!" He laughed and dodged as she went to hit him. *It's funny,* she thought, *but I feel like I've known him a long time.*

"What on earth possessed you to go running off on your own like that?" Grandma demanded as Laura flopped exhaustedly onto the hotel bed. "And to get yourself arrested?"

"I wanted to see if the letters and diaries were still in the attic, that's all," Laura said. "And they were, and I sat there reading them until it got dark! I brought Emma's diary back for you, but they said I was stealing it. I tried to tell them it was ours by right, but I don't think they believed me. Anyway, they've taken the diary and I've got to appear in magistrate's court on Thursday. You'll come with me, won't you? Maybe if they knew that you really were born in the house . . ."

"Of course I'll come with you, although I don't know that I'll make much difference. Whoever bought the house bought it with the furnishings and fixtures, Laura. That means they legally own everything. I think you'll still end up paying a fine."

"Simon doesn't think so," Laura said.

"And who is Simon?"

"The guy who called you. I met him at the house. He's just started as a newspaper reporter. He was so nice. He came to the police station and then he drove me to the train. I'm going to meet him again and tell him about our family and what I've discovered. He thinks I'll make a good story, especially now that I've been arrested."

"I see," Grandma said. "No wonder he was so helpful then."

"Oh, he's not like that at all," Laura began.

"Newspapermen all are," Helen countered. "They'd do anything for a good story."

"But he seemed genuinely nice," Laura insisted. "And he's going to try to contact the owners for us to see if they'll let us go back up to the attic and look through the rest of the papers."

Helen Sutcliffe sighed. "I almost wish I'd never started this now. You've become obsessed with your ancestors."

"Of course I have," Laura said.

"And may one ask why this is suddenly so important to you, after you told me very clearly that the past was all boring and irrelevant?" Helen looked at her with amusement.

Laura had wondered the same thing herself. Why was it so important to find out everything about her family? She had a suspicion that it had something to with being very ordinary Laura Sutcliffe, with an unemployed father, destined for a junior college and a nothing sort of life. Somehow having a family of exciting, daring ancestors and a legacy of diamonds would turn her into a different person, worthy of inheriting all this. But how could she put that into words?

"You can't start off a story and then not finish it." She shrugged. "I have to know what happened to everybody and whether they lived happily ever after. And I have to know what happened to the diamonds. Does our family still own them—in which case, how come we're not rich?"

Helen shook her head. "They were all lost, child," she said. "All squandered away for the wrong reasons."

"Do you know how they were lost?" Laura asked.

"For the most part," Grandma Helen said. "The rest I can guess."

CHAPTER SIXTEEN

TESSA FARNWORTH, AUSTRALIA. 1878

The coach came to a halt on the dusty road under a stand of tall gum trees. Their strong, medicine-chest odor hung in the air, reminding Tessa Farnworth that she was home long before she caught a glimpse of the house. She hadn't realized how she'd missed the gum trees. Putting her head out the window, she breathed deeply.

"Here you are, miss," the driver said, coming around to help her down. "My regards to your parents."

"Thank you," Tessa replied stiffly. She allowed him to carry her bags to the side of the road, where a big brick gateway had been built and the carved sign across the gate read THE SUTCLIFFE HERD. PRIZE MERINOS. OWNER JOSEPH FARNWORTH.

The driver climbed back on board and sounded his horn, and the coach drove away in a plume of yellow dust. Tessa waited impatiently, and pretty soon another cloud of dust could be seen coming up the driveway from the white house in the distance. Tessa jumped out onto the track as the buggy approached.

"About time," she called. "I thought you'd forgotten that your only daughter was coming home today! I was being roasted alive and I'll be covered in horrible freckles now, and it's all your fault!"

The dust settled, and Tessa was surprised and embarrassed to see that the driver was not her father, as she had assumed, but a strange young man.

"Who are you?" she demanded.

"Ted Henderson, miss," he said.

"Wonderful," Tessa said dryly. "I've been away for six whole months, and he sends a farmhand out to meet me."

"Ah, well, your dad's tied up at the moment," Ted said, throwing her two bags aboard before offering his hand to help her up. "He's got the shearers in a week earlier than planned, so he couldn't leave. That's why he sent me."

"Stupid sheep," Tessa said. "They're more trouble than they're worth. Always something with them. I bet he still won't leave them to take me to Europe!"

"Your father's built up a very fine herd here, Miss Tessa," Ted said solemnly. "He's got a lot of money tied up in this place."

"Then it's about time he sold it and moved somewhere more civilized," Tessa snapped. She was still annoyed that her father couldn't spare two minutes away from those precious sheep to meet her. "I don't know what he thinks I'm going to do with myself out here."

"I think he's hoping that you'll learn to take over one day," Ted said. "You're the only heir, aren't you?"

Tessa tossed back her dark hair. "I might be the only heir, but I'm certainly not going to find myself stuck in this horrid place."

Ted looked around. "I think it's one of the most beautiful spots I've ever seen," he said. "Reminds me of the Garden of Eden."

"Then I don't suppose you've traveled very much, Mr. Henderson," Tessa said. "Nor have you ever seen the Garden of Eden."

"Have you, Miss Farnworth?" he retorted. "I hadn't realized your name was Eve."

Tessa flushed angrily. One thing she hated was being made fun of. She put on her most superior voice. "Mr. Henderson, if you had been to some parts of Sydney—to the great houses at Darling Point on the harbor, or to Manly on the North Shore—then you'd know what beauty really means. Those spots are truly elegant—not full of gum trees and sheep. I shall absolutely shrivel up and die if I can't go to Sydney once a week." She looked around her in desperation. "How can one exist fifty miles by coach from the nearest department stores and cafés and concerts?"

Ted Henderson said nothing but urged on the horse to a lively trot until the elegant columns of the main house sparkled in the bright sunlight. Tessa could see her mother come running out onto the porch, waving wildly. The three aboriginal housemaids and the Irish cook followed her.

"My darling child," Nora Farnworth said as Tessa sprang down from the wagon. "How very good to have you home again. This time for keeps. I can't believe it. You're through with school. I won't have to break my heart sending you off to Sydney after a couple of weeks with us."

Ted started to lift down the first of the bags. Nora protested: "Oh, no, please leave those, Mr. Henderson. One of the men will be up shortly to get them. And I do hope you'll take tea with us. It's all ready."

"Thank you, Mrs. Farnworth, but I should be getting back to see if your husband needs some help," he said. "Maybe some other afternoon, after Miss Tessa has settled in."

He touched his hat to both of them and walked away. Tessa turned to her mother and raised her eyebrows. "Since when do we invite farmhands to take tea with us?" she demanded indignantly.

"Farmhands? Tessa, don't be so rude," Nora Farnworth said. "Mr. Henderson is a graduate of the agricultural college down in Melbourne. Your father has brought him here as estate manager to improve the breeding quality of his sheep."

"Oh," Tessa said, her cheeks flaming as she remembered how she had spoken to Ted Henderson. But it was his fault, she decided. He hadn't introduced himself. And he had acted like a farmhand!

They were just finishing the last slices of plum cake when big boots could be heard running through the house, and Joseph Farnworth appeared. He was still handsome, like his father, Tip, and his grandfather Roland had been, but his black hair was now streaked with gray. His face broke into a delighted smile, and he opened his arms to his daughter. "Here she is. Here's my precious one," he said. "Come and give your old father a big hug."

Tessa complied, but she wrinkled her nose. "Father, you smell of sheep," she said.

"Of course I do. What do you think I've been doing all day but dragging a couple of hundred sheep out of holding pens to shearing sheds?" he said, laughing. "You should see the quality of the wool this year, ladies! Top grade, all of it. We should get a pretty penny at the wool markets in London. And we need it too—have to pay for all that expensive schooling Tessa has had." He held her away from him, looking at her. "So you're now an educated woman, are you?" he asked. "You can spout Latin and Greek and do square roots in your head?"

"And algebra and geometry and French and Italian," Tessa said with a grand gesture.

"Bloody marvelous," Joseph said, beaming at her proudly. "I told you she was a sharp one, didn't I, love? I told you she'd be a credit to us. So what do you plan to do with yourself now?

How are you going to put all this education to good use?"

"Most of the girls in my class are going to Europe, Daddy," Tessa said hopefully. "Some of them are going to finishing schools in Paris and London. Hetty Mannard said that she's probably going to be presented at court. Imagine that, Daddy. We've got noble relatives in England, haven't we? So maybe I could be presented at court too."

"What for?" Joseph sounded amused. "Lot of fuss about nothing. I suppose it's all right if you were going to live over there and marry some lord, but that sort of stuff doesn't mean a thing in Australia."

"But I want to go to Europe, Daddy," Tessa said, grabbing his arm. "Couldn't I go and visit our relatives or go to a finishing school in Paris like Florence Buckley?"

Joseph Farnworth snorted, giving his wife an amused glance. "What do you need a finishing school for? You're educated and you've learned what you have to learn, and that should be good enough. I'm not wasting good money to have you taught how to drink tea with your pinky in the air or how to dance the minuet."

"Then what am I going to do?" Tessa demanded. "I can't stay here."

"Why not? Why can't you stay here?" The smile had gone from Joseph Farnworth's face. "This is your home. This is where you belong."

"But it's so far from civilization, Daddy,"

Tessa said. "Nothing exciting happens for miles. No theater. No concerts, nothing."

"We can have musical evenings," Nora said, looking at her husband. "The Murphy girls play the violin, and I hear Mr. Henderson is supposed to be a fine pianist. We could get an amateur theater group together, if you'd like, or arrange dances. . . ."

"A bunch of farmhands clodhopping around is hardly my idea of bliss," Tessa commented dryly. "I'll die of boredom, I know I will."

"Not if you start taking an interest in the farm," Joseph said.

"The farm? Why would I want to take an interest in the farm?"

"What do you think you've been educated for?" Joseph asked. "Not so that you can spout Greek. You've been given the best education in Australia so that you'll be ready when you have to take over all this someday. I know you won't be able to do the physical side of it, like a man would, but you'll be smart enough to keep an eye on your estate manager and not let this place go downhill."

Tessa was staring at him in horror. "You think I'll run this place someday?"

"Who else?" Joseph asked angrily. "I know you're only a woman, but you're our heir, Tessa. If one of your brothers had survived the diphtheria epidemic, things would have been different. You could have gone where you wanted and marry whom you wanted. But now you've got the responsibility. You have to learn how to run this place, and when you marry, you have to choose someone who knows about sheep."

Tessa didn't say any more because she was scared she might lose her temper or, worse still, start crying. She had always known that she was the heir and she'd get the property someday, but she'd never really stopped to consider that she'd be running it—stuck out here with millions of sheep. She shuddered. There was no way that she'd ever want to live out here! She'd sell up and go to live somewhere civilized as soon as she inherited, but in the meantime it sounded as if her father was going to give her an intensive course in sheep rearing.

"I'll just have to make him see," she told herself. She knew her father adored her and decided she'd just have to work on him gradually, so that he came to realize that she could never spend her life on a ranch. But she hadn't been home for very long before she began to suspect that her parents had her future planned out for her. In fact they actually had someone in mind for her future husband. When they had dinner parties, she was seated next to Ted Henderson. He was her partner in charades and at bridge. Her mother had him accompany her singing on the piano. Gradually the truth began to dawn on her: Her father had not just brought in Ted Henderson because he knew about sheep. He had chosen him because he was a clean-cut, good-looking young man and would make a suitable husband for the future owner.

She told her friend Florence Buckley about it when she went into Sydney for an eighteenth-birthday party. Florence's family lived in a big house on the North Shore, overlooking the harbor. Lawns stretched down to the water's edge, and lanterns had been strung across the lawns, their lights reflected in the dark waters. A band was playing, and there was the sound of laughter from inside the house as Tessa took Florence's arm and led her away from the party noise.

"What is it, Tessa, you sounded so upset," Florence whispered.

"I feel like one of his sheep, Florrie," Tessa muttered, glancing over her shoulder to see if anyone was listening. "Chosen for breeding with the prize ram. Whatever am I going to do?"

"Tell them you'd like to see Europe before you settle down and learn the business," Florrie said. "That will make you sound willing, won't it? I'll ask Papa if you can come with us. Maybe they'd let us share a cabin. Wouldn't that be fun?"

"Oh, Florrie, that sounds marvelous," Tessa said, clasping her friend's hands. "We'd have a ball, wouldn't we? Dances on the ship, lots of young men to flirt with, new dresses in Paris. If only he'd let me go. . . ."

"He might if he thought that my parents were chaperoning you," Florrie said, "and if you promised you'd come home in six months."

"I might not want to come home in six

months." Tessa gave Florrie a mysterious smile. "I might like it there better. I might meet a handsome prince or one of my lordly cousins. I'm sure they'd be less boring than clodhopping Ted Henderson. He is such a bore, Florrie. When we're together he tells me things about sheep and nature. He brought me a koala cub he'd found in a downed gum tree. It was sweet enough, but what do I want with a koala cub? Nasty little thing peed all over me!"

Florence started to laugh and Tessa had to join in. "It wasn't funny at the time," she said. "I had on my white muslin with the embroidered flowers. The girls had to scrub it for hours to get out the stain." She touched Florence's arm again. "You can see, Florrie, that I'm just not a farm girl at heart. By accident of birth I was born out in the country, but I really belong in society, where there is music and laughter and life!"

"Then you must come to Paris," Florrie said. "Come on, we'll speak to Papa tonight."

Next day Tessa rode back in great excitement. When she told her parents the news they did not look overjoyed.

"But darling, what were you thinking?" Nora said. "We couldn't let you go to Europe alone, even if we could afford it."

"Of course you could afford it. We're rich, aren't we?" Tessa looked confused.

"But all our money is tied up," Nora explained. "We've put every penny into the improvement of the breeding stock. One day it will really pay off, when everyone in Australia wants one of our rams, but just at the moment . . ." She let her voice trail away.

"And anyway, as your mother said, we'd not let you go with people we don't know," Joseph added.

"But I know them. They're lovely people," Tessa insisted. "Invite them up here for a weekend. Look them over. Then if you still find they're unsuitable, fine. But I know you won't. You'll love them."

"You're not going, Tessa, and that's final." Joseph slammed his fist down on the table.

"You don't care about me at all!" Tessa shouted. "All you care about is this stupid damn farm."

She ran out of the room. As she went upstairs she heard her father say to her mother, "Of course we've spoiled her horribly, and this is what we've got for it—a thankless, headstrong daughter with fancy ideas above herself. I can just see her acting the lady in Europe. If she got there she'd never come back."

"But won't she blame us forever if we don't let her go?" Nora asked.

"She can think what she likes," Joseph said. "I've broken many a young colt in my time. I'll get her in line, if it's the last thing I do. What she needs is a good, strong man to take charge of her. We'll get young Ted to speed up his courting, and let's plan on a wedding by the end of the year."

Tessa listened in horror. They were going to make her marry Ted whether she wanted to or not! She went over to her writing desk and sat down. "Dearest Florrie," she wrote. "It is with great pleasure that I write to tell you my parents have agreed to our trip to Europe together. Please have your father book my passage with yours, and I'll reimburse him when we meet in Sydney. Yours in haste, your loving friend, Tessa."

After she sent the letter she appeared to behave like the devoted daughter, but all the time she was carefully planning. She had all her dresses suitable for travel cleaned and pressed. She took her jewelry into Sydney and sold the most valuable pieces. But when she had paid for her ticket, she realized that she still wouldn't have enough money to support herself once she got to Europe. The more she thought about it, the more there seemed to be only one solution: She'd have to take the diamonds. Her mother had shown them to her once, on her twelfth birthday, before she left for boarding school. She had opened a secret panel in the fireplace and brought out a small cloth bag.

"These are your inheritance," she had said to Tessa. "If your brothers had lived, we would have divided them between you, but now they will all come to you someday."

Tessa had let the diamonds spill through her fingers, noting how they glinted with rainbow fire in the sunlight. "They're so pretty," she had said. "Why don't you have them made into a necklace so you can wear them, and then I can wear them when I'm grown up?"

Nora had laughed. "They're too valuable for that. I'd feel strange with thousands of pounds around my neck. And we don't want thieves to know they exist, so please don't mention them to anybody!"

Tessa slid out of bed and tiptoed silently down the stairs. The big living room was bathed in moonlight. Outside, wallabies flitted like ghostly shapes across the lawns. She went straight across to the fireplace and pressed the knot in the wood. A panel slid back with a loud click and a black cavity was revealed. Tessa's heart was beating very fast as she put in her hand and drew out the pouch.

"These are just for emergencies," she told herself. "I'll bring them back safely with me."

CHAPTER SEVENTEEN

Tessa Farnworth looked at herself in the ornate gilt mirror. She could scarcely believe that she was the elegant young woman who looked back at her. The dress was of white satin, very low cut, with a tiny waist and huge bustle. A white egret's feather decorated her hair, and she had had one of the diamonds fashioned into a choker around her neck, where it now sparkled dramatically in the lamplight. She had thought of herself as fashionable back in Sydney, but here in Paris her Australian dresses had seemed hopelessly dowdy and out of style. As soon as they had settled into a hotel, Florence and her mother headed straight for the houses of haute couture.

Tessa tried to remind herself that she didn't have unlimited money like Florence's family, but she couldn't resist going with them. She didn't want to appear as the ugly sister when they went to the opera or a ball. And so she ordered the most gorgeous gowns she could imagine and closed her eyes as she handed over her rapidly dwindling money. One day she opened her purse and it had all gone. She told herself severely that the diamonds were only for emergencies, but she had to go on living. She had already sold three of them, and her stay was not even half over . . .

"Are you ready, Tessa?" Florence tapped on her hotel door.

"Almost," Tessa called back. "Come on in and tell me how I look."

Florence came in, then stood by the door with her mouth open. "Tessa, you look stunning! Where did you get that dress?"

Tessa beamed with pleasure. "I had it made at the Salon Flaubert. Mme. Rochefort recommended them. Isn't it the cat's whisker?"

Florence was still staring in admiration. "Such a tiny waist. However do you manage it?"

"New corset too," Tessa said. "I had the maid lace me in. I had to hang onto the bedpost for dear life! Of course I won't be able to breathe all evening, but it will be worth it."

"I should say," Florence said. "None of the men there will be able to take their eyes off you."

Tessa crossed the room and grabbed her friend's arm. "Florrie, I am so excited. Imagine us—two girls from the colonies, actually being invited to a chic Paris soiree. Don't you just adore Europe? It is so civilized compared to Australia."

"Yes, but all the same," Florence said. "I miss Australia. I know I'll be looking forward to going home when our stay here is finished."

"I won't," Tessa said. "I'd love to stay forever."

"In which case," Florence giggled, "you'd

better land yourself a suitable husband while my parents are still around to take us to parties."

"Why do you think I bought the dress?" Tessa said, laughing.

Tessa held her breath as she and Florence and Florence's parents were announced at the dance. For a second she felt panic at the sight of so many strangers, all exquisitely dressed. What if someone spoke to her and she didn't understand? What if nobody asked her to dance all evening? What if somebody asked her and she didn't know the dance steps? She stayed close to Florence as they made their way across the dance floor.

She had not been sitting long when she felt someone looking at her. Through the blur of whirling couples she saw a young man eyeing her with undisguised interest. He was lean, dark haired, and incredibly handsome. As he caught her eye he bowed, then made his way across the floor to her.

"I ask myself why it is that the most beautiful woman in the room is not dancing," he said. "And I tell myself because she is very discriminating. She waits for me."

He held out his hand. "Nicholas de Verrance at your service, mademoiselle."

"Tessa Farnworth," Tessa said, extending her own hand, which Nicholas brought to his lips. "Enchanted, mademoiselle," he said. "And now would you do me the honor of dancing with me?"

Tessa's heart was hammering as she allowed

Nicholas to lead her onto the floor. He held her very close as he guided her into a waltz.

"You are not French, mademoiselle? Although you speak our language very well," he murmured into her ear.

"I'm from Australia, although I don't suppose you even know where that is," she said, laughing.

"Ah, but I do. It is where the kangaroos come from," he said. "How amazing. I have never before thought I would meet a kangaroo lady!" He laughed, his dark eyes never leaving hers. Tessa had never been looked at with such frank desire before. It made her legs feel as if they wouldn't hold her up.

"You have a magnificent figure, mademoiselle," he said, "and that dress shows it off to perfection. What a tiny waist. I feel that I could span it with my hands. And the exquisite diamond you wear at your lovely throat . . ."

"One of my family heirlooms," Tessa said proudly.

Nicholas's eyes registered this. "Are all the girls in Australia as lovely as you? In which case, I will pack my bags and get on the next boat."

"Most girls in Australia don't bother about their appearance," Tessa said. "They work on farms and get too many freckles."

"How distressing and how boring," he said. "I think farms are very boring, don't you? There is a farm on my family's estate, but I only visit when the asparagus are fresh. Apart from that, I prefer Paris!"

The dance ended, and Nicholas steered her to a small table in an alcove. He snapped his fingers and champagne appeared. Tessa had never drunk it before and made a funny face.

"You don't like it?" Nicholas asked, concerned.

"Oh, yes, I like it very much," she said, "but the bubbles tickle so."

"You are quite adorable," Nicholas said, gazing at her with delight. "So tell me, mademoiselle," he continued. "If everyone else in Australia is a farmer and has many freckles, how come that you are as beautiful as any European girl and travel overseas?"

Tessa laughed. "Because my father has one of the biggest farms in the country," she answered. "He has thousands and thousands of sheep. We send our wool direct to London."

"So he is rich, your papa?"

"Oh, yes. Very rich."

"Splendid," Nicholas exclaimed, laughing loudly. "We shall make a lovely couple. You see, I am poor. I am a count and my family has a delightful château on the Loire, but we lost most of our wealth in the revolution. So a rich woman suits me very well, because I do like the good things of life, don't you?"

"I haven't had a chance to enjoy the good things of life yet," Tessa stammered. His boldness had thrown her off guard. "In Australia life is very simple."

"Then I will be delighted and honored to be your teacher." Nicholas took her hand and brought it to his lips. "Together we will explore the best that Paris has to offer!"

Nicholas came to their hotel on the Champs Elysées every day after that. He took her for rides through the Bois de Bologne in his open carriage. They dined together at restaurants where orchestras played and smartly dressed waiters appeared with one exotic dish after another. They went to art exhibits and concerts. And one night, as they came home from the theater, he kissed her for the first time, in his carriage. As his lips caressed hers, gently, his hand slid down her bare neck and lingered over her breast. Feelings stirred inside Tessa that she had never dreamed could exist. She turned toward him, her mouth seeking his as he began to kiss her more intensely.

"Do you really have to go home now?" he whispered. "My apartment is close by, and nobody will disturb us."

"I . . . that is, they will be expecting me," she said, flustered. At school they had been told what men thought of women who were fast and loose.

Nicholas smiled. "I understand perfectly," he said. "I will come calling in the morning then."

That night Tessa lay in bed, reliving every moment in that carriage and aching for him. Next day they took a picnic out to St.-Germain-des-Près on the banks of the Seine. A spring breeze was blowing, scented with blossoms, and Nicholas lay back contentedly in the grass.

"You don't know how good it feels to be in the open air like this, away from the grime of the city," he said. "I imagine that the wide open spaces in your country must be magnificent. What a feeling of freedom! You must take me to see them someday, and we will go find the kangaroos together."

Tessa's heart skipped a beat. Was this a proposal? After all, you didn't go all the way to Australia with a girl unless you were married to her. She lay back beside him and closed her eyes, slipping into a pleasant daydream in which she returned home with Nicholas at her side. "I am now a French countess, Mummy," she'd say. "We have a château and a house in Paris, but we're going to divide our time between the two countries." Everyone would look impressed, especially Ted Henderson.

At the end of the day, Nicholas didn't ask her what she wanted to do but took her back to his apartment. "Now I shall be delighted to teach you the mysteries of love," he whispered as he reached for the top button on her dress.

In April, Florence went to her finishing school near Fontainbleau on the outskirts of Paris, and her parents wanted to move on to England, but Tessa refused to go with them. "I'll stay on here at the hotel," she told Florence.

"Alone?" Florence looked horrified. "But Tessa, it's not done."

"It will be fine," Tessa said. "I won't leave Nicholas now, and I'm sure it won't be too long before we get married."

Florence's parents, too, were very concerned. "It's not suitable for a young lady to be all alone in a city," Florence's mother said. "What would your parents think of us if we just abandoned you?"

"Please don't concern yourselves," Tessa said. "I am staying at a respectable hotel, after all, and I have Nicholas to take care of me."

"But how will you manage for money? Living in Paris is so expensive."

Tessa tried not to let her anxiety show. "Oh, don't worry. I have quite enough," she said. This wasn't exactly true. She had already used five of the diamonds. Nicholas had come to take it for granted that she would pay for opera tickets and banquets.

Florence's mother said no more, and Tessa watched them pack and depart. In a way she was relieved, as she wouldn't have to worry about slipping in and out at odd times. She was free to come and go as she pleased. She put on her bonnet and went out, determined to make the most of this newfound freedom.

She was admiring perfume in one of the boutiques along the rue du Faubourg-St. Honoré when she heard a high-pitched laugh. She looked around to see who was making such a stupid noise and froze. The girl was sniffing at perfume bottles. She was very ordinary looking, but standing beside her was Nicholas.

Tessa clutched one of the high-backed chairs in the store, feeling that she was going to faint. It couldn't be true. She closed her eyes and when she opened them again, the man was still unmistakably her Nicholas.

When Nicholas showed up at her hotel that evening, he seemed in no way embarrassed or flustered.

"You are ready, my love?" he asked, then stopped, looking at her face. "You are not even dressed for the opera! What is wrong?"

She had promised herself that she'd remain calm but now that she saw him, smiling and relaxed, her anger and fear spilled out. "You are, you two-timer," she snapped. "I saw you today—in Panache with another woman."

To her complete confusion, he threw back his head and laughed. "But that was only Sylvie. You don't have to be jealous of her. She is no threat."

She could feel the tension draining. It had all been a silly mistake. She had let herself get upset over nothing. "And why not?"

"Because she is only my fiancée. She is in Paris for her yearly visit, so it would have been rude not to show her around a little."

"Your fiancée?" Tessa stammered. Maybe the word meant something different in French. "You're going to marry her?"

He shrugged. "Someday, I suppose. Our families expect it. But not for many years, I hope."

226

The color had drained from Tessa's cheeks. "I don't understand," she stammered. "I thought you loved me."

"But I do, *chérie*," he said. "I'm madly in love with you."

"And yet you're going to marry another woman?"

He looked amused. "Of course. That's the way things are done. You and I could never marry. You are not a French aristocrat, for one thing, and you are not Catholic, for another. Such a match would not be correct. So I marry the woman my family selects for me and for love I turn elsewhere. That is the way in France."

"Not where I come from," Tessa said angrily.

"Ah, yes, but there it is so primitive . . . so uncivilized, as you said yourself," he said, walking over to stroke her cheek. "Now let us forget all unpleasantness and go out for a delightful dinner."

It was taking every ounce of her composure not to yell and tell him that the delightful dinners and enchanting carriage rides had been at her expense, bought by her legacy, her diamonds. She saw now that he had used her, and that she had squandered the diamonds in an attempt to buy happiness.

But she wasn't going to make a scene. She was going to let him remember her as dignified and noble, so that he was the one who looked back with regret.

"Not tonight," Tessa said, turning away from him. "I'm not feeling well." And this was true. The room was hot and clammy, and she was suddenly feeling nauseated, as if she were going to throw up at any moment.

"Then I'll call on you in the morning," he said easily. "Au revoir, my petite. Sleep well."

As he turned toward the door she said, "Just a moment, Nicholas, there's something I must tell you."

He paused, his handsome face still smiling. "What is it?"

When she came to say the words, she couldn't. She shook her head. "Nothing. Nothing at all. Good-bye, Nicholas," she said softly as he closed the door.

She went up the hotel stairs and into her room, closing the door softly behind her before she threw herself down on the bed and cried. When she could cry no more she started cramming her clothes into her cabin trunk and ran down to the hotel desk. "Please find me the first passage on a ship to Australia," she begged the desk clerk.

"Mademoiselle is going home?" the clerk inquired, raising his eyebrows. She realized now that they had all known about Nicholas, and that all disapproved of her. She'd sensed the coldness all along but tried to ignore it.

She nodded, very much afraid that she might cry in pubic. How stupid that she had thought that she never wanted to see Australia again. At this moment, all she wanted was her mother's comforting arms, her father's big hug, telling her that everything was going to be all right. She sat down and wrote a letter:

"Dearest Mummy and Daddy,

I'm so sorry for everything I've done. I miss you so much, and I'm coming home. Please forgive me. I'm ready to be the daughter you wanted now. I didn't realize before how wonderful you both were. I've learned my lesson. Don't turn me away, please.

I'm catching the next boat home. I'm hoping this letter will go out by navy ship and get there before I do."

She paused with her pen poised above the paper. She wanted to tell them more, but she couldn't. After all, they might not be so willing to forgive her if they found out that she was going to have a baby.

Amid the crowd on the dock of Sydney Harbour, Tessa caught a glimpse of her mother, standing with Ted Henderson beside her. Daddy must be tending the sheep, as usual, she thought, her heart swelling at the prospect of seeing her father again. But then she gasped as she saw her mother's pretty hair, singed to a short crop, and burn marks on her face and arms.

"Mummy, it's me, Tessa!" she yelled. She pushed her way down the gangplank and threw herself into her mother's arms. "What happened, Mummy? Are you all right? Your poor hair," she cried, tears streaming down her cheeks.

"Hair grows again, child," Nora said, wrapping her daughter in a fierce embrace. "It's your poor father we should cry about. There was a terrible bushfire, Tessa. The ranch was wiped out completely."

"Oh, Mummy, where is he? Is he all right?"

"He insisted on trying to save the flock. Of course it was useless. The fire was jumping whole valleys, and we were lucky to get out with our lives. I only escaped because your father told Mr. Henderson to get me out of there and he galloped us through a curtain of flame. Then he tried to go back for your father, but it was too late."

Tessa turned serious eyes to Ted Henderson. "Thank you," she said quietly. He nodded, and she noticed for the first time what a kind, gentle face he had compared to his big, well-muscled body.

"It's not the homecoming we would have wished for you, Miss Farnworth, but welcome back," he said softly.

"Can I see Daddy?" she asked in a small voice.

"We'll go straight there," Nora said. "You know, I believe he's only stayed alive to see you again."

Joseph Farnworth lay swathed in bandages. Tessa dropped to her knees beside him.

"Daddy, it's me. It's your Tessa come back to you," she said.

The bandaged figure stirred. "My little girl?" he asked in a croaking voice. "Really here?"

"Really here, Daddy," she said, gently touching his fingers. "I'd kiss you, but I don't want to hurt you more."

"I didn't think I'd see you again," he said. "Europe's so far away."

"I'm done with Europe now," she said through her tears. "I've come home. I'll help you rebuild the ranch. We'll make it even better, eh, Daddy."

The ghost of a smile crossed his lips. "That's my girl," he said. "Ted knows as much as I do now. He'll get it going again."

"No, not Ted. You," she implored. "You're going to get better and build up the ranch again."

"Too late for me," he whispered. "Only wanted to see you again."

"Don't say that, Daddy," she sobbed. "I love you so much. Mummy loves you. We want you to get well. Please get well for us."

Joseph's fingers tightened around Tessa's hand. "Look after your mother for me," he whispered. "She's been a good woman—good wife, good mother . . ."

"And you've been a good father," Tessa said. "The best, Daddy. I didn't realize before how wonderful you both are. I love you so much."

A slow smile spread across his bandaged face. In the background she heard her mother give a little sob, and she realized that the hand holding hers had gone limp.

After the funeral, Tessa and her mother stood together at the edge of the graveyard. "I promised Daddy we'd start rebuilding right away," she said.

Nora turned a hopeless face to her

daughter. "There's no money, Tessa."

"But we're rich, " Tessa stated incredulously.

Nora sighed. "We own lots of land, but what use is that? All our profits went into upgrading our herd. Apart from a small bank account we have nothing. Of course, the diamonds could help us get through, but they were lost in the fire. We had people sift through the rubble, but we couldn't find them."

A big sob formed in Tessa's throat. "I took them, Mummy," she said. "I used most of them. I wasted them on stupid, meaningless things that only brought me unhappiness. . . . I'm so sorry."

Nora sighed. "What's done is done. We'll just have to sell the land and live quietly on the proceeds."

Tessa put her arm around her mother. "Don't worry. I promised Daddy I'd take care of you and I will," she said, leading her mother back to the little guest house where they were staying.

The next day she asked Ted to drive her out to the ranch. She had been determined to be strong, but she was not prepared for the extent of the devastation. When she came to the place where the gum trees had stood at the end of the drive and she saw just blackened earth stretching in all directions, she couldn't hold back the tears. Ted's arms came around her and she didn't push him away.

"It's okay. Go ahead, cry. It's good for you," he said softly.

"I thought we could rebuild, but it's hopeless," Tessa said. "If I hadn't taken the diamonds . . ."

"I suspected that maybe that's where they'd gone to," he said softly.

She buried her head in his shoulder. "I've been so stupid, Ted. So stupid and selfish. How can I bring a child into this world when I can't even get my own life straight?"

She felt his arms stiffen. "You're going to have a baby?" he whispered.

She nodded, looking away. She hadn't meant to tell him; it had just slipped out. "I haven't told my mother yet. I thought she couldn't take another shock."

"And the father?"

"He's marrying someone else," she said simply.

"I'm sorry." She heard the compassion in his voice and looked up to find his clear, gray eyes gazing at her tenderly.

"Don't be. He'd have made a terrible husband," she admitted. She managed a weak smile. "He was even more selfish than me. He would have been quite devoted to me as long as I had diamonds left to pay for all his luxuries. God, what a fool I've been, Ted. How you must despise me."

Ted didn't answer. He was looking around. "You know, I think we could make a go of this place again, you and I," he said. "On a small scale, of course. Start off with a few sheep, a little house . . ."

She lifted her head from his shoulder, looking up at his face. "Are you suggesting . . ."

"That we get married," he said, "and right away, judging by that bulge there!"

She didn't know whether to laugh or cry. She put her hands up to her face. "Oh, Ted, you are very sweet," she whispered, "but you don't have to do this."

"Tessa, I've wanted to marry you since the day I set eyes on you," he said simply. "In those days I admired your beauty and your fire. Now I think you've turned into a far nicer person. We've both come through fire, you and I. I really think we could be happy together."

"With another man's child?" she asked. "You wouldn't resent that?"

"Plenty of time for our own later," he said, smiling down at her tenderly. "Right now we've got work ahead of us: building, reseeding, getting this place going again. What do you say?"

Tessa stared out across the blackened land and slipped her hand into his. She felt the strength of his grip, the warmth of his hand in hers, and it was as if she were emerging from a long dark tunnel into the light. A few moments before she had believed that nothing would ever be right again, that she had nothing to live for or look forward to. But now she realized that she had a whole exciting life ahead with a man who had strength enough for both of them.

"I say we can do it, Ted," she said. "I think we can be happy together here."

CHAPTER EIGHTEEN

"How could Tessa have been so stupid!" Laura said angrily as she got up and began pacing around the room. She and her grandmother were sitting in the hotel room, the lights of London twinkling out their window. "Surely she could have seen through that creepy Nicholas!"

"Young girls don't always want to see through the man they love," Helen commented with a knowing smile.

"What's that supposed to mean?" Laura demanded. "Are you talking about me and Brian again?"

"Not at all," Helen said. "But this has been true for rather a lot of the Sutcliffe and Treadwick women, I'm afraid. We're strong, we're afraid of nothing, but we are the most awful judges of character."

"Weren't there any Sutcliffe women who instantly fell in love with suitable, sensible boys?" Laura asked.

"Well, Sierra was the closest, but I'm afraid that like Emma's Thomas and Margaret's

Peter, Sierra's Arthur met with disapproval. And they both met with a tragic end. . . ."

"Sierra? Who was she?"

"An American Sutcliffe, just like you," Helen said. "Let me see. She would have been the grandchild of Margaret and Peter, who made their fortune in the gold rush."

"So they did make a fortune and get the diamonds back from the pawnshop?" Laura asked excitedly.

Grandmama Helen smiled. "Oh, yes, they made a fortune. They became one of the great families of San Francisco. . . ."

CHAPTER NINETEEN

SIERRA SUTCLIFFE, SAN FRANCISCO. 1906

Sierra Sutcliffe made her way down Market Street, picking up her skirts daintily as she stepped over puddles. She held her head proudly and pretended she didn't notice when passersby gave her admiring glances or stepped aside for her. She knew she was pretty, she knew she was rich, and she enjoyed both. Even her black school uniform dress with its white lace collar could not disguise her budding beauty. Her hair flashed with red-blond lights as it hung in curls over her shoulders, and she walked as if she owned the city, which, in a certain sense, she did.

She paused outside the imposing building that took up a whole city block and smiled when she saw the sign SUTCLIFFE'S EMPORIUM above the main entrance. It always felt good to see that sign up there and to know that she was the daughter of one of the richest families in San Francisco. Other girls at Miss Pinkerton's academy envied her. She knew that they pointed her out to new girls. "That's Sierra Sutcliffe," they'd say. "You better get on her good side. Her family owns the biggest store in town."

Sierra grinned to herself again and stepped into the building. The doorman rushed to open the door for her, and she swept through into the main floor of the store. All around her was bustle and activity. A young salesgirl came past, her arms full of boxes, and almost bumped into Sierra.

"Watch where you're going, girl," Sierra said sharply.

The young girl's face flushed. "Oh, I'm so sorry, Miss Sutcliffe. I didn't see you," she said.

"I might have been a customer," Sierra said. "What's your name, girl?"

"Rose Blenchly, miss, but please don't report me," the girl begged.

Sierra looked at her with distaste. "I'll have to think about it," she said. "Just watch your clumsiness in the future." She continued her way to the elevator, riding up to her father's office on the top floor. His clerk, Arthur Phillips, sprang to his feet as she came in. He was tall, slim, and blond-haired. His fair skin turned bright red as he addressed her.

"Good afternoon, Miss Sutcliffe. Good day at school?"

"Boring day, thank you, Arthur. Every day is boring at school. I can't wait to be out."

"Your father hopes you'll stay on and go to college," Arthur said.

"College, good grief," Sierra said. "What do I want with college? It isn't as if I'll have to earn my living. In fact, I'm sure the men of the city will be lining up to marry me."

"I'm sure they will," Arthur said, his fair face flushing to an even deeper red. "Any young man would be honored to have your attention."

"Why, Arthur," she said, smiling, "I do believe you have a crush on me yourself!"

"I'm only human, Miss Sutcliffe," he said.

Sierra laughed. "And you're only a clerk, Arthur."

"Even a clerk can have ambitions in America," he replied.

"I'd be the laughingstock at school if I were ever seen with a clerk."

"Maybe one day I'll be more than a clerk," he said.

"A store owner, maybe?"

"No, a writer," he said. "I aim to be a writer someday."

"I never thought of you as another O. Henry or Walt Whitman," she said, still laughing.

"Then I might surprise you someday, Miss Sutcliffe," he replied, going back to his work.

"Stupid boy," she thought, sweeping through to her father's office. "How stupid these boys all are!"

James Sutcliffe looked up from his desk. The lines melted from his worried face as he saw his daughter. "Why, sweetheart, what a lovely surprise. What brings you here?"

"Secret mission, Papa," Sierra said. She went across to her father and kissed him on the cheek. "I wanted to come to you before I spoke to Mama. It's about Daisy Melbourne's party."

"What about it?"

"I'm sure Mama won't let me go, and it's going to be so wild and such fun, Papa. They're bringing in a ragtime band and there'll be dancing all night. I can go, can't I?"

"Why do you think your mother might not want you to go?" James asked.

"Because of what happened at her last party," Sierra said. "Remember how they stole a cab and brought the horse into the front hall? The police came and there was all that fuss!" She giggled, then fought to keep a straight face because her father was frowning.

"Ah, yes," James said. "You know, Sierra, Daisy's crowd is a little old for you. I understand that there is drinking at those parties. I agree with your mother."

"But Papa, if I promise not to drink. If I promise to be home by midnight. Then can I go?" She wound her arms around his neck. "All the girls in my class are going. I'll be the only party pooper if I can't go too. Please say yes. Please . . ."

"We'll see," he said, patting her arm. "Now run along home. I've work to do. We're thinking of adding another floor to the emporium and I'm meeting the architect this afternoon."

"Love you, Papa," she said, kissing him again.

"Do your homework," he called after her. "We want to make sure you get in to Mills College, don't we?"

Sierra didn't answer, but she made a face at Arthur as she ran out. At least she was pretty sure now that her father would allow her to go to the party. She usually got her way with her father. It was so easy to get around him. After three sons, she was the only daughter, and she knew that he loved to spoil her. "Maybe he'll even let me have another new dress for the party," she thought, "a grown-up dress in emerald green velvet with one of those hourglass waists and draped at the hips. It wouldn't do any harm to stop by the dressmaker's on the way home and pick out some fabric, just in case."

She caught a cable car and rode up Powell Street to the top of Nob Hill, where her family's imposing brick home stood across from Grace Cathedral. Elegant Grecian columns flanked the flight of steps leading to the front door. Sierra bounded up them, forgetting for a moment to look elegant and dignified. A trunk stood in the entrance hall. Her brother Richard must be home from Harvard.

"Richard!" she yelled.

Mrs. Sutcliffe's face peered around the drawing room door. "Sierra. Don't shout. It's not ladylike."

"Mother, you know I'm not ladylike." Sierra laughed. "Where is he?"

"Up in his room, unpacking his books," Mrs. Sutcliffe said. "Come in here and have some tea. He'll be down."

"Sorry, Mama, can't wait," Sierra said and

rushed up the stairs to the top of the house.

"You're back. How wonderful!" She flung herself into her brother's arms. "Now I won't be bored to death around here."

"Sierra, whoa. You're knocking me over," Richard said, laughing. "What a terrible child you are."

"I'm a young lady, for your information," Sierra said haughtily. "I'm almost done with school and of marriageable age, so there."

"Pity the poor man who gets you," Richard said, ruffling her hair. "What a dance you'll lead him."

"Not if he sits adoringly at my feet and does what I want."

"Then you'd be bored with him in a week," Richard answered.

"So are you really home for good?" Sierra asked.

"Seems that way," Richard said. "Father wants me to learn the business, although I had hoped to go to Berkeley and work on my Ph.D."

"Oh, Richard, not more boring books. How could you?" Sierra said. "Start working in the store. Then I can come and visit you every day."

"I wish you were a man and you could learn to run the store," Richard said. "Then I could get on with my own life."

"And what would your own life be, pray?"

Richard frowned. "I feel torn between continuing my own studies, for my own gratification, and putting my knowledge to work for the good of others." He began pacing across the room. "So much needs to be done, Sierra. Do you know how many immigrants come to the city speaking no English? I wouldn't mind being an English teacher to the Chinese children."

Sierra wrinkled her nose. "Oh, pooh, Richard, what a stupid idea. As if they matter. All they're ever going to be is servants, anyway."

"Poor people deserve an education too, Sierra," he said quietly.

"Poor people are utterly boring." Sierra dismissed this topic with a wave of her hand.

"What a snobby, insufferable little creature you've become." Richard laughed, ruffling her hair.

"Don't, Richard, you're spoiling my hairstyle," Sierra said, but she laughed too. "Maybe I don't always mean everything I say," she agreed. "I do feel sorry for poor people, but you have to admit they're very dreary."

"Nevertheless, I'd really like to devote my life to education, only it doesn't seem as if I'm to be given that option," Richard said.

"Too bad Henry and Peter died so young," Sierra said. "If they hadn't caught meningitis, one of them might have had Papa's marketing genius."

"Well, I certainly haven't," Richard said. "I guess you'll just have to marry a marketing genius."

"Me? I'm going to marry a prince," Sierra said, "or at least a Roosevelt."

Richard laughed. "You don't aim low," he said.

"Why should I?' Sierra demanded, her eyes teasing him. "I'm a very eligible commodity, Richard. I'm going to pick the very best. I might even get Papa to take me to Europe so that I can meet a few princes. I rather see myself with a crown on."

"I'll crown you if you don't get out of here and leave me in peace," Richard said, giving her a playful hit on the head with a book.

That night Sierra was strangely restless, tossing and turning in bed as if she were waiting for something to happen. "Am I excited because Mama agreed to the party?" she wondered. "Or because Richard's home or I'm almost out of school?" But it was a different sort of anticipation, almost like the night before an exam.

She drifted off into troubled sleep early in the morning hours and woke around five o'clock to find herself thrown out of bed. For a moment she wondered if this was part of her nightmare, for she had been dreaming of being on a ship that turned over in high seas. Then a jug bounced off the dresser and smashed onto the floor beside her, showering her with broken china, and she knew she wasn't dreaming. She tried to get up but she couldn't. The whole room was shaking with a rumbling noise like a passing train.

"Earthquake," she managed to say at last. "It's an earthquake."

All over the house she could hear the crash of falling objects—the terrible clank as the grandfather clock in the hall toppled over, and the splintering of glass. Someone was screaming up above in the servants' quarters. She managed to crawl across the floor and slide under her bed, just before the heavy gilded mirror came down from the wall.

The horrible rumbling seemed to go on forever, but at last the shaking subsided to a gentle rocking, then a shudder, then stillness. Cautiously Sierra climbed out from her hiding place. Her floor was strewn with broken glass and water from the jug. She grabbed her slippers before she ventured any farther. She had just reached her door when she heard her mother's frantic voice: "Sierra? Are you all right? Oh, James, my baby. Is she all right?"

"It's okay, Mother, I'm fine," Sierra said, appearing at the top of the stairs.

Richard's tousled head appeared from his door. "Boy, that was some shaker," he said. "Better than the roller coaster at Coney Island."

"It's no joking matter, Richard," James Sutcliffe said. "That was a pretty powerful quake. I wonder what the damage was like at the store? We're on firm ground here, but Market Street is on landfill. I must get down there right away."

"Oh, James, do be careful," Mrs. Sutcliffe begged.

"I'll come with you, Pop," Richard said. "Just let me get on some clothes."

"I'll come too," Sierra added.

"No, you stay with your mother," James said. "We won't be long."

The servants came down cautiously from their rooms in the attic. The younger maids were crying, and Mrs. Sutcliffe had to calm them. "No real harm done," she said. "Just a lot of glass to sweep up. So put some shoes on and get busy. And, Cook, I suggest you get the coffeepot going. We could all use a hot drink."

Sierra went back to her room to get dressed. She was annoyed to find so many of her favorite ornaments and knickknacks smashed, and she sorted through the pieces on the floor to see which ones could be stuck together again. It was while she was busily occupied with this that she first noticed the noises coming from the city below. She opened her window and looked out. Outside it was just getting light. Smoke and dust clouds were hanging over the lower portions of the city. Fire engine bells were clanging furiously. And through the shifting smoke, Sierra saw for the first time the devastation down below. Houses going down the hill had collapsed like a pack of cards. The streets were covered in rubble. Through the sound of the fire engines came the higher notes of human cries and screams. Hastily Sierra shut her window again.

"Don't let Papa go," she called down to her mother. "It's dangerous out there."

"He's already gone, darling," Mrs. Sutcliffe said.

Sierra ran down the stairs. "Mama, I'm scared," she whimpered. "Is everything going to be all right?"

"I do hope so, dear," Mrs. Sutcliffe said.

"The houses down below have all collapsed," Sierra said. "There's nothing left of them but rubble."

"Oh dear, poor people," Mrs. Sutcliffe said. "We should get dressed and see what we can do to help. I'll have Cook make a big jug of coffee and maybe some soup . . ."

But at that moment Cook reappeared. "Sorry, Mrs. Sutcliffe, but there's no gas," she said. "I can't make coffee."

"Of course. I should have thought," Mrs. Sutcliffe said. "How silly of me. The gas mains would have broken, wouldn't they?"

"Fires," Sierra thought. That's what was causing the fires. She had a vision of all those ruptured gas mains, all leaking gas, waiting to explode. She ran to the window again and looked out. This time the smell of smoke made her cough. She could actually see the flames racing through the small buildings down by the waterfront. The fire bells were still clanging but the cloud of smoke just kept getting bigger and bigger.

"I wish Papa would come back," she said. She wrapped her arms tightly around herself because she was shivering.

One of the maids came running down the stairs, crying. "Oh, Mrs. Sutcliffe, ma'am, it looks like the whole city's burning down there. What are we going to do?"

"We'll be safe enough up here," Mrs. Sutcliffe said firmly. "Don't worry, Ethel." But she went to peer anxiously out the window. Even though the sun should now have been up, the sky was still dark, and through the darkness was a red glow and the sound of roaring.

Up in her room, Sierra could not leave her window. She watched the flames racing through the lowlands. She saw fireballs go up as more gas mains exploded. There were fires down in China Town, there were fires down toward Market Street. Slowly it came to her that they might find themselves caught in a ring of fire on their hilltop. She put on her coat and went to find her mother.

"We should get out while we can," she said.

"Get out, what do you mean?"

"I mean we could soon be trapped," she went on impatiently. "The fires are spreading so quickly. If they move around to Van Ness, we've no way out."

"They won't come up here," Mrs. Sutcliffe said, her voice indicating that no fire would dare consume a rich neighborhood.

"But they might, Mama. We don't want to leave it too late," Sierra insisted, fighting to stay calm. "I think we should have the coachman bring round the carriage and tell the servants to be ready too."

"I don't know what to say," Mrs. Sutcliffe said, waving her arms ineffectually. "We shouldn't leave until your father gets back."

"He might not be able to get back. It looks like Market Street is in flames," Sierra said.

"Come on, Mother. Get your coat on. Now."

Even as she was talking another fireball went up directly beneath them. "Come on, Mama," Sierra pleaded, frightened now. "It's moving so fast!" She grabbed her mother's arm and propelled her out to the carriage. Mrs. Sutcliffe allowed herself to be led. Sierra told the terrified servant girls to climb in too. The horses stood trembling as soot rained down on them.

"Head down California Street, Frederick," Sierra commanded. "That seems to be the only direction not burning."

The horses broke into a gallop, anxious to get away from the swirling smoke. But progress was not easy. The streets were buckled and full of debris and rubble. Sierra gasped as she saw the collapsed houses, with their former occupants standing on the sidewalk, not knowing what to do next. At one house children were clawing at the rubble screaming, "Mommy, Mommy!"

Sierra almost opened her mouth to command Frederick to stop, but she didn't see what they could possibly do to help. A fire truck sped past them, its bell ringing furiously. At last they came to a halt at Aquatic Park—a little oasis of green beside the bay.

"We should be safe enough here, miss," Frederick said. They sat between two worlds. Out over the bay the sun was shining on green hills. Behind them the black smoke of hell was consuming the city.

"Oh, James, Richard!" Mrs. Sutcliffe

wept. "Why did I let them go?"

"Don't worry, Mama. They're not stupid. They wouldn't stick around if the fire was coming," Sierra said.

The park filled with more and more people. Some were pushing everything they had managed to save on carts or in baby carriages. Many were blackened with soot or wounded from the earthquake. They each found a spot on the grass and sat there, just waiting to see what would happen.

All morning the fire raged on. Even down here they could feel the heat of it and hear the roar. They were covered in falling soot.

Then at last the flames died down. There was a line of blackness just above the green of the park, and where the city used to be there were only scorched ruins. Later in the day Sierra and her mother walked back up the hill. They wouldn't risk taking the horses because they didn't know what they would encounter. It was almost impossible to find their way because street signs were down and there were no recognizable landmarks. Then Sierra gave a happy shout. On top of Nob Hill, houses were still standing.

"It's okay, Mama. Come on," she called. "Look, nothing got burned up here."

But when they came to where their house stood, there was now only a blackened shell. Mrs. Sutcliffe put her hand to her mouth. "My home, my lovely home," she whimpered. "And my husband and my son." She started to sob uncontrollably. "We've lost everything, Sierra. Everything. What am I going to do? Who's going to take care of us?"

Sierra was shivering violently but she put her arm around her mother. "Don't worry, Mama," she whispered, "I'm here. I'll take care of you."

Then right behind them there came a shout and up the hill Richard and James came running.

"Papa, you're safe!" Sierra cried, flinging herself into his arms.

"Yes, thank God, we're all safe," James said, wrapping his arms around her.

"And the store?" she asked.

"Gone," he said. "All gone. Burned to the ground, Sierra. We've lost everything."

CHAPTER TWENTY

"Is this it?" Sierra asked in a voice that trembled slightly. She took in the tall grimy brick building with barred windows and locked spiked gates.

"Looks like it," her father said. He consulted the street address. "Yes, here we are. See, here's the brass plate on the wall: Northwood Academy for Young Ladies."

Sierra shivered. She had been cold ever since they landed in England. She often wondered if her past life before the earthquake had been a beautiful dream. It seemed so unreal now that she had lived in a great house and gone to parties and been envied by all the other girls. The days since the earthquake had been either frightening or dreary. First there had been the chaos following the quake, the attempts to salvage something of their former lives, and then the realization that her mother had suffered a complete mental collapse. When she didn't recover, they had come to Europe, seeking a change of scene and the best specialists. They had taken an apartment in London, and Sierra's life had become that of nursemaid and companion, sitting with her mother, chattering cheerfully while she felt her heart was breaking.

Finally there had been some response. Her mother emerged from her depression and began to take an interest in Sierra's future. She became obsessed with turning Sierra into an English lady and having her launched into the cream of English society, where she would definitely meet a prince. So she'd got it into her head that Sierra must go to a finishing school, and Northwood Academy had been highly recommended. Looking at it now, Sierra couldn't imagine who had recommended it, apart from the director of prisons! Sierra felt as if doom had struck when the doors closed behind her.

She had made up her mind that she wouldn't like any of the snobby, standoffish girls at Northwood, but she couldn't help liking Emily Devonshire. Emily arrived, overweight, shy, clumsy, and was put next to Sierra at meals. "I thought my heart would stop when I saw those terrible gates outside," she whispered to Sierra. "It's just like prison, isn't it? I really think this place might finish me off, but not in the way my parents hoped." And she smiled at Sierra, such a sweet, hopeful smile that Sierra smiled back.

"The food will get the job done quickly enough," she whispered back.

Emily prodded the lump of steak and kidney pudding. "Is it always as bad as this?" she asked.

Sierra nodded. "I've tried complaining, but they say it builds character to eat it," she said. Sierra glanced around and noted some of the other girls nudging each other and giggling about Emily. She decided that she wasn't going to let Emily be pushed around. When they went to ballet class the next morning, M. Robert, the ballet master, looked at Emily with distaste. After a few minutes of warm-ups he began criticizing her. His put-downs made some of the other girls giggle.

"We are not dancing the dance of the elephants but the dance of the swans," he said. Emily blushed scarlet.

The other girls looked away, embarrassed, but Sierra could take it no longer. "She's doing her best," Sierra said, going over to put an arm around Emily. "We can't all be prima ballerinas, you know. It's not nice to hurt her feelings."

M. Robert's face darkened. "Who gave you permission to speak, young lady?" he asked.

Sierra tossed back her hair. "Our fathers pay for this," she said. "They wouldn't like it if they knew their daughters were being insulted."

"Go!" he shouted. "Go, leave my class at once."

Sierra was sent to the principal and had to write a letter of apology to Monsieur, but as she was writing it, the other girls crowded around her. "We're going to let you in on a little secret," Anne said. "We've found this marvelous coffeehouse in Chelsea. We're planning to go there this weekend, when we're supposed to be home with our parents."

Missy giggled and grabbed Sierra's arm. "We're each planning to say that we're going to supper with the other," she said, "and then we're all going to meet at Sloane Square. Isn't it too, too exciting?"

"And we'd like you to join us," Constance said. "We think you're an absolute brick."

"Thanks," Sierra said, not knowing if this was a compliment or not.

"All the young poets and writers come to this café," Missy said excitedly. "And communists, and Irish freedom fighters! Anyone who's anyone is seen there."

"Say you'll come," Constance begged.

"Of course I'll come," Sierra said, grinning. "I've been dying to break out of this place since I got here."

The other girls nodded in sympathy. "Yes, it is a frightful place, isn't it?" Missy agreed. "We all hate it, but we all have to be finished or we'll never get presented at court. We look on it like army service for the boys."

They linked arms and went out of the room, laughing.

That Saturday night Sierra caught the train to Sloane Square, feeling excited for the first time in months. The danger and the deception had made the adventure even sweeter, and the four girls looked at one another in delight as they each emerged from the grimy underground station.

The café was in a dreary basement. It consisted of simple wooden tables, each with a candle in an old wine bottle on it. The girls would have liked to order wine, but they felt almost as daring ordering black Turkish coffee. Anne handed around cigarettes, and they tried to look as if they came here every day.

After a while, a poet got up and read his work—strange meterless ramblings about decay and death. Then the café owner signaled for quiet again. "We're privileged to have with us tonight the promising young novelist Terrence Flannery. He'll be reading from his soon-to-be-published book *Mirrors of Madness*."

There was enthusiastic applause, and a young man stepped into the spotlight. Sierra felt as if she had stepped into an unreal dream, because she recognized his face. He was wearing his fair hair longer now, and he was dressed in an elegant black velvet jacket with a white frilled shirt, but it was Arthur Phillips, her father's clerk from back home. He'd been transformed from shy clerk into confident young novelist. The words he read were deep and poetic, and she listened to them, spellbound. At last he sat down to loud applause. Sierra got up. "I have to go speak to him," she said.

"You and every other female in England," Anne said, laughing.

"But you don't understand. I know him," Sierra said. "He used to work for my father."

Missy jumped up. "Then what are we waiting for? Introduce us too," she said, pushing Sierra in the direction of the crowd around Arthur.

The crowd drove her forward until she

found herself right beside him. He looked up, recognized her, and was at a loss for words.

"Hi," she said airily. "You don't have to look at me as if I'm the ghost of Christmas past!"

"Sierra? What in God's name are you doing here?" he stammered.

"We're in London for mother's health," she said.

"You're living here now?"

"If you could call it living." Sierra made a face. "I hardly think that rice pudding and lumpy beds count as actual living. *Existing* would be a better word."

"You're in an orphanage?"

Sierra threw back her head and laughed. "I'm sure orphans would be treated better," she said. "I'm at an expensive finishing school. Rice pudding is apparently how the English toughen up their future empire builders." She turned to the girls clustered behind her. "These are my roommates."

Arthur nodded politely, but turned back to gaze at Sierra. She had never noticed before what clear blue eyes he had. "How about you?" she asked softly. "You seem to be doing very well."

He smiled shyly. "Yeah, things do seem to be looking up. After the earthquake, when I had no home and no job, I told myself that I could see this as an ending or an open door. I chose the latter. I came here and almost right away magazines started buying my work. My first novel got great reviews. Funny to think I have an earthquake to thank for all this."

"I'm so glad you're finally doing what you wanted to," she said simply.

"How did you know what I wanted to do?"

"You told me."

"I didn't think you'd even remember," he said dryly. "I thought that I was just another piece of furniture in your father's office to you in those days. But I'm glad to see a friendly face. I don't suppose you'd like to get together some time for a stroll in the park or something?"

Sierra glanced back at her roommates. "I'm pretty much a prisoner at this horrid school, but I suppose there are ways of escaping, if one really tried. If there was a worthwhile reason."

A broad smile spread across his face. "We'll try to arrange something then. Will you give me your address? I'd love to sit and talk right now, but it seems that I'm in demand at the moment." He looked up at the large crowd that still pressed around his table.

"It's okay. I understand," Sierra said, handing him her card. "I'd better let you get back to your fans then."

"We'll make that date soon," Arthur said. "We Yanks have to stick together in foreign lands."

They smiled at each other, and Sierra began to turn away. "And Sierra," he called after her. She looked back. "You're looking more lovely than ever," he said softly.

After that they saw each other often—usually only a carefully arranged moment of conversation in an art gallery while the rest of the girls disappeared to the next room.

Sierra liked his interesting, witty conversation and the way he made her laugh. Their swift, secret meetings were the exciting highlights of her week. She hadn't thought beyond that, but as they walked together one Sunday afternoon, Arthur suddenly said, "Let's go back across Kensington Gardens." He took her hand and led her into the leafy park. Once they were across the street and in the park, Arthur didn't let go of her hand, and she didn't try to pull it away. She liked the way his hand felt in hers, warm, comforting. She glanced up and her eyes met his.

"I've often thought the earthquake was the best thing that ever happened to me," he said softly. "Now I know that it is. Back there I'd always have been a lowly clerk and you'd have been a rich young lady."

"And pretty insufferable too," she had to admit. "A few months at Northwood Academy has certainly taught me to count my blessings."

He nodded. "You're so much nicer, Sierra. You always were beautiful and lively, but now you're soft and warm as well. You're . . . just perfect."

"You're not so bad yourself," she said, her eyes teasing his as she gazed up at him.

They paused in the middle of the leafy walk, and he bent to kiss her gently on the lips. The kiss was so restrained and polite that Sierra had to laugh. "Even Miss Hutchinson, our principal, couldn't disapprove of a kiss like that," she said.

"You think I should give you one that she would disapprove of?" he asked huskily.

Without speaking, she slid her arms around his neck and raised her face for him to kiss. This time it was no gentle brushing of lips. It was a kiss of pent-up desire, and people hurried past them, embarrassed, as they stood there in the middle of the park, unaware of the rest of the world.

"Oh, Sierra," Arthur whispered afterward. "I can't believe this is happening to us. The whole thing is like a miracle."

She was gazing up at him, her eyes shining. "The very best sort of miracle," she said. "I get out of that terrible school in a couple of months, and then we can see each other whenever we want!"

School came to an end, and Mr. Sutcliffe started making plans for going back to America and reopening his store. Mrs. Sutcliffe announced that she was going to stay on in Europe with Sierra, while Richard went home to help his father.

"This is what the school was for," she told Sierra. "Now comes the fun part. Your classmates will be presented at court, and you'll have a chance to attend all those lovely balls and meet all the eligible young men. If you play your cards right, you'll be able to snare yourself an upper-class husband and live in a castle."

"What if I don't want to, Mama?" Sierra asked cautiously. "What if I've already found the man I want?"

"If you're talking about that young writer,

forget it," Mrs. Sutcliffe snapped. "He's a no-body, Sierra. He might have achieved a sort of fame as a writer, but he'll never be rich. He'll never be able to support you properly."

"Maybe I've realized that there are things more important than money," Sierra said simply. "He makes me happy, Mama. I like being with him."

Mrs. Sutcliffe snorted. "See how much you like being with him when you have to scrub the floors," she said. "You were born to comfort, child. Anyway, you're still so young. Everyone falls in and out of love a dozen times in these years. You'll have forgotten him after a few months of dances and parties and trips to Paris." She jumped up excitedly. "I tell you what: We'll take the family diamonds to a jeweler and have them set into a new necklace for you. That should dazzle all the right young men."

"The family diamonds?" Sierra asked. She'd heard about them but had never actually seen them. She had always assumed they were in a bank vault, but her mother went across to the bookcase and got out a book, which opened like a box. "Look," she said. "Your legacy, Sierra."

In spite of herself, Sierra gasped as the dia-monds cascaded into her hands in a flash of multicolored fire. "Mama, they're incredible," she whispered.

"And so will you be, my darling, with these around your neck," her mother said. "You'll have all Europe at your feet."

*　　　*　　　*

Sierra was excited about the diamond necklace, and she loved the admiring looks she got when she wore it. She truly felt like a princess as she went into a ballroom with the diamonds sparkling at her throat, but after a season of glittering balls, she knew that she didn't want to marry a prince or a duke or any of the young men she met. She found them shallow and condescending. Arthur talked to her as if she was an intelligent person. These young aristocrats treated her as if she were a china doll. She found that she had to meet Arthur mostly in secret, as her dates with him always upset her mother so much that she had to go to bed for days.

As the months went by and Sierra showed no signs of falling in love with any of the young lords she met, Mrs. Sutcliffe got more and more angry. "You're doing this to spite me," she snapped. "All your friends from the finishing school are already married—to the most suitable young men. You know I want to see you happily settled before I die and yet you won't make the effort."

"If you'd only learn to like Arthur, you might see me happily settled," Sierra said.

"I will not see you married to a clerk," Mrs. Sutcliffe snapped. "We're wasting your father's money staying on here. If you refuse to try to and meet suitable young men, then we'll simply go home again and we'll find you a boy in San Francisco."

Sierra's heart lurched. She didn't want to go home again and be half a world away from

262

Arthur. So she tried to act as if she was enthusiastic about the next dances, but she knew her time in England was limited. Eventually they'd have to go back to San Francisco. Every day she looked at the calendar and counted the months to her twenty-first birthday, when she would be free to do as she pleased.

Then one day she came home to find her mother busy packing.

"I've had a cable from your father," she said. "The store is back in operation, the house is ready for occupation, and we are going home."

"Not yet!" Sierra begged.

"We've wasted long enough in a country I don't even like," Mrs. Sutcliffe said. "You're no nearer to finding an acceptable husband than the day we arrived. I've told your father to start seeking out suitable boys back home, and that's where we're going, just as soon as I can book us a passage on a ship."

Sierra tried changing her mother's mind, but she wouldn't listen. In desperation she went to Arthur. "She's making me go home," she said. "What are we going to do?"

"There's no friend you could stay with for the few months until your birthday?" he asked.

"She won't let me. She's already got my father looking for husbands for me in California," Sierra said, gazing at him desperately. "I can't bear to be parted from you, Arthur." Suddenly she jumped up, flinging her arms around him. "I know, why don't you come with me? We'll secretly book you a passage on the ship and we'll stroll around the decks together and kiss in the moonlight. Doesn't it sound wonderful?"

"But sweetest, for one thing I could never afford a first-class ticket, so we wouldn't be allowed to stroll on the same deck, and for another, I don't want to live in America again," Arthur said. "I really don't think I could write there. It's the lively atmosphere in London that sets all those creative juices flowing."

"Only until I'm twenty-one," Sierra begged. "We'll get married on my birthday and come back here. Do say yes, Arthur, please! Otherwise I'm scared they'll get me married off to a rich banker and I won't be able to stop them."

His eyes softened as he looked at her. "For you I'd do anything. You know that," he said. "It will mean using my savings to buy my ticket, but I'll just have to write the next book all the faster."

Her arms tightened around his neck. "Oh Arthur, I do adore you," she whispered. "We'll be so happy together."

"So how long have I got before this ship sails?"

"Three weeks," she said. "It's going to be her maiden voyage. She's a wonderful new ship, and everybody wants to sail on her. I do hope they've still got a cabin somewhere."

"What's her name?"

"The *Titanic*," Sierra said.

CHAPTER TWENTY-ONE

"The *Titanic*?" Laura asked, her eyes wide.

"The *Titanic*." Her grandmother nodded solemnly.

"So . . ."

"So Sierra and Arthur perished with the rest of the people who went down when it was struck by an iceberg."

Laura looked out of the train window so that the other passengers wouldn't see tears in her eyes. "Why did you have to tell me a story like that now?" she demanded of her grandmother, who was sitting beside her.

Helen Sutcliffe smiled. "Because you asked me," she said, "and because I could tell you needed something to take your mind off the court appearance."

"I'm not really worried," Laura said bravely. "I mean, they couldn't really do anything to me, could they? The American Embassy wouldn't let them throw me in jail, would they?"

"I'm sure it's just a formality," Helen said, patting her granddaughter's knee, "but we

English are sticklers for upholding the law, you know. You might have to pay a fine."

"Any idea how big a fine?" Laura asked cautiously. "I'm not exactly flush, you know."

Grandmama shrugged. "Not the price of the crown jewels, I should imagine."

"I suppose those diamonds went down with Sierra," Laura commented, almost to herself. "They never recovered her body?"

"No, the bodies were never recovered," Grandmama said.

"So she wasn't really my direct ancestor," Laura said thoughtfully.

"No. It was her brother, Richard, who was your grandpa Jimmy's grandfather," Grandmama Helen said.

"Oh, Richard. I'm glad it was him," Laura said. "He sounded nice. He wanted to do something useful with his life."

Grandmama Helen went to say something to Laura, but instead gave her a long look, then smiled.

Laura took her grandmother's hand. "I'm glad you're coming with me to this," she said. "Thanks for not making more of a fuss."

Helen nodded. "It's all I could expect of a Sutcliffe woman," she said. "Impetuous, headstrong, will stop at nothing to get what she wants. You're just like the first Laura, my dear, in more ways than the portrait."

Laura grinned. "So you really think I would stop at nothing to get what I want?"

266

"When you've decided what you want," Grandmama said.

Laura looked out the window. They were passing Cotswold scenery: rolling hills dotted with sheep, stone walls, windswept trees, square stone farmhouses. "That's the problem," she said. She didn't know what she wanted out of life. Right now she wanted to get through the appearance before the judges, but after that. . . . The only thing she really wanted was something that didn't exist anymore. She wanted to get her hands on the diamonds, to have the necklace whole again and back in the family. Then she could make everything right for her father and go to a good college and live happily ever after. . . .

The train jerked as it pulled into Cirencester station, where the magistrate's court would be meeting. Laura took a big breath. "Be brave," she told herself. "Remember how brave the other Laura would have been!" She kept telling herself this over and over until she was actually standing before the three magistrates. All the Sutcliffe and Treadwick women had had spunk. They had faced horrible sea voyages and crossed continents and had babies in the middle of the wilderness. So how could she, descendant of both Sutcliffes and Treadwicks, be scared of three old fogies?

She glanced across at them, an elderly man with a toothbrush mustache, a horse-faced woman wearing mannish tweed clothing, and an old woman who smiled all the time and looked as if she was really out of it. To think that her fate depended on them! In the darkness at the back of the courtroom, she could see her grandmother's face.

"You are up on a charge of trespassing and petty theft, I understand?" the toothbrush man said, glaring at Laura. "You are an American visitor to this country and decided to help yourself to a little souvenir?"

He nodded across, and the security guard from Treadwick stood up to give evidence. He reported how Laura had slipped away from a tour, had triggered the alarm system, and had been caught with the valuable diary in her possession. Laura saw three hostile faces looking at her.

"I'd like to explain," she began, but the toothbrush man wagged his finger at her and went on. "You Americans seem to think that we have so much history in England that we won't even miss little morsels if you take them. You try to chip off bits of Stonehenge and help yourself to stones from a Roman wall, just because they're open and available for all. But I would like to point out to you that these are our heritage and this is not the Wild West!"

"If I might say something at this point," came a commanding voice that echoed through the high-beamed, drafty hall.

The three magistrates looked up, too surprised to comment as Grandmama Helen strode down the center aisle. The bailiff jumped up but she pushed him aside. "This young woman acted under the assumption that the property belonged to me," she said clearly.

"And you are, madam?" the toothbrush man asked.

"Helen Sutcliffe, formerly Helen Henderson of the Treadwick family and owner of Treadwick Hall," she said. "This young person is my granddaughter. I had told her about my ancestors' diaries and letters, which I used to read as a child. My granddaughter got it into her head that they might still be up in the attic. She found my ancestor Emma Treadwick's diary and wanted to bring it back for me."

"Wait a minute," the toothbrush man said, peering over his steel-rimmed glasses. "I know you. Helen Henderson of Treadwick. We used to go to pony club meetings out at Treadwick Hall. You and your sister . . . Remember me? Cedric Molesworth?"

"Good heavens. Cedric Molesworth. You got stuck in that tree when your pony went on without you."

Suddenly Laura felt as if she didn't exist anymore. The three magistrates were chatting with her grandmother as if they were at a tea party and not in court. At last the tweedy woman caught sight of Laura's face and nudged Cedric Molesworth, who cleared his throat.

"This does seem to be a case of misunderstanding rather than of deliberately breaking the law. I'm afraid, young lady, that any item in

Treadwick Hall would seem to be the property of the current owners and should not be touched without their permission."

"I understand that now, sir," Laura said, trying to look repentant and humble.

The man smiled kindly and leaned over the table toward Laura. "We might suggest that you contact the family if you wish to browse further among old documents. I can't see that they would refuse such a reasonable request." All three magistrates smiled.

Grandmama prodded Laura to approach the bench, and they all shook hands. Then Laura found herself emerging into bright sunlight. As she stood, dazzled, in the entrance hall, a flashbulb went off in her face, startling her.

"Got it," Simon said, grinning delightedly. "That should look good with my story. Heiress escapes jail in search for past? Yeah, not bad. Adds that touch of drama to the story. Might even make the front page!"

Laura's pent-up fear came spilling out. "My grandmother was right," she said. "You were only interested in me for your stupid story! You don't care about me or my feelings at all. I might have been put in jail and you wouldn't care. Go away. Leave me alone!"

She pushed past him into the fresh air. As she walked down the steps, not waiting for her grandmother to catch up with her, a distinguished gray-haired man stepped forward. "Miss Sutcliffe?" he asked. "I am Mr. Mandrake of Mandrake, Wetheram, and Mandrake. We represent the Cooper family, who now own Treadwick Hall. We were approached by a Mr. Simon Davies who told us your story. Mr. and Mrs. Cooper were sorry that you have been caused any distress and ask me to convey to you that you are welcome to continue your investigations in the attic whenever you wish. Their only stipulation is that nothing is removed from the house without my permission. They actually have no interest in any item in the attic, so feel free to take what you want from up there."

"Oh," Laura stammered, painfully conscious that Simon had gone to all that trouble for her and she had been so rude to him. "Thanks very much."

The man actually blushed. "Always happy to help a member of the Treadwick family," he said. "My father used to be your family lawyer. It was a sad day when the house was sold."

As he melted away, Laura looked around for Simon. She saw the familiar tweed jacket as he walked dejectedly down the street and ran after him. "Simon, wait up," she called.

He stopped, his face so miserable and embarrassed that she wanted to laugh. "You arranged all that with the lawyers for me," she said. "I wanted to thank you."

"And I wanted to tell you that you've got it all wrong," he said softly. "I didn't mean to exploit you, honestly. I know it's a good story, Laura, and it could mean a lot to my career, but if you tell me not to publish, I'll tear the whole thing up."

"You don't have to do that," she said. "Now that I'm not going to be a jailbird, I don't mind at all."

"Really?" His whole face lit up again. "Then I'd love to hear the rest of the story sometime."

"You better plan on a whole free day," she said. "And you might find that your newspaper story stretches into a whole series of articles."

"Hey, that sounds super," he said. "Can I take you for a coffee, to celebrate your freedom?"

"My grandmother's here too," Laura said. "I left her on the steps. I'd better go back for her, but maybe you could come up to London and we can tell you the whole story."

"And I could take you somewhere in the evening, if your grandmother doesn't mind," he said, his eyes shining now. "I know some fun things to do—some good dance clubs and that sort of thing. What do you say?"

"I'd love it," Laura said. "I've spent three weeks exclusively with suits of armor and old portraits. It would make a change to spend the evening with somebody living and breathing."

"Oh, I can assure you that I'm very much alive," he said, his eyes holding hers for a second.

Laura was grinning to herself as she went back to her grandmother.

The next day it rained steadily, and Laura was happy to sit in the hotel parlor with Simon and her grandmother, drinking tea and talking. Simon was a good listener, and Laura didn't mind hearing the stories over again.

At last he said, "I'm confused about one thing, Mrs. Sutcliffe. You say you were born at Treadwick but your name was Henderson and your married name is Sutcliffe. Where did the Treadwicks come into this and how come you ended up a Sutcliffe?"

Laura's grandmother smiled. "I suppose I'm the thread that joined all the stories together," she said. "My mother was a Treadwick but my father was Australian . . ."

"Henderson!" Laura said excitedly. "That was the name of the guy who married Tessa when she came home to Australia and there was the terrible fire."

"He was my grandfather," Helen said. "Or at least, I suppose my real grandfather was a scoundrel French count. No wonder my granddaughter resorts to breaking and entering!"

"How did your father meet your mother?" Simon asked.

Helen Sutcliffe smiled. "His name was Hugo, and he was very handsome," she said. "He came to England in the army during World War One. He had the address of his English relatives, the Treadwicks of Treadwick Hall, and he came to look them up. He took one look at my mother, Sylvia, and they fell helplessly in love. I understand that Sylvia's father was furious, and rightly so. Sylvia was the only child and was going to inherit all the property. I loved my father dearly, but he was a very unreliable man. He had no head for money, for one thing. He invested everything on Wall Street before the great crash of twenty-nine and lost it all. That's when we had to move out of Treadwick and into a cottage. The shock killed my mother, and my father killed himself."

"Grandmama, how terrible," Laura said. "What an awful childhood."

"I survived," Grandmama said. "I'm a Treadwick and a Sutcliffe, remember. We're born fighters."

"And Grandpa Jimmy?" Laura asked. "You said he was one of the American Sutcliffes, Richard's children. . . ."

Helen Sutcliffe nodded. "That's right. Richard married and had children. He also gave up the business when his father died and became a schoolteacher just like he always wanted. He had no head for business, and the store never really prospered again after the earthquake."

"And you met Grandpa Jimmy in the war as the bombs were falling," Laura prompted. "You've told me that story before. Did he come to visit his English kin, just like your father did when he met your mother?"

Grandmama Helen smiled, as if reliving an old memory. "No, that was the strange thing," she said. "We met entirely by accident, or rather by fate, if you like. . . ."

CHAPTER TWENTY-TWO

Helen Henderson picked her way through the rubble of what had once been Oxford Street. It had been a bad night, with one air raid after another, and store dummies lay like corpses among the broken glass of shop windows. Helen hardly noticed them. All she wanted was a hot cup of tea and then to get home to bed. She had been volunteering at a first aid post all night, and what she had seen made her feel sick. She had started two months earlier with so much hope and purpose and enthusiasm, but night after night of no sleep with so much useless loss of life made her feel far older than her twenty years.

She was still a good distance from Oxford Circus underground station when another air raid warning went. Away in the distance, the staccato fire of antiaircraft guns began, and Helen could just make out the trembling drone of an enemy plane. She looked up briefly, then kept on walking. Suddenly she was grabbed by the arm so forcefully that she was spun around.

"Hey, lady, didn't you hear the air raid siren?" a deep American voice demanded.

Helen looked up, surprised. The speaker was a tall, lean American serviceman, wearing the leather jacket and peaked cap of an airman.

In normal circumstances, Helen would have reverted to good old British tradition and told him frostily that they hadn't been introduced—a polite way of telling him to mind his own business. But these were not normal circumstances. The war and the bombing of London had made old customs seem stupid. Why did it matter anymore if a person had not been introduced or wasn't of the right class when the bombs didn't care if they took strangers or friends?

"It's okay," she said easily. "They're still quite a way off. Listen."

The tall stranger shook his head in disbelief. "I've only been in this crazy country one week," he said, "and in this crazy city for two hours. If I hear an air raid warning, I get to a shelter, and so should you if you know what's good for you."

"You soon get used to it," Helen said. "If everyone stopped what they were doing each time there was a warning, nothing would get done. You just have to learn to take your chances."

He shook his head again. "I take enough chances up in that plane," he said. "I aim to stay safe on the ground, if possible."

"Oh, you're quite safe," Helen said amiably. "If we can't even see the planes yet, we're in no big hurry. We can make it to Oxford Circus. I do this every morning."

He looked amazed. "How can you be such a cool customer?"

"Practice," she said.

She continued walking at an even pace, and the young airman tried not to seem in a hurry at her side, but they had gone only a few steps more when there was a whooshing noise, and a blinding flash, followed by a huge explosion. The young man barely had time to say "What the hell . . ." when they were flung backward in a shower of debris and glass. They didn't have time to see if they were all right or not. As they looked up, one of the decorative columns outside Selfridges department store toppled toward them.

"Look out!" the American shouted. He grabbed Helen and flung himself on top of her, shielding them both with his leather-jacketed arm as the column broke into a thousand pieces right beside them.

As the dust cleared, he sat up awkwardly and began brushing himself off. "You okay?" he asked.

"I think so, thanks to you," Helen said breathlessly. She also sat up and started brushing the dust from her uniform. "You saved my life," she said.

He gave a crooked grin that she found very endearing.

"What the hell was that, anyway?" he demanded. "There weren't any planes. . . ."

"It must have been one of those new V-2 rockets they've been talking about," Helen said. "They're supposed to be the new secret weapon—completely silent until they hit. The element of surprise."

"Well, I'd say it worked pretty well this time," he said, chuckling as he got to his feet. "It surprised us all right."

"It certainly did," Helen said, laughing too as he helped her up. "If I hadn't stopped to talk to you but kept going toward Oxford Circus, I'd have been blown to pieces by now. The least I owe you is a cup of tea at the services canteen."

"A double whiskey would make more sense," he said, "but I suppose at nine o'clock in the morning I'll have to settle for that horrible thick stuff you British call tea." He gave her a friendly smile, then held out his hand. "Name's Jimmy Sutcliffe," he said. "From San Francisco, California."

"How odd," Helen said.

"Me, or that I'm from San Francisco?"

"Your name. We must be related way back. I have Sutcliffes on both sides of my family and it can't be too common a name."

"I was the only one in my school," Jimmy said. "My folks left England and made a fortune in the gold rush."

"Then I bet it's the same ones," Helen said excitedly. "My great-great-aunt ran off to America to marry a groom, and they changed their name to Sutcliffe."

"I bet it is the same ones, then," Jimmy said, "because I heard tell that we once came from a real swell British family." He held out his hand again. "Glad to meet you, cousin, although I still don't know your name."

"I'm sorry. I was so excited that I forgot," Helen said. "I'm Helen. Helen Henderson. How do you do?"

Ambulances and fire trucks had begun arriving at the crater site, and black smoke billowed ahead of them. Helen hardly looked at it, but Jimmy shuddered. "This is all still real hard for me," he said. "I want to rush over there and see if they need any help."

"I know how you feel," Helen said. "I felt exactly the same way when I first came to London, but I'm afraid it happens so often that you do your own bit and leave the rest to others. I've just got off duty at a first aid post, and I've been patching up victims like this all night."

He looked at her with admiration. "That's quite an order for a little bit of a girl like you."

"I'm not a girl; I'm almost twenty-one," she said.

"Quite an old maid then," he said and chuckled when she made a face.

They went down the steps into the underground station and over to the kiosk that had been set up to serve tea and snacks. Helen ordered two teas and two bacon sandwiches and insisted on paying for them through Jimmy's protests.

"You saved my life and I've just met my long-lost cousin," she said. "That deserves at least a bacon sandwich, and they're pretty tasty here."

They took their food and sat down at a makeshift trestle table beside a couple of ambulance workers and nightwatchmen.

"I think this is just amazing," Jimmy said, gazing at her with undisguised interest. "In the middle of the London bombs, feeling lost and scared and half a world from home, I meet a long-lost relative."

"It is pretty amazing," Helen agreed.

"Do you have any time off in the next couple of days?" he asked. "I've got a three-day pass and I am determined to see something of London before I start flying bombing missions to Germany. I could sure use a guide who knows her way around."

"I'd be happy to," Helen said. "I was about to go home to sleep, but sleep seems rather a waste of time these days. In fact, everything seemed rather a waste of time until you showed up. I was beginning to get very depressed by the whole thing."

He nodded as if he understood. "War does seem kind of overwhelming, doesn't it?" he said. "Like two little people can't make much difference, so what's the point."

"Exactly," she said. "I was so keen when I first came to London a couple of months ago. My sister went off to join the navy and I was all alone in the country, where it was deadly dull, so I decided to come to London and see where they needed help."

"Your folks still live in the country?" he asked.

"My folks are both dead," she said. "It's just me and my sister."

"I'm sorry."

"It's okay. We're used to it," she said. "They've been dead for quite a while."

"So you volunteered as a first aid nurse?"

Helen nodded. "A friend from school had started doing it and said it was exciting, so I came up to London to join her. And it was exciting to begin with. My friend is sort of high society, and we had all these crazy parties when we danced on the rooftops while the bombs were falling. It was like defying death, I suppose. It made the war seem terribly unreal, until a certain young man . . ."

"Your young man?"

"In a way." She looked down at her mug of tea. "He could have been if we'd had enough time. I danced with him one night, and the next morning he was shot down over the channel. It made everything seem so useless."

Jimmy reached out his hand and covered hers. "I know how you feel," he said. "Every time we take off we have to face the fact that we might not come back. It's hard."

"War's so stupid!" she said angrily. Already she was having fearful thoughts about losing this new found relative and friend.

"To hell with war, that's what I say," he said,

thumping down his empty mug. "Let's go have a good time. Show me the best that London has to offer."

They spent two crazy days, visiting all the sights, walking by the Thames, and in the evening they danced at the Allied Officers Club to the music of a swing band. Jimmy was the perfect gentleman and insisted on escorting her home to her front door in Hampstead, even though the last bus had already gone.

"Don't worry. I'll hitch a ride. I always do," he said and waved a big, friendly hand.

After that he called and wrote to her often. He came down to London whenever he had a day pass, and Helen began to feel alive and hopeful again. It was like discovering a brother she had never known. Then one day he invited her to visit him at the base.

"We're having a kind of dance," he said. "My landlady says she can put you up for the night."

Helen spent two freezing hours in the train going to Lincolnshire. Jimmy met her, looking his polished best, and escorted her proudly into the dance. "I'd like you to meet my buddies," he said.

That's when she found herself staring into the handsome face of Tony Alioto. He was laughing at someone else's joke, his dark eyes flashing and his perfect teeth sparkling. Helen thought she had never seen anything as perfect as Tony's face. Suddenly he was aware of her. He looked at her appraisingly and then winked. Helen felt herself blushing down to her shoes, but her heart was beating very fast as he got up and came over to her.

"So this is the long-lost cousin we've been hearing so much about," he said. "No wonder we haven't seen you before. If I had a cousin who looked like you, I'd keep her locked away too. Wanna dance?"

Without waiting for an answer he took her into his arms and swirled her onto the floor. He was a wonderful dancer, and his arms held her so tightly that she could feel his heart beating through her thin dress. He told her stories about Brooklyn and he made her laugh. Later they went for a stroll outside, and he kissed her.

"You and Alioto seemed to hit it off pretty good," Jimmy commented casually as he walked her back to his house.

"Isn't he a wonderful dancer?" Helen said breathlessly. "And so funny."

"Look, kid," Jimmy began. "Take it easy, okay? I mean, he's not your type of guy at all. He's fine to dance with for one evening, but don't get any ideas."

Helen looked up at his face and laughed. "Why, Jimmy, I do believe you're jealous," she said.

"Not at all," he said hastily. "I just don't want to see my favorite cousin hurt."

"I'm a big girl," she said haughtily. "I can take care of myself."

She made an excuse to stay down there a day longer and spent the whole afternoon with Tony. He borrowed a Jeep and they drove out to the ocean, where they parked, watching the waves through the barbed wire. He began kissing her again, but then broke away with a laugh. "This damn climate is too cold for making love," he said. "Any more of this and our lips will freeze together. Tell ya what, kiddo. I've got a three-day pass coming up. Why don't I come up to London and we'll find someplace way more cozy? Then I'll show you that Brooklyn guys know a thing or two about the birds and the bees."

Inside her head a voice was reminding her to watch her step, that smooth-talking Yanks had acquired a bad reputation with the way they treated English girls. But she didn't want to watch her step. She knew that nobody had ever made her feel the way Tony did. This had to be the real thing, the great love that only happened once in a person's life, and she'd be crazy to turn it down.

"All right," she said, not a trace of hesitation in her voice.

He hugged her fiercely to him. "You're a great girl, Helen," he said. "I'm sure glad I found you."

Jimmy didn't say much when he discovered that she'd spent the afternoon with Tony, but she could tell he was angry. He hardly said a word as he drove her back to the station.

"Don't be angry, please," she said, gently

touching his cheek. "I can't help whom I fall in love with."

"I know I have no hold over you," Jimmy said in a tight voice, "but just don't believe everything he tells you. He's one of those guys who lie whenever they want something. Don't get me wrong; the guys here like Tony. He's good for a laugh. But we don't trust him and nobody likes to fly with him."

"Huh!" Helen said. She was sure now that Jimmy was making this up, just to keep her away from another man, which must mean he was interested in her himself. In the train going home she thought about this. She had never considered Jimmy in that way before. He had never given any indication that he was attracted to her. He had never tried to touch her in anything but a brotherly way. And what did she feel for him? Definite warm feelings, the sort of feelings distant relatives should feel for each other, but not the sort of rush of ecstasy she felt when she thought of Tony's kisses.

"I'm a sensible girl," she told herself. "I know what sort of reputation these Americans have got. I'm not going to let him go too far. . . ." But then she wondered just how far she wanted him to go. She'd heard about a lot of whirlwind marriages and girls who had gone to America as brides. What if Tony wanted to marry her? Would she want to live in Brooklyn? The thought of being in Tony's arms excited her. It didn't matter where she lived as long as she was with a man she loved, she decided.

She had her hair permed and bought a new dress the day before Tony's three-day pass. She knew she was looking her best as she went to the station to meet him. The train from Lincolnshire arrived but no Tony was on it. She waited for the next train, thinking that he must have missed it. Maybe there had been a last-minute emergency. If his leave had been canceled at the last minute surely he would have called her. . . .

Then she saw a familiar face in the crowd. Jimmy was walking down the platform toward her. "Hi," he said.

"What are you doing here?"

"I came to tell you myself," he said.

A cold shiver ran down her back.

"His plane didn't return from yesterday's raid."

"Oh." She didn't know what else to say.

"I'm really sorry," he said. "I know this can't be easy. . . ."

"Thank you for coming," she said at last. "It was sweet of you to travel all this way in the cold."

He gave that endearing, half-sad smile. "I'd do anything for you. You know that." He reached out and touched her sleeve. "It's okay to cry if you want. You don't have to keep that stiff British upper lip."

Without warning she flung herself into his arms. "Oh, Jimmy. What am I going to do?" she sobbed. "Every time I fall madly in love with a man he's killed. I can't bear it."

He held her close and stroked her hair as if she were a little child. "It's going to be okay," he whispered. "I'm here. I'll take care of you."

Then he took her for coffee and they walked across Hampstead Heath. A bitter wind was blowing, and he held her hand.

"I don't want to rush you," he said, "but maybe you'd do better with a guy like me. I know you don't love me the way you loved Tony, but I'd sure take good care of you and cherish you all your life. Ever since we first met I've known we belong together. And I think that deep down you know it too. It had to be fate that brought us together in the middle of five million people . . . two distant cousins from halfway around the world, from a family that was broken up a hundred years ago. . . . It broke my heart to see you with him, knowing what I know . . ."

"What do you know?"

"I won't say it now, seeing that he's dead," Jimmy said. "I only know that no good would have come of it, and I'm not just saying that because I want you for myself. You see, I think you and I have got the makings of a real relationship: We're friends, we trust each other, we care about each other. That's the sort of love that lasts."

As he talked, she looked at his kind, rugged face, and she knew this was true. Her feelings for Tony were like wonderful fireworks ready to explode into a thousand stars, but her feelings for Jimmy were like a fire, glowing in a fireplace—a fire that wouldn't go out or leave you cold.

They were married three months later, and Helen left on one of the special ships full of English brides bound for America, waiting anxiously for the end of the war when he would come home to her.

CHAPTER TWENTY-THREE

"It's a terrible thing to say, but it was lucky that Tony fellow got killed or your grandmother might have made a big mistake," Simon said to Laura.

They were walking together that evening along the Thames embankment. The rain had stopped, and lights twinkled in the dark waters. The melancholy hoot of a tugboat cut through the muted roar of traffic.

"I might not be here," Laura said. "That's a scary thought. Funny, I always thought Grandmama Helen was so sensible too. I guess all the Sutcliffe women have that streak in them that makes them choose the wrong man."

"What about you?" Simon asked, giving her a sideways look. "Are you like that?"

"I . . . of course not," Laura said quickly.

"You seem to like me a little, which shows the beginnings of good taste," Simon said, laughing. Then, as she didn't laugh too, he asked: "Do you have a boyfriend back home?"

"Yes, I do," Laura said at last. "He's a really

interesting person. You should interview him; he's done so many things."

"Is it serious, you and him?"

"Pretty serious. He wants me to join him in Europe as soon as I can. He's touring and staying in hostels. I'm hoping to go across when my grandmother goes home."

"I see," he said. They walked along in silence, and Laura got the impression that he was disappointed she had a boyfriend.

"What about you?" she asked to break the silence. "Do you have a girlfriend?"

"Sort of. We dated in high school and we haven't officially broken up, but we don't have much in common anymore."

"I guess that's important, having something in common." Laura frowned. She was wondering what she and Brian would have in common when they met again.

They walked on. "Where are we going?" Laura asked cautiously. The river was no longer bordered by glittering high-rises and stately monuments. Tall brick warehouses now lined the waterfront. Dark alleys ran between them. There was the sound of water dripping, and a cat shot across the path in front of them.

"I'm luring you onto a ship to take you to Australia," Simon said, laughing. "This is the old dock area. Maybe one of your ancestors sailed out of here."

"Is it safe to be here?" Laura asked.

"You have to take some risks in life, don't

you?" Simon said with a grin. "Your ancestors certainly took their share of risks."

"And it didn't always turn out well for them," Laura said.

"Don't worry. I'll take good care of you," Simon said. He gave her the sweetest smile that made his whole face light up.

"He's nice," Laura thought. "I really do feel comfortable with him, as if I've known him forever."

They cut through an alleyway and found themselves outside an old pub.

"This is what I brought you to see," Simon said. "It's the Prospect of Whitby. One of the oldest pubs in London." He opened the door to music and laughter. The bar was brightly lit, with beamed ceilings and lots of brass. Simon led the way through the bar and out onto the terrace over the river. Lights were strung around the deck and danced in the dark water below.

"This is the heart of London," he said. "All sorts of smuggling and criminal deals used to go on here. Now it's just businesspeople and tourists."

They sat on the deck, and Simon ordered a beer for himself and a shandy for her: a pint of beer mixed with ginger beer.

"Don't worry; it's legal to drink at eighteen over here," he said.

"It's good too," she said. "I wish we had something like pubs in America. They're much more social and friendly than our bars and clubs."

291

They sat sipping their drinks and bombarded each other with questions. Simon was really curious about life in America, especially Laura's life in high school, and she was amazed by his revelations.

"I can't believe it. You had to wear a uniform even when you were eighteen years old? How dumb." She laughed, shaking her head.

"At least we didn't have to decide what to wear every day," he said, laughing with her. "But I'd have loved your choices in high school. We got stuck with the subjects we needed for our exams."

"I'd have hated that too," Laura admitted. "One set of exams to decide your whole fate and where you could go to college?"

"You're right. Judging a student on four years of work is much fairer," he agreed.

After a while it got too cold to sit outside.

"I'd like to take you somewhere nice to dinner," Simon said, "but London restaurants cost a fortune. You'll have to wait until I'm a famous reporter. Then I'll whisk you away in a taxi to Julie's or Simpson's."

"To tell you the truth, I'm dying for a hamburger," Laura said. "I've had to eat English food since I've been here and I've got real french fry withdrawal symptoms."

"Easily done." Simon smiled.

They hopped on an underground train and came up next to a McDonald's. Then they walked through Chelsea, looking at the latest fashions, talking nonstop until they came to a distinguished-looking house.

"Not a late-night museum," Laura said, looking up at Simon's face. "I couldn't bear another dose of armor and portraits."

"Not even close," he said, laughing at her expression. "It's my favorite dance club. It's called the Purple Onion. Let's go."

He took her hand and led her down the steps to the basement. The hallway was vibrating to a deep bass beat. At the end of the hall, Simon pushed open a door and they were in a big underground room full of moving bodies, with laser lights playing on the ceiling.

Simon turned out to be a great dancer and knew dances that Laura hadn't even heard of. In the slow numbers he held her very close, and it seemed natural for her cheek to rest against his shoulder. In the early hours of the morning, they walked hand in hand through the deserted streets.

"I had a really great time," she said as they stood outside her hotel.

"Me too."

"You're some dancer."

"So are you." He looked at her tenderly. "I think we made a great couple."

She nodded.

"Correction," he said in a low voice. "I think we make a great couple." Slowly his arms came around her. He drew her close to him and kissed her. It was such a tender, gentle kiss that Laura thought it was the most beautiful thing that had ever happened to her.

"I'll always remember tonight, all my life," she whispered. "It was really special, Simon."

"I hope there will be other nights," he said. "There's so much I want to show you—so many things I want to share with you." He looked at her shyly. "I think I'm falling in love with you, Laura. Is that a very stupid thing to do?"

She smiled at his hesitant face. "I don't think we can choose who we fall in love with."

"So you're saying you don't feel the same way about me?"

"I didn't say that," she stammered. "I . . . it's just too soon to know how I feel. I've been looking forward so much to being with Brian again. I have to think about this, Simon."

"It's okay. I understand. I'm not going to rush you," he said, "but can we do something tomorrow? Do you think your grandma would mind?"

"She can spend the day in Harrod's," Laura said, grinning delightedly. "She's been dying to browse in the linens department!"

"I thought that maybe we could hire a rowboat and row up the Thames to Hampton Court Palace," Simon suggested. "And we could take a picnic and tie up our boat under willow trees. . . . How does that sound?"

"Pretty good, as long as you do the rowing," Laura said. "I've never tried it, and I might tip us over."

"Actually I pictured myself lying back on pillows while you rowed me along like a faithful slave," he said, then dodged, laughing, as she tried to hit him. "Of course I was intending to be rower in chief. I used to row for my school and I've got the muscles to prove it."

"I'd better go in," Laura said reluctantly. "It's getting late."

He took her face in his hands and kissed her again. "Tomorrow morning, then. I'll come for you about ten?"

"Wonderful." She had a sudden thought. "But Simon. How will you get home tonight? Do trains still go down to Gloucestershire at this hour?"

"Don't worry about me. I've got a friend who lets me use his floor whenever I'm in town," he said. "See you in the morning. Sleep well, sweet dreams."

Laura blew him a kiss as she ran inside.

"Message for you, Miss Sutcliffe," the desk clerk said as he handed her her key.

"Oh . . . thanks." She took the folded piece of paper and opened it. "Arriving Friday on boat train. Be at your hotel before noon. Can't wait. Brian."

The next morning Laura walked down the stairs rather than riding the elevator. She still didn't know how she was going to face Simon. She saw him before he saw her. He was standing looking out the window. His fair hair still flopped boyishly forward across his forehead. His blue eyes were looking around with interest. He turned instinctively as she crossed the room.

"Hi!" he said, picking up her Americanism. "Ready to split?"

"Simon . . ." she began.

"Something's wrong?"

"I can't come with you today. My boyfriend, the one I told you about . . . he's arriving this morning."

"Oh . . . I see," he said. "Well, all right. I'd better be going then. Maybe I'll see you again when you come down to Treadwick. You could give me a call if you need someone to go through the attic with you . . . if you want to, that is."

He started to walk to the door.

"Simon!" she called after him.

He looked back, so hopeless and vulnerable that she didn't want him to go. "I'll call you," she said. "I have your number."

He nodded.

"I'm really sorry about this."

"I understand. Bye, Laura."

"Bye."

She gave a halfhearted wave as he went through the revolving glass door and out into the busy street.

For the next hour she was torn between guilt and anticipation. She had done the right thing, hadn't she? Of course she was dying to see Brian again. Simon was very sweet and kind and fun, but, after all, he didn't make her feel like Brian did. She didn't actually love Simon. In her mind she went over every exciting moment with Brian, everything they had done together, every word he had said.

"Brian's coming back," she told herself over and over again like a chant.

He walked into the hotel around eleven thirty, making two elderly ladies hastily stand aside as he came in. She had forgotten how different he looked. In San Francisco his dress and hairstyle blended in, but here, in a sedate London hotel, he stood out like a peacock in a henhouse. His hair was combed back into a ponytail and he'd grown a full, shaggy beard. He was wearing a Mexican shawl thrown over his shoulders, bright surfer pants, and Birkies. On his back was an enormous backpack with a guitar strapped to it.

His eyes lit up when he saw her. "Hey, babe," he said. He grabbed her and kissed her passionately, right in the middle of the lobby.

"How you been?" he asked.

"Surviving," she said, happy to be in his arms again, "and you?"

"Great. I've been great. I've seen some terrific stuff in Europe—neat hostels, met a lot of really great kids, hung out, smoked some dope, played some music . . . just great. Kept thinking of you, though. You must be bored out of your skull."

"It's been okay," she said pulling back from him. "I got arrested."

"Cool, what for?"

"Breaking and entering, if you can believe it," she said, laughing. "I went to look at the attic at my ancestral home. There were all these letters my ancestors had written, Brian, and diaries . . . I now know all my past. It's incredible . . . there was another Laura Sutcliffe, and she followed the man she loved to Australia back in the convict days and that . . ."

"Sounds cool," he said. "So are you ready to split?"

"What?"

"I thought we'd catch the two o'clock train back to France."

"You what?"

He looked amazed. "What do you think I came for? Not to see London. Too many old fogies over here. Too much history crap. I came to take you away from the old dragon. Get your stuff."

Laura gave an embarrassed laugh. "Brian, I can't leave now. Not just like that."

"Why not?"

"I can't just leave my grandmother here alone, for one thing."

"Why not? She's not an invalid or something, is she?"

"No, but . . ."

"But?"

"She paid for the trip. . . ."

"She's gotten her money's worth. She's had you for three weeks." He looked at Laura critically. "What's with you? I thought you wanted me to rescue you."

"I thought so too," she said. "But now I don't."

"Are you saying you don't want to come to the Continent with me?"

"I've got things to do here," she said hesitantly. "I can't come right now. Maybe in a week or two, when we're finished up here . . ."

She saw his dark eyes flash with anger. "Forget it," he snapped. "It's now or never, Laura. I don't wait around for any girl. You either want me or you don't."

She looked at him steadily. "You'd better go, Brian, or you'll miss your train."

He looked at her with disgust. "You've changed, Laura," he said angrily. "The old Laura would have come with me in a minute flat."

"Yes," she said, surprised at herself. "Yes, I have changed. I think I've grown up a lot this summer, and I think you've got some growing up to do too."

He was still eyeing her angrily. "Me? I am the most together person I know, but that's your loss. You're missing out on a lot of cool stuff."

"I'll risk it," she said, amazed at her calmness.

"You're not ever going to find a guy like me again," he threatened.

"Probably not," she said, "but I'll risk that too. Good luck, Brian. I hope you find what you're looking for."

He didn't say another word, just swung around and pushed his way out through the revolving door. Laura bit her lip as she watched him go.

"I almost made a big mistake," she muttered to herself, amazed that she hadn't seen it before.

Then a thought sprang to her mind: Simon! He might not have left London yet. There weren't too many trains down to his part of the country.

She hailed a taxi and sped to Paddington station. The next train to Gloucester was leaving at noon. If only he hadn't managed to catch the one before . . .

The platform was crowded. Passengers were pouring out of a train that had just arrived. Laura had to dodge past luggage carts and strollers and porters. She had almost gone the whole length of the platform when she spotted the familiar light brown hair. He was sitting on a bench, bent over a magazine. A great rush of delight and relief swept through her. She crept up to him.

"Excuse me, but is this the right way to the river Thames and Hampton Court Palace?" she asked. "I'm looking for a strong, reliable man to row me to a picnic."

He looked up, his jaw dropping open in amazement.

"Where's your boyfriend?"

"You mean Brian? My ex-boyfriend?" she asked. "I imagine he's getting on the boat train back to France about now."

"What happened?"

"He wanted me to go with him, and I decided I liked it better here," she said.

"Oh." He still looked dazed.

"I like everything better here," she went on. "The stupid suits of armor and the dumb portraits and even the people. Especially the people."

He got to his feet. His eyes were shining. "Does cold chicken and crusty bread and peaches sound all right for a picnic?" he asked.

"Sounds wonderful," she said, smiling up at him. She grabbed his hand. "Come on, what are we waiting for?"

They ran down the platform, hand in hand.

CHAPTER TWENTY-FOUR

"It's just as I remember it," Helen Sutcliffe gasped as she followed Laura into the attic at Treadwick. "I don't think anybody's touched it since we were children." She laughed uneasily. "We were always a little scared that there were ghosts under the sheets."

"I felt the same thing, Grandmama," Laura said, laughing. "It was really spooky up here alone." She smiled fondly at her grandmother's face as the housekeeper came, wheezing and out of breath, up the last few steps.

"They do say the house is haunted," the housekeeper said. She told them she had had her instructions from the estate manager that she was to let them look at what they wanted, but to keep an eye on them. "Although I've never seen a ghost myself, but I've definitely felt cold sometimes, got the shivers and had to turn around quickly."

"I know what you mean," Helen said. "I had that feeling several times."

"I must say it would be really interesting to

see a ghost," Simon commented. "It would make a great front-page story, especially if I managed to capture it on film."

"Does everything have to be a scoop with you?" Laura teased, slipping her hand into his. "I'd rather not see the ghost, thank you, even if it is my own ancestor."

"So it's true what they say, that you folks really are from the old Treadwick family?" the housekeeper asked.

"Oh, yes. I was born here," Helen Sutcliffe answered, before Laura could say anything, "and my husband is from this family too, only his side left England over a hundred years ago."

The housekeeper shook her head in amazement. "Fancy having Treadwicks back here," she exclaimed. "Who would have thought it. My grandma worked here and she said they all cried the day the old family had to leave."

"What was your grandma's name?" Helen asked.

"Tilly, ma'am. Tilly Hopkins."

"Tilly!" Grandma exclaimed delightedly. "She was the new parlor maid. She got in terrible trouble once for knocking over a vase of flowers. We felt so sorry for her that we sneaked her a chocolate biscuit from tea!"

"Fancy that," the housekeeper said again, looking pleased now. "How about I leave you folks to your looking and I go and make you a nice cup of tea?"

"You've certainly charmed her," Simon

commented, as the heavy feet departed down the stairs.

"Let's get started," Laura said impatiently. "Do you think there's any hope that the last diamond is somewhere in this house? The big queen stone that Emma said was too big to sell?"

"Oh, I doubt it," Grandma said. "I never saw it in my lifetime, and I'm sure my father would have pawned it if he had found it."

"This looks as if it could be your famous doll," Simon suggested, lifting up a huge, exquisitely dressed doll from a chest. "It has to be French with all that jewelry and lace."

"Let's see if its head comes off," Laura said excitedly.

"It does," Simon said.

"And what's inside?" Laura demanded, trying to peer into the doll's body.

"Nothing. It's empty."

"Oh."

She felt absurdly disappointed. At the back of her mind had always been the hope of finding the last diamond. If only someone had mislaid it or hidden it so well that it was waiting to be found . . . but, of course, a hundred and fifty years was a long time.

Trying to hide her disappointment she went to join her grandmother at the piles of letters. They spent a pleasant morning poring through stories they already knew, reading out interesting parts to each other, and putting the letters and diaries into piles.

At the bottom of what they had come to think of as Emma's trunk, they found another diary, wrapped in a lace handkerchief. It was dark leather and locked with a heavy silver clasp.

"This one looks as if it's never been opened," Laura said in a shaky voice. The diary looked very, very old.

"Oh, yes, I remember that one too," Grandma Helen said. "We never could find the key to it."

"I wonder if . . ." Laura began. She jiggled the clasp, hoping to make it come loose. Instead the aged leather ripped free of the heavy silver. "Whoops," Laura said.

"You'll go to jail for that one," Simon whispered. "Good job the housekeeper isn't here right now!"

"It was an accident," Laura said, giggling nervously, "but at least now it's open. Not that I can read it. It's in another language . . . oh, it must be French."

"Then it has to be the countesse's diary— Emma and Laura's mother. No wonder Emma kept it so carefully."

"Can you read it, Grandma?" Laura asked.

Helen adjusted her glasses and took the book close to the window. "A little," she said. "The whole thing will take time to translate. My French is rusty, of course, and they wrote differently in those days. It seems to be from the time when the girls were young. I can read 'My dear Emma sang so prettily . . .' "

As they turned over the pages a sheet fluttered to the floor. Laura picked it up. "Hey, this is in English," she said. "It looks like a letter. Yeah, listen to this:

'To be given to my dearest Emma in the event of my death.' I bet it never was given to her. . . . "

"Maybe because they didn't have the key to the diary and nobody ever opened it after her death," Simon suggested. "Maybe they didn't like to pry into someone else's diary. . . . "

"What does it say?" Grandma asked, coming to look over Laura's shoulder.

"My dear, sweet child:

I fear my days are numbered. The doctor does not hold much hope for me. I want you to know how much I cherish both of you and how much I long and pray for your happiness. I have been greatly troubled about the diamond necklace, which I told you to think of as an inheritance. This letter is meant for your eyes only, Emma. You are growing up to be such a sensible young person, I feel I have to trust you.

Emma, I worry about your sister. I fear she shows signs of a reckless, fearless nature that can only lead to trouble. I had a dream that she took the diamonds and they led her to ruin. I don't want that to happen, Emma, which is why I did what I did.

Charpentier, the queen's own jeweler, escaped from France and now lives in England. He is the most skilled man at his trade in the whole of Europe. I am telling you this because I had him make a copy of the necklace. It looks so perfect that I'm sure nobody can tell the difference except for the most expert of jewelers. I have also had another doll made, like the first, and the real necklace is now safely inside her.

I leave it to your discretion when you decide to tell her the truth and reveal the true necklace. Now, as I face death, I come to the belief more and more that the necklace should be kept safe for its rightful owners: the eventual return of the true government to France. It is not ours to use, dear child, and I fear that its use can only lead to destruction.

God keep you, my child, and preserve you all your days. Your loving and devoted Mother, Gabrielle de Chamboury Sutcliffe."

The silence in the attic was electric.

"Is it possible," Laura whispered at last, "that the real necklace was never discovered and is still around?"

"I never knew there were two dolls," Helen Sutcliffe said. "That's what the countess must have been saying on her deathbed. Do you remember in Emma's diary she wrote that her mother kept repeating over and over something about a new doll and nobody knew what she meant?"

"I wonder where it is now?" Laura said. "Do you think that in some museum or antique shop there's a doll with half a million dollars inside it?"

The housekeeper's heavy feet could be

heard, laboriously climbing the stairs again with a tea tray. "Here we are, my lovelies," she said, moving the doll to put the tray on an old trunk. "Oh, I didn't know that doll was up here," she commented with interest. "Last time I saw her, she was on the shelf in the nursery. Maybe they changed the display around . . ."

She didn't finish her sentence, as Laura was already pushing past her, leaping down the stairs two at a time. "Where's the nursery?" she called.

"One floor down, East Wing," the house-keeper called back, "but what's the big hurry?"

There was a whole shelf of antique dolls sitting over the Victorian crib. Laura reached up to take down the copy of the queen's doll.

"Do you think it's okay to take its head off?" she asked Simon.

"I think maybe we should wait for the Coopers' lawyer," Simon said.

"I'm so excited, I don't think I can wait," Laura said. "But I suppose you're right. Come on, let's call him to come over right now."

Half an hour later they sat together in Emma's old sitting room. Mr. Mandrake read the letter, then looked at the two dolls.

"I think, under the circumstances, that it would be permissible to see if the head comes off," he said. Carefully he twisted the china neck. "Look, it unscrews," he said.

He tipped up the doll and a faded velvet pouch slid onto the polished table. He pulled open the ancient leather drawstring and a string of liquid fire cascaded onto the polished tabletop.

"Wow," Laura muttered. Cautiously she picked up the diamonds, the queen stone shooting out rainbows as it lay heavy in her hand. "They're as bright as they were two hundred years ago!"

"They're even more beautiful than I imagined," Grandmama said huskily.

"Exquisite," Mr. Mandrake commented.

"Hold it, let me capture this moment," Simon instructed, adjusting his camera as Mandrake and Laura held the diamonds between them.

"So who do these belong to now?" Simon asked.

"Interesting legal question," Mr. Mandrake said. "The house was originally sold with furnishings and fixtures. A diamond necklace left behind inadvertently would not, I think, qualify. I would say that the family has a pretty good claim on its ownership."

"You mean the diamond necklace is ours?" Laura exclaimed, picking it up and letting the stones spill through her fingers exactly as the first Laura had done. So many exciting thoughts flashed through her mind . . . buying her parents a new house, touring Europe, going to a private college, new wardrobe . . .

"I wouldn't like to speculate on that without more documentation," Mr. Mandrake said, "but there's a strong possibility . . ."

"We're rich!" Laura shouted, dancing around. She had her legacy, as rightful heir to the Treadwicks and the Sutcliffes. Anything was now possible! She caught up Simon and her grandmother into the dance and they spun around, laughing crazily.

"I hate to leave England with the matter unsolved," Helen Sutcliffe said to Laura. They were due to leave the next day and had come down to Treadwick for a last time. Mr. Mandrake had hinted that it could be a lengthy court battle to prove ownership of the diamonds. The Sutcliffe diamonds were now a hot topic in the English press. Simon's photo had made the front page of all the big dailies, and Laura had been interviewed on British TV and radio, standing beside the portrait of her ancestor-namesake and look-alike. She had become a popular heroine, and it was generally felt that the diamonds should go to her without question.

"Maybe I could stay on," Laura suggested. "Simon said I could stay with his family. . . ."

She looked hopefully at her grandmother.

"What about starting junior college?"

"Grandma, if we get these diamonds, I can afford to take a year off and go to a really good college next year," Laura said. She looked around her at the stately oaks and beeches in Treadwick park. "Or I could maybe go to school in England. I understand that English education is supposed to be the best," she went on, giving her grandmother a sideways glance.

Helen chuckled and gave her granddaughter a nudge. "Go on with you," she said. "We all know your real reason for wanting to stay here, and it's not the diamonds!"

"You're right," Laura said. "I really don't want to leave Simon right now. Not when things are going so well. Will you speak to my parents and ask them if I can stay on? You can tell them that Simon is okay."

"Not another Brian, you mean?"

Laura grinned. "Not another Brian," she said. "I wonder where he is now? Hanging out on a beach in Spain, wasting his life, I bet."

They turned down a quiet, shaded walk, heavy with the scent of roses. "Wouldn't it be great if we did get the diamonds? Do you think they'd be enough to buy back Treadwick for you?"

"Heavens, child, that's the last thing I'd want now," Grandmama Helen exclaimed in horror. "Think of having to heat and clean all those rooms—and mow all this grass!"

"Then what would you want?" Laura asked.

"Enough to be comfortable," Grandma Helen said simply.

Laura looked surprised. "I thought you *were* comfortable," she said. "You took my sister, then me to Europe."

Helen looked embarrassed. "I used up the last of my savings to do this," she admitted.

"Grandmama, you didn't! Why would you do a thing like that?"

"Because I thought you needed to know your heritage, and I thought now was the time to do it. I saw the family temperament coming out in you and I thought you might make some serious mistakes."

"I might have," Laura admitted. "I was all set to go with Brian."

She went over to the old woman and put her arms around her. "Thank you," she whispered, planting a kiss on the papery old cheek.

An hour later they called on Mr. Mandrake again. "I've been on the phone to one of the best legal counsels in the country," he said, "and he is of the opinion that the necklace probably would legally belong to the French government."

"But it can't!" Laura blurted out. "It belonged to the queen and she didn't want it to fall into the government's hands."

"Nevertheless, they are the rightful government of France, and the necklace is definitely a national treasure," he said. "It's far too beautiful and special for one person to own and keep shut away. It should be in a museum for everyone to admire."

"I suppose you're right," Laura said slowly, fighting against her disappointment. She had sensed all along, deep down, that the necklace would never be hers. "What would I do with a necklace like that anyway?" she said lightly. "Sell it to some rich Arab sheik for his wives to wear? Or have it broken up and sold stone by stone? It *is* a national treasure, and I'd rather let everybody admire it."

Mr. Mandrake glanced from Laura to her grandmother. "Of course it would be up to the courts to battle it out, if you wanted the expense of a lengthy legal battle," he said. "The Coopers have hinted that they are not interested in fighting this in court, which leaves you versus the French government."

Laura made a face to her grandmother. "Great. I don't think we'd have much chance of winning that one. Anyway, I think the necklace should wind up in a museum. Anything as lovely and historic as that should be enjoyed by everybody."

"Well said, Laura," Grandmama exclaimed. "My own feelings exactly."

Laura gave a little smile. "I mean, can you see me wearing it to the Purple Onion with Simon? We're no longer the sort of family who needs stuff like that, and we no longer live in that sort of world. Although the money sure would have been nice . . ."

"I'm sure the French government would not be ungenerous with a finder's fee," Mr. Mandrake said.

"Really? There would be a finder's fee?" Laura asked, beaming at her grandmother. "My parents and Grandmama could sure use the money."

"What about you?"

"Oh, I'll be fine," Laura said confidently. "I

want to go to college over here if my parents will let me, and I can always get a job giving tours around Treadwick while I research the book I want to write about the family. Don't you think I'd give the tourists a shock when they see my portrait on the wall and they think they're seeing a ghost?"

She got up to go. Mr. Mandrake shook hands with her. "Good luck, young lady," he said. "I'm sure it will be a smashing success. You strike me as the kind of young woman who will do well with your life, whatever direction you take."

"Thank you," Laura said. She realized that this was true. She didn't need a necklace to make her a Sutcliffe. Her legacy from her ancestors had not been some precious stones; it had been the Sutcliffe strength and stubbornness, and the Sutcliffe story. She was a Sutcliffe woman with a strong will that couldn't be crushed, who would succeed against all odds and not give in to fear or doubt. With that kind of Sutcliffe stubbornness she couldn't go far wrong, could she?

She followed her grandmother out of the dusty office and into the bright sunshine of the busy street, where Simon, and her future, were waiting.